Praise for
House of Shadows

"…an energized tale of adventure, which keeps the reader on the edge of their seat. The suspense and danger are balanced exceedingly well with Rowan and Rick's relationship, which is explosive. This is one book that I will be remembering for a long time. There is never a boring moment and it's a one-sitting read. Highly, HIGHLY recommended!!"
—Tracy West, *The Road to Romance—Recommended Read!*

"If thrills and suspense is what you are after pick up this book quick!"
—Angel Brewer, *The Romance Studio Blue—*5 Hearts!

"…An amazing paranormal erotic romance!"
—Dani Jacquel. *Just Erotic Romance Reviews—*5 stars!

"This story line is amazing and will certainly keep you on your toes while reading it!"
—Lia Carla, *THE LAIR—The UK's No.1 Vampire Community*

"Everything you could hope for in a vampire erotic romance…"
—Miriam, *Sizzling Romances—*5 Flames!

Acknowledgements:

Without your help, encouragements and ashtrays, this novel could not have been written.
Thank you.

Lava Java Coffee House - Charlotte NC

For giving me gallons of coffee, and the loan of your power cord for my laptop all summer.

The Common Market - Charlotte NC

For letting me write, drink Butterscotch Toffee coffee and smoke indoors all winter.

Mike — *Pre-editor and saving grace.*
Randwulf — *Proofreader and Scholar Arcanum*
Derrick — *Inspirational research assistant*

A very special thanks to **Daria**—*for all the help with Russia & the Ukraine.*

And most especially, thanks to:
Michelle B. & Jane H.
Who slogged through the whole thing repeatedly, and encouraged me anyway.

House Of Shadows
Enchantment in Crimson—Book 1
Copyright 2004 Morgan Hawke
ISBN: 1-55410-155-7
Cover art by Angela Knight
Cover design by Martine Jardin

Published by eXtasy Books, a division of Zumaya Publications, 2004
Look for us online at:
www.zumayapublications.com
www.extasybooks.com

Library and Archives Canada Cataloguing in Publication

Hawke, Morgan, 1963-
        House of shadows / Morgan Hawke.

(Enchantment in crimson ; bk. 1)
Also available in electronic format.
ISBN 1-55410-155-7

I. Title. II. Series: Hawke, Morgan, 1963- Enchantment in crimson ; bk. 1.

PS3608.A83H68 2004   813'.6   C2004-903494-4

Also By Morgan Hawke

Demoness

Phantasmagoria: A Collection of Darker Passions

Passion's Vintage — Tarot key: The Star

Available at:
www.extasybooks.com

With inhuman speed the vampire grabbed her by the shoulders and pressed his lips to hers. Startled, her mouth opened and his tongue surged in. He turned his head, angling his mouth to cover hers, then thoroughly and expertly kissed her with long slow swipes of his tongue.

Without thought, she kissed him back, her tongue moving against his, exploring his mouth. He tasted of darkness and shadows, but it was surprisingly warm and wet. *He doesn't taste dead.* Her body clenched in sudden and voracious carnal response. *He's a very good kisser.* Rowan let out a small sound. Her hands fisted in his coat and her eyes fluttered closed. His arm closed around her waist, pulling her tightly against him.

She felt a small, sharp prick. She'd jabbed herself on one of his teeth. The taste of sweet copper bloomed. *Uh, oh.* She felt herself lifted from her feet and he sucked at the small burning wound on her tongue. He seemed to be getting warmer.

He broke the kiss and stared at her from barely an inch away. "Damn, I haven't fed this well in years." His eyes were pools of fire surrounded by thin rings of beaten copper. A tiny smear of blood escaped the corner of his mouth. He chased after it with his tongue.

I don't feel like part of my soul has been sucked out, or even dented. Rowan frowned. "It was only a scratch. You barely had any."

"Apparently your quintessence is super charged. I only needed a little." He grinned, showing the sharp points of his teeth. "I won't need to feed again for a few days."

Rowan glared at him. "What the hell was that kiss for anyway?"

"I swore not to harm you." He grinned. "I never said I wouldn't seduce you."

"What?" Her mouth fell open.

"I have a few hours before I have to go." He let her slide down his body, then pressed her back against the car.

She could feel the firm strength of his body and the rigid length of an impressive erection letting her know, in no uncertain terms, that he was more than interested in something other than food. His hips swiveled against hers with a slow, suggestive roll. Her panties became embarrassingly moist.

"I'll make it good, I promise." He licked his reddened lips and smiled.

House of Shadows

Enchantment in Crimson

Book 1

By

Morgan Hawke

✤ One ✦

Auspice

The witch stepped out onto the narrow back porch of her small second story apartment. A chill gust of wind, carrying the scent of rain, curled under her waist-length copper mane and blew the fine, straight strands across her pale brow.

"Hmm, I forgot that it would be a new moon tonight." She brushed the spider-silk strands of hair from her face, narrowing her eyes. The radiant silver smile appeared to sit as though perched behind the twisted branches of the winter bare oak tree by her porch in the darkening twilight.

"Other people have nice, normal lives full of random events," she mused out loud, shaking her head with a tight smile. "Me? I randomly catch a moonrise and it's an email from the Powers That Be." She pulled the lapels of her plush black velvet robe closer to her throat, then slid the glass door closed behind her with a soft thump. "I guess this means I'm about to start something new. Damn..."

Absently, she dug a slender black cigarette from the pack and lit it on the unwavering blue jet of flame from her silver, ultra-modern lighter. She exhaled the rich, clove smoke with luxurious relish, and the wind carried the thick, perfumed cloud away. "Let's see what else appears. Maybe I can figure out what's coming to get me before I get myself cornered."

With a rustle of black feathers, a crow dropped from the darkening sky and landed in the tree right by her porch. Not an uncommon occurrence. However, this crow balancing on the slender branch was framed perfectly by the horns of the rising moon.

"One crow for sorrow," she quoted softly. "And perching in the horns of the new moon." She smiled sourly. "Terrific. Whatever adventure I'm about to start is going to involve some form of angst and very likely drama." She drew on her cigarette. "Well, that means it's not going to happen at the library." She snorted. "Nothing with angst or drama ever happens at the library, and certainly not at my reference desk."

The crow turned his head to the side and peered at her from one bright eye. It released three harsh cries then mantled its wings and flew straight at her. It banked sharply upward and over the roof.

"Oh, goody, this is going to be personal," she said in complete disgust. "But with one crow in a tree framed by a new moon, I can't tell if it's just a random nasty event I walk into, or if someone is pissed off and out to get me." She drew on the cigarette and stared at the smiling crescent. "On second thought, this is a new moon, so it's a new problem, something that is not rooted in the past." She closed her eyes and groaned. "Damn. That means it's something I'm going to stir up all by myself." She shook her head. "This is getting uglier by the second. Why can't I just get nice clear visions like all the TV psychics say they do?"

The tree rocked in the breeze. Her eyes narrowed sharply as the moon began to change. Slowly, the entire bottom half of the crescent became tinted a definite red. The tilted silver smile suddenly looked a lot more like a curved fang stained with blood. A fang trapped among branches that looked like groping skeletal fingers.

The witch blinked at the view and felt the hair on her neck shiver to attention. "That does not look good," she said very softly to the universe at large. "I need…" Carefully she took a mouthful of smoke, then exhaled. "A second opinion."

Abruptly, the neighbor's black collie-mix dog lunged energetically from one the first floor apartments, towing her neighbor Caroline from the end of his leash.

The witch leaned over the rail of her porch. "One second opinion, right on cue," she said softly. "Hi, Caroline!" she called and stubbed out her cigarette.

Caroline, her sandy curls swept up into a bobbing ponytail, turned her soft green eyes upward. "Oh, hi!" She smiled. Her dog towed her directly under the overhanging porch. "It's Rowan, right?"

"Yep, that's me." Rowan smiled and made a wry face. "I know this is going to sound weird, but I think I need new glasses. Can you tell me what color the moon is?"

Caroline obligingly looked up at the moon. "It's a bluish-white." She turned back to Rowan. "Why? What color do you think it is?"

Rowan squinted up at the moon. "Does it look a little...reddish to you at all?"

"No, not at all." Caroline shook her head and smiled. "You do need glasses."

Rowan smiled in return. "Well, thanks, and have fun on your walk."

"Glad to be of help." Caroline laughed. "I gotta go! Take care!" She waved, then allowed her dog to tow her across the frost-seared lawn toward the next apartment complex over.

Rowan stared at the moon and lit another cigarette. "Great," she grumped. "My nice quiet life is about to be invaded by scary, weird shit." She flopped down on one of the plastic lawn chairs on her small porch. "As the only working witch in town, I get all the midnight 'help, my house is haunted' phone calls. Why do I have a feeling that this means I'll be running into something a lot nastier than a simple haunt?"

After a while, she crushed out her cigarette and sighed. "Time to get ready." She stood up, then jerked the sliding glass door open. "With that omen hanging over my head, I really don't want to go out tonight." She looked back at the moon floating among the tree branches. "But I have bills to pay." Her lip curled in disgust. "I wouldn't have to pimp out my witchcraft by playing fortune teller if the pay didn't suck as a librarian." She stepped inside and closed the door firmly behind her.

ꝏ ᴛ ꞔ𝓌𝓅 ∾ ꝏ Two ∾

ᴏ𝓇𝒶𝒸𝓁ᴇ Oracle

Rowan shoved open the heavy door marked: 'Employees Only' with one hand. She pushed with her shoulder, wrestling with her large, black brocade shoulder bag and grabbing at her long, pitch-black, ground-sweeping coat to avoid trapping the hem at her boot-heels in the closing door.

She wove her way through the crowd while nodding in time to the familiar brooding and violently loud music. It was a typically crowded Friday night at the club Gothic Noire. As usual, she had to practically shove her way across the main room, heading toward her fortune-telling booth. It was on the other side of the dance floor near the main entrance door. Waves and smiles greeted her from patrons in varying outfits of plastic, leather and black fishnet. They swarmed, conversed, smoked and drank while endeavoring to look both sexy and intimidating. The music was loud and throbbed with deep, rich inflections. The air was scented with clove smoke from all the black cigarettes.

While passing the long bar, she smiled at the two harried handsome and barely dressed bartenders. Stopping briefly, she gave a quick passing hug to Tony, the big, gruff club manager, then continued deeper into the club, her heels clicking on the hardwood floor. She spared a glance in the ornate mirror behind the bar. Rhinestones twinkled in the smoked metal headband that held her waist-length, pin-straight copper mane back from her brow. She stopped and took a moment to tuck an errant lock back into the glittering band, then continued onward.

As she passed the far edge of the bar, Rowan felt a shimmer of otherworldly chill. *That feels a little like magic and death.* She stopped on the edge of the dance floor and looked over at the very end of the bar. *Holy shit,* Rowan thought in astonishment. *There should be a law against a guy being that beautiful.*

A blindingly handsome young man was sitting on one of the barstools nursing an imported beer. His dark, straight hair was pulled back into a tight tail that fell over his shoulder and brushed his forearm. His pale, chiseled face was pared to the bone, showing fine, sharp features and full lips that belonged on the cover of a pulp vampire novel.

He turned slightly and saw her. His pale brown eyes seemed to collect the light from around him, reflecting a soft, shimmering green the way a cat's does in the shadows. Slowly he twisted around in his stool and looked her full in the face. His silky, sleeveless black shirt framed his broad shoulders while showing off the ropes of muscle in his arms and hugging his flat stomach and narrow waist. The black leather pants he wore looked as though they had been tailored to fit. A long, typically Goth coat was flung over the bar. He smiled.

Rowan felt her heart thump in reaction and the warm roil of her libido sitting up and taking notice. *This one is definitely too pretty for anyone's good,* she thought in bittersweet admiration, then realized that the cool brush of subtle danger emanated from him. She gave him a tight smile, then sharply turned on her heel and marched toward the small corner booth on the other side of the dance floor.

I am not running away, she told her fast-beating heart. *I just don't have time for incredibly cute metaphysical weirdness. I have work to do.* A glance in the mirrors behind the bar showed that he was watching her. She walked away and felt her body clench in greedy longing. *Ahem, brain to sex-drive —we already have a 'too cute for his own good' boy-diva,* she told herself sternly. She bit her lip and climbed the three small steps that led to her corner, set aside for the house fortuneteller. *We don't need another potential heartbreak.*

Rowan dropped her black leather satchel on the curved, red plastic bench of her semi-private booth. She shrugged out of her long coat and straightened her long, beaded black skirts. She pulled her silver pentacle from where it had tucked itself into her corset, then adjusted the black fishnet that stretched across the pushed-up fullness of her cleavage. The deep black velvet of the tightly laced, Victorian style corset accentuated her unusually narrow waist and framed her rounded hips.

Tugging at her full skirts, she settled into the booth, then pushed the fishnet sleeves up to her forearms. *Time to set up shop...*She opened her satchel, then laid out the tools of her trade. A red velvet cloth covered the small, bare and drink-stained table. A small gargoyle holding a short, squat red candle, her oversized Tarot sign and the small, freestanding pricing list completed her setting. Rowan pulled her set of tarot cards from the sandalwood box. She was open for business.

A flurry of friends came in and paid to have their fortunes told.

Rowan was kept busy for a long while, smiling and counseling as needed, bestowing congratulations or comforting hugs to soften emotional bruises delivered by her readings.

The stream of friends and new patrons finally died down, and Rowan was able to sip at her ginger ale in relative quiet. Every last one of her readings had involved someone's love life, which of course depressingly brought to mind her own. *Plenty of sex, not one drop of real affection...* She grimaced. *I need a hobby that doesn't involve men.*

She stood up in her booth and signaled one of the waiters that she needed another soda. Catching sight of her reflection in a small smoked mirror by the opposite bench, she leaned over and absently checked her make-up. *Hmm, I've been talking all this time, might want to put on a bit more lipstick…*

She slid back into her booth, settled her skirts, then dug her small purse out of her satchel. She reached in and pulled out her compact. A small, framed photo slid from her bag. It hit the corner of the table with a crack of breaking glass, then fell to the floor. A shiver of foreboding raced up her spine. *Someone is coming. Someone I don't want to see.*

Looking carefully under her table, she found the photo of her current boyfriend. She picked the fallen photo out of the glass and frowned. A sharp shard had gouged a long tear though the picture's mouth. Instinctively she understood what the symbolic rip meant.

Lies…

Suddenly another shiver skimmed up her spine, raising the hairs on her arms. *Trouble is coming and if the photo is any indication, it's probably him that's going to bring it.*

There was a heavy thump on the stairs to her booth.

She closed her eyes. "Please don't be him. Please, make it somebody else. I don't want to deal with this tonight." She opened her eyes to find her boyfriend glowering from the side of her table.

"We need to talk," he said, practically spitting the words out.

"I am working, can it wait?" Whatever the hell he wanted, she just knew it was going to be ugly. He wasn't supposed to stop by until after she'd finished working the club, but his short hair was slicked back with gel and his designer clothes were neatly pressed. Rowan frowned. *Do I smell beer on his breath, and cologne? Where the hell has he been?*

"You're using me—for sex!" His hand cracked down on her table. "You, and your witchcraft!"

She raised her brow and slowly stood up. "This is a public place, can't you wait to shout at me in private?"

His face turned an ugly mottled red. "You're not a witch, you're a goddamned vampire!"

"I'll take that to be a: no, you want to have a shouting match right here," she said softly. Over his shoulder she caught a glimpse of one of the larger bouncers making his way toward her booth. Behind him, the cute gothic hunk at the bar was standing and watching.

"You screw me every time you use your magic, and suck me so dry that I can't…"

Her gaze shot to her boyfriend's and narrowed. "Can't what?" She could feel the truth hovering unsaid in his mouth. *Wait a damned minute. I've heard this complaint before… And that's not cologne, that's some girl's perfume.* Her lips curled up in a sour smile. "Let me guess, you just got back from playing with some other chick and you couldn't get it up."

His face went bone white.

She felt her lips curl back from her teeth in a parody of a smile. "You wanted to ball somebody and couldn't."

He jabbed a finger toward her. "Because you sucked everything out of me, like the damned vampire you are!"

"You weren't complaining last night!" she shot back. "Now get out of my club."

He jerked back. "What?"

"You want to go screw other people? Fine, go do it." She flung a hand out and pointed toward the door. She watched the thoughts race across his face. Apparently, he hadn't meant to admit that he was sleeping around, which meant that he hadn't meant to get thrown out of her bed, either. She snorted. *Idiot…*

"Look, I don't mean that the way it sounded," he said as though in apology. "You're the best I ever…"

"Best ride that you ever had? I know." Her smile was feral. "And now you can forget about ever having it again."

He frowned. "Did you just curse me?"

She hadn't, of course. "Sure," she said out of pure spite. "And if you don't want your dick to fall off, you'll get the hell out of my club, and never show your piss-ant face here again."

"You fucking bitch," he snarled. He turned on his heel and stalked toward the door. She watched the bouncer meet him on the floor. He spoke a few soft words, then escorted her brand-new ex-

9

boyfriend out.

She swiped a hand across her cheek, wiping away a tear she refused to acknowledge. "Damn, now I have to find another boyfriend." Rowan raised her ginger ale and frowned at the pale-gold soda in her glass. *A pity alcohol kills my talent; I could really use a beer right now.* Absently, she swiped at the chill moisture on her other cheek. She dug a black cigarette from the pack. "Cheating moron..."

Her lighter clicked. She lit the clove, then exhaled the sweet smoke. "I really need to find a guy that's older and less stupid," she muttered softly, then sighed. *You'd think the library would attract a smarter selection of guys.* She shook her head. *I have got to stop using work to pick up men when I need to get laid. I'm so sick and tired of insecure idiots that can't handle my being a witch.* She sipped at her ginger ale. *I definitely need a vaguely decent man in my life...* Her eyes drifted back over to the unsettling hunk at the bar. *Or a distraction...*

He had turned his back to her and was chatting with a small group of enthusiastic girls in black plastic, fishnet and heavy eyeliner. Stools were dragged over and he shifted to make room for them.

Rowan frowned, mulling over the impressions that she was picking up from his presence. *He can't be what I think he is...* Even from this far away she could feel the shimmer of disquiet that drifted from him. *There's no such thing.* She shook her head. *I'm going to need to check the cards for this.*

Rowan focused on the guy at the edge of the bar and shuffled her tarot cards. *Okay, is he or isn't he?* Two cards slipped through her fingers, the Ace of Swords, *yes,* and the Devil, subtitled: the Vampire.

So this guy really is a vampire. She made a sour face. *Terrific. There's a for-real vampire sitting at the bar in with all the vampire wannabes.* She smiled tightly. *Talk about protective coloring.*

Jennifer, her tastefully made-up face wreathed with a deep scarlet smile, came thumping up the tiny staircase in her shiny, black plastic platform boots. She practically danced with excitement into the circular booth.

"I just met this really gorgeous guy and you have to tell me all about him!" Jennifer's earnest, deep blue eyes were framed with heavy black eyeliner and dark blue shadow that would have looked atrocious on anyone else.

"Anything for you, Jenn." Rowan smiled and pulled her long black skirts to one side, making room for Jennifer on the red plastic seat of the booth. *Terrific, another love-life reading...*

Jennifer giggled, struggling to sit in her exquisitely short, super tight, red plastic skirt. Daintily she crossed her legs, exposing a long line of trim, black-fishnet-encased thigh.

Rowan shuffled the oversized cards, then spread them across the table. "How detailed a reading can I give you?"

Jennifer leaned over the small table, her breasts swelling over the neckline of her sheer black blouse. "Just a quickie, I want to know if this guy is, well... You know..."

Rowan's brows shot up. "You want to know if he's 'The One'?" She smiled and nodded her head. *Jeeze, how many times do I get asked this question? When are they going to learn there is no such thing as a One True Love?*

"Well, um." Jennifer licked her artfully painted lips and darted a look over her shoulder, tossing the short and stylish bright blond bob that curled around her ears. "Yeah, is this guy the one for me?" She smiled, then bit into her painted lip.

Rowan let her draw five cards at random, then set them in her Answer spread. Center card, the Devil; subtitled: the Vampire, meaning manipulation and compulsion. *Uh, oh. This guy is a user.* The card on the right was the Page of Wands. *Well, that pretty much describes Jennifer, immature and talkative.* The card on the left was the Tower, subtitled the Dragon, meaning personal and possibly mental destruction. *Definitely not good...* Crossing at her feet was the Seven of Swords, meaning lies and theft. *Oh, boy, he doesn't just use them, he throws them away.* The very last card at the root or outcome: Temperance, subtitled: the Alchemist, also known as the

Physician, indicating a visit to the hospital. *Oh, shit.*

Rowan blinked, realizing what she was looking at. She had seen this same exact set of cards in this layout with a few of her friends before. She had ended up visiting each of them in the hospital a few days later for shock and blood-loss. *Shit, shit, shit...* According to the tarot cards, Jennifer was the vampire's next intended victim.

Rowan glanced over at the vampire and noticed that the crowd of Goth girls had left him alone, surrounded by empty stools. He had put on his long coat and was obviously waiting for someone. He turned and peered into her booth.

He's looking at Jennifer... Rowan nibbled on her lip, wondering what to say. *Being the Goth chick she is, if I tell Jennifer that he's a vampire, she'll beg him to turn her into one. He'll probably kill her instead for knowing what he is, after finding out that it was me that told her. I do not need a pissed-off vampire after me, but I am not visiting another friend in the hospital, either.*

Rowan caught Jennifer's eye and held it. "Jenn, you are in danger. I really think you should go home early and not tell anyone that you are leaving."

Jennifer's scarlet mouth fell open in shock. "What?" She blinked her bright blue eyes. "But there's this guy I just met, that's why I'm having you do this reading. He's—"

Rowan cut her off. "According to my cards, the guy you just met is a rapist." She cringed inwardly. She was bending the truth. An outright lie was a serious no-no and would cost her divination talents for a least a week. *Vampire, rapist, there's not a whole lot of difference.* She tapped the cards with a finger. "If you stay, you will leave with this guy and you will end up in the hospital." That *was* the truth.

"But..." Jennifer's eyes darted to the bar, then back. "Are you sure?"

Damn it, Jennifer is already hooked on him. Rowan sighed inwardly. "It's your choice to ignore my warning, but how often have I been wrong?"

"As far as I know, never." Jennifer frowned. "But he's so cute." She was, of course, referring to the vampire, who was painfully cute.

Rowan bit back her frustration. "Of course he is." She smiled coldly. "It makes it easier to find people willing to walk out with him."

Jennifer bit her lip. "But he seemed so nice."

"Of course he did." Rowan gritted her teeth, but kept smiling. Jennifer was proving stubborn. "The last thing he wants to do is alert his victim as to what's in store for them." *Time to press the point.* She trapped Jennifer's wide-eyed gaze with her own. "Jenn, I told Donner and Tess the same exact thing last month. They chose to ignore me."

Jennifer locked on the one thing guaranteed to catch her attention. "Donner? He does guys, too?"

Rowan nodded solemnly. "Rapists don't really care who they hurt."

Jennifer leaned forward in her chair. "Donner is in the psych ward," she whispered.

Is that a chink in Jennifer's armor? Rowan leaned across the table, closer to Jennifer. "Yes, he is. And this guy put him there."

"You're sure?" Jennifer's lower lip was trembling. "That it's *this* guy?"

"Absolutely." Rowan nodded firmly. "These are your choices: leave now and avoid the whole thing or stay and wake up in the hospital, possibly the psych ward. Game over."

Jennifer bit her lip. "All right, I'll leave." She sniffed and there was a shimmer of tears in her eyes. "Just let me tell Susan—"

Rowan shook her head. "No, don't tell Susan that you're leaving." Jennifer and Susan were best friends and fierce rivals. Both were about the same height with similar blond bobs and style of dress. The only real difference was that Susan was a little more aggressive in her approach to men.

"Remember," Rowan continued, "Susan probably thinks he's cute, too."

Jennifer bared her teeth. "That's right. If Susan knows I've left the field open, she'll go straight for him."

Rowan felt the sudden swell of jealousy boil up in Jennifer. *Oops, gotta nip that in the bud.* She placed a hand over Jennifer's. "Jenn, if you tell her that you're leaving and she goes after this guy, she'll end up in the hospital and it will be your fault."

Jennifer's eyes flew wide. "Oh."

"Why don't you tell Susan that you have to make a call, then just don't come back? You can always tell her tomorrow that you had a minor emergency and had to leave. This way she won't make a bee-line for the rapist."

Jennifer tilted her head to one side. "Um..." Her eyes slid to the vampire at the bar. She bit her heavily-painted lip, then looked at Rowan with indecision. "Are you really, really sure it's this guy?"

Jeeze, Jenn and her appetite for cute guys... Rowan closed her hand around Jennifer's. "It's your choice, Jenn, but I really don't want to visit you in the hospital. Or the psych ward..."

"I don't want people to think I'm crazy," Jennifer whispered.

Let's apply a nail to that coffin. Rowan smiled sadly at Jennifer. "Jenn, no one thinks they're crazy, just a little unconnected with reality." *Which is to say, they think they're crazy.* "Tell you what, go visit Donner and Tess tomorrow and ask them what the guy looked like. They'll tell you."

Jennifer's cheeks blanched. She rose from her chair. "All right, I'm going."

"Good girl." Rowan rose with her and gave her a hug. "I just don't want anything to happen to my favorite Jennifer."

Jennifer hugged her back. "I'm the only Jennifer you know." She smiled and slid from Rowan's embrace.

"That doesn't make you any less my favorite." Rowan squeezed her hand then let her go with a lopsided grin. "Take care of yourself, sweetheart."

Jennifer smiled back, then darted a nervous look over her shoulder. "Okay, I'm going." She nodded firmly, then turned and left the booth. Jennifer's chin went up. She passed the vampire, marching straight for Susan, who was chatting with a weightlifter by the dance floor.

Okay, looks like she's going to do it. Let's see if she was smart enough to keep her mouth shut to Susan.

Susan and Jennifer exchanged words briefly, then Jenn turned on her heel and marched for the front door. Rowan saw the vampire look up. Jennifer pulled her cell phone from her purse, then walked out the front door with the phone jammed tight to her ear, without a single glance toward him.

Bravo, Jenn! Rowan saw Susan drag the weightlifter onto the dance-floor, ignoring the vampire. *Looks like Jenn kept quiet.* She watched the vampire nurse his beer while watching the door. Several long minutes passed and Jenn stayed gone. The vampire began showing obvious signs of building frustration.

Rowan couldn't help the self-satisfied grin on her face. *That's right, you blood-sucking parasite, your meal ticket has left you high and dry.* Rowan nodded to herself. *Fortuneteller one point, vampire zero.*

A little while later, Rowan had settled back in her booth with a fresh ginger ale after yet another 'love life' reading when she heard the main entrance door open behind her booth. An icy shiver crawled up her spine, making the hair on her arms stand up. *That's an aura of bad magic.* Her stomach did a slow, sickening turn for good measure. *Really, bad magic...* Frowning, she looked over toward the door. A very tall, very broad, completely bald man in a dark suit stalked purposefully past her booth.

Rowan blinked. Her eyes were having trouble focusing on him. She frowned in concentration, then confusion. *Well, that's weird...*

The man had two distinct shadows. One of them wasn't even remotely human in shape.

What the Hell is he? She squinted to blur her eyesight, focusing her inner-vision. Rays of light, sort of like heat curling from hot pavement, became immediately apparent. *Okay, he's definitely magical...* There was a hint of colors in the wavering rays, but they looked wrong, a moldy gray-green and pus yellow. *Ugh, that is really nasty magic. A sorcerer?* Rowan absently shuffled her cards. *What the hell am I looking at?*

Three cards slipped through her fingers and settled on the table. The Hermit, subtitled the Scientist, meaning solitary or secret knowledge, and the Magician; control over forces. The last card was the Hanged Man, the willing sacrifice, meaning a quest for dangerous knowledge. *Yep, that's a sorcerer all right, and he is definitely up to no good.*

She slid the cards back in the deck and watched the sorcerer make his ponderous way across the dance floor. On every side, dancers shifted to avoid him, unconsciously making a path across.

What the Hell is that second shadow from? Another pair of cards slid through her fingers onto the table; the Devil; manipulation and the Tower; destructive force.

Demonic possession? The Ace of swords just about leapt from the deck. *Yes.* She slid the three cards back in the deck. *The Hanged Man proves that if he's housing an actual demon, the sorcerer is a willing participant. Either way, what the Hell is it doing in here?*

The Empress, with her display of bounty, slid to the table. Rowan eyed the card. *The Empress means procreation.* Nothing hit the table. She continued to shuffle. *I guess he's not looking for a date. Wait, the Empress also means food.* The Ace of Swords slid to the tabletop once again. *Yes.*

Rowan raised her brow. *Food? So he's looking for a meal... Hmm, according to my books, demons are supposed to feed on the souls of the corrupt. Gee, let's see. Who has the most corrupt soul in the club?*

The sorcerer spotted the vampire sitting dejectedly at the bar, smiled and abruptly took the abandoned stool beside him.

Well, imagine that. Rowan bit back a smile and watched.

The hungry vampire glanced up in surprise, said something, then fell under the sorcerer's sway almost easily. One minute he was smiling and the next he was wide-eyed and frozen in place on his bar stool.

Rowan could just make out a swirl of color pinning him to where he sat. She choked on outright laughter. *Let's see how you feel about being on the menu for once, vampire.*

A small breeze from the door behind her blew some cards from the small table. With a huff of annoyance, Rowan retrieved the cards from the floor. The Tower, the Devil, the Magician, the Hermit and the Ten of Swords. Rowan felt the blood drain from her face. *Piss and firewater!* Together these cards meant imminent and massive destruction. The Ten of Pentacles slid out of her fingers; the establishment—the club!

Rowans held the cards and her hands shook. *Son of a bitch! That sorcerer is going to slaughter everyone in the club with the power he's draining off the vampire.* She glanced around at the crowded club. *Damn it! There's no way to warn all these people. Even if I called the police right now, people will die before they even get here. Mother of us all, what am I thinking? The police don't stand a chance against something like this!* She bit her lip and tapped a finger on the cards. *Shit, something has to be done before the sorcerer can cause his bloodbath, but what?*

The High Priestess card, subtitled: the Witch, fluttered to the floor followed by Justice, subtitled: the White Knight, meaning rescue. *Damn it! I can't stop that—I'm not anywhere near magically strong enough. That monster is way outta my league...*

The Devil, also known as the Vampire, slid to the tabletop followed by the Five of Wands, meaning argument. *The vampire can fight the sorcerer?* The Ace of Swords flipped almost to the floor. *Yes.*

Rowan looked over at the trapped vampire. *The vampire may be sending people to the hospital, but from everything I've heard, they're still in one piece and still breathing when he's done with them. This guy intends to leave nothing but bodies. Or rather, body parts. I guess this is a case of 'the lesser of two evils'.*

The vampire will have to be released from the sorcerer's spell first... The Ace of Cups slithered through her fingers. *True love?*

Rowan frowned. *What does love have to do with it?* She shook her head. *Never mind, I'll just take that as an ace, which means yes, I have to rescue the vampire. Terrific.*

She frowned at the two at the bar. That vampire was going to be pissed once released and the following battle would be messy. *Their fight will at least clear the bar of innocent bystanders in a big hurry. I better pack up.*

She put her cards together and wrapped them in her cloth, then set the cards in their sandalwood box. Quickly and efficiently, she tucked her entire setup, signs, candles and gargoyle statuary into her large leather satchel.

Now, what do I need to break that spell? She reached into the small red brocade Magikal Arte bag that she had tied onto her belt and rummaged around. Her fingers touched small paper twists of various herbs and small, randomly collected trinkets. She stabbed her finger on something sharp. She took out a tiny, silver-dipped, horseshoe nail. *Ah, yes. This will do nicely. I can always get another one made, so I can just leave it behind.*

Unknotting the small bag from her belt, she tucked it into her satchel and pushed her kit behind the booth, out of casual view. She grabbed her long-skirted coat from the back of the booth and shrugged into it.

Gritting her teeth in a tight smile, she sauntered out of her booth and over to the bar. *Why do I have to do all the rescuing tonight? First I rescue the vampire's victim, now I get to rescue the vampire. Karma must be after me.*

Gingerly, she sat in the stool directly behind the broad back of the sorcerer who sat facing the trapped vampire. *Let's begin by invoking the element of Fire.* She turned her back to the sorcerer and lit a clove cigarette. Slowly, she turned around on the barstool and leaned an elbow on the bar to peek past the sorcerer's shoulder.

By squinting her eyes, she could see that the vampire's vitality was being unraveled in bright skeins of power. To the rest of the bar, it looked as though they were sharing a conversation, with the sorcerer doing all the chatting. The vampire was beginning to look a bit too pale, almost gray. His full lips had a bluish cast to them. *He's going to be really pissed off and hungry once I set him loose. Too bad for the sorcerer...*

The vampire spotted her behind the sorcerer. She smiled grimly at him. His eyes widened, but other than that, he obviously couldn't move a muscle.

Okay, I need to invoke Earth. Very softly, Rowan whispered. "I need salt." One of the bartenders accidentally spilled bar salt right in front of her. She smiled. *Well, Lord Karma may be pissed at me for some reason, but Lady Fate is still on my side.* With her index finger, she sketched a pentacle in the spilled salt that conveniently lay in a portion of the inhuman shadow. *There, earth.... Now, Air...* She held up her horseshoe nail and winked at the vampire. *And finally, the element of Water...* She licked the nail.

The vampire looked at her in puzzlement. The sorcerer was so involved in what he was doing that he didn't notice the changes of expression on the vampire's face.

She took a deep suck on her clove cigarette. Gently, she whispered, "Blessed be," while blowing the fragrant smoke on the pentacle drawn in salt. Abruptly, she stabbed the damp, silver nail deep into a crack on the bar top. It stuck upright in the center of the pentacle that lay well within the sorcerer's second and inhuman shadow.

Rowan watched the colorful webbing around the vampire suddenly dissipate. *That ought to make things interesting.* With a grin, she quickly ducked under the bar, then peeked out.

The vampire took a deep breath and abruptly realized that his binding was gone. His eyes ignited into pools of flame and he smiled, baring long fangs.

Rowan's eyes opened wide. *Great Mother, that is definitely not a human—he is a real vampire!*

The vampire lunged for the surprised sorcerer's throat with both hands, his long coat flying out like a cape. The sorcerer roared and they went over together, hitting the floor with the furious vampire on top.

Pandemonium ensued. Screams and shouts erupted all over the bar. People jostled each other in their rush to get out of range. The fight quickly escalated, with furniture being thrown. Bodies pressed for the front and back exits.

Fortuneteller two points, creatures of darkness still at zero... Rowan chuckled, crawling along the underside the bar as fast as she could. Darting away to her corner, she grabbed her satchel, then dashed under the bar to slip out the side door with the escaping employees.

❧ Three ❧

Copper Kiss

Rowan trotted down the alley behind the club. The alley itself was dark and narrow, but short, and led straight to the brightly lit main street. The whistling late autumn wind was sharp and cold, biting right through her light coat. Her waist-length copper mane and her flared coat sailed behind her. A growing urgency skittered with warning along her senses. She had learned long ago to listen to her instincts.

Her satchel tucked over her shoulder, Rowan stepped from the dank alley, then walked briskly across the city street. Luckily traffic was light, so she didn't have to dodge cars. She stepped up on the sidewalk that ran by the small, fenced churchyard diagonally across from the club. She strode quickly along the fence surrounding the church graveyard, headed for the parking lot behind it and her car. Her booted heels clicked sharply on the cement.

Something big exploded behind her with a loud roar and the crash of glass. The ground shook under her feet and a hot wind shoved at her back, pushing her forward. Car alarms screeched from all over the place and sirens suddenly wailed in the streets around her.

She whirled to look and winced.

The Goth club was in flames.

I guess I'll have to find a new club to work in. Rowan smiled sourly. *Looks like the vampire took out the sorcerer, forcibly releasing the demon. Vampire one point, sorcerer; still at nothing.* She turned around to continue on to her car.

The vampire stepped out of a pool of deep shadow, tall, elegant and slightly singed, but still heartbreakingly handsome in his long and somewhat tattered coat. His long hair, loosened from its neat tail, spread over his shoulders in a soft cloak of darkness. He was a lot taller than she had originally thought. The top of her head was barely even with his shoulder. He turned and stared straight at her.

Piss and firewater. Rowan shouldered her bag, pinned a smile on her lips and moved to walk around him. Very deliberately, he stepped into her path, blocking her. She'd have to walk into traffic to get around him. *Stay calm. Don't panic.* She raised a brow at him. "Can I help you?"

"Do you normally take on demons?" His voice was deep and rich, with a slightly clipped German accent.

Rowan shrugged nonchalantly and looked pointedly past him. "No, not normally. If you'll excuse me?"

"How did you figure out what it was? Hell, what I really want to know is how you knew what to do about it?"

Rowan shrugged. "Just one of the hazards of being a fortune-teller. The rest of it sort of comes with the territory." She snuck a quick peek at his face. She swallowed and felt her heart rate kick up a notch. *Gods, he's cute up close. No wonder Jennifer kicked up a fuss when I made her go home.*

He frowned. "Weren't you afraid that it would come after you and kill you?"

Rowan shook her head. "I'm a pagan—reincarnation and all that. If I die, I come right back."

He raised a skeptical brow. "You're sure?"

Rowan nodded firmly. "Oh, yeah, I'm sure." She tapped her temple with a finger. "Got the memories to prove it, too."

"I see…" He gave her a lop-sided smile. "Well, thank you for releasing me. You saved my life."

What an ego! Rowan turned her head and pinned him with an angry stare. "I didn't do it to save you, I did it to keep everyone else from dying. The sorcerer intended to suck you dry, then use your power to slaughter everyone else. I figured if I released you from his spell, that a fight between you two would be scary enough to clear the bar of innocent people."

He blinked. "You know what I am."

"Yes." Rowan smiled coldly. *You blood-sucking parasite…*

"It was you that sent Jennifer home early." His look was accusatory.

"Of course I sent her home," Rowan snapped. "Once I saw what was in her cards, what else was I supposed to do? Let her get killed?"

"Look, I don't kill them." He crossed his arms defensively across his broad chest. "I'm the one that usually calls the ambulance after…"

Is that guilt I'm sensing? Rowan frowned, then jabbed a finger at him. "It *was* you that put a few of my other friends in the hospital for blood loss and shock." She narrowed her eyes. "Two of them are in the psych ward for extreme paranoia." She raised a sarcastic brow. "For some reason, they think that the shadows are going to get them."

He winced. "Sometimes the hypnotic trance doesn't take completely."

"Oops? Your bad?" she said with venom.

"Hey, take it easy." He frowned. "I haven't killed anyone." He gave her a slight smirk. "Well, until tonight, but that sorcerer had it coming…"

"You just drink them dry enough to put them in the hospital instead?" Rowan rolled her eyes. "Oh, that's so much better."

He rolled his eyes then made another face. "Lately I haven't found much value in what I have been drinking. The quality of their essence, spirit, soul, whatever, is so poor that it takes a lot of blood to get anything out of it, though I have gotten a few interesting buzzes." He gave her a lopsided smile while she continued to stare angrily at him. He shrugged.

Rowan raised a sarcastic brow. "I feel so bad for you," she said in complete deadpan. "Can't you drink from animals instead of people?"

"Hell no, that stuff's nasty." He made a sour face.

"Not at all?" She tilted her head in curiosity. "Blood is blood..."

He shook his head and sighed. "Not exactly. I can drink from animals to keep from dropping dead, but there is literally nothing in it for me. Animals don't have the quintessence or vitality that humans have." He made a face. "That humans are supposed to have, anyway."

"If you were truly grateful for your life, you would find another town to hunt in."

He smiled and nodded. "Very well, then. I'll hunt in another town."

Her eyes opened wide. "Just like that?"

"Sure." He nodded again. "However, I only have four hours to be settled for the daylight hours."

"Then you'd better hurry."

"I intend to." He raised a brow and gave her a tight smile. "But I need to feed before I can leave." He took a casual step toward her. "And since you chased off my original quarry..."

"What?" Rowan took a startled half step back, then jabbed a finger at him. "Hey, I saved your undead ass from that demon!"

"Which is why I agreed to hunt elsewhere." He shrugged and casually stepped closer. "After tonight." His smile grew sharp and pointed.

Rowan took a step back. "Didn't you snack on the sorcerer?"

He made a face. "Hell, no, that would have been pure sewage." He took another casual step toward her. "And I'm starved."

Rowan started backing away in alarm. He followed her with long slow strides. "You are *so* not feeding on me." His approaching steps were unnervingly silent.

"Stop me." His eyes kindled and blazed like coals.

Shit! She turned to bolt. Faster than she could see, he reached out and captured her upper arm. She was jerked to a halt and whirled to face him. She twisted to break his grip, but his hand was wrapped around her arm like steel.

"Don't try to fight, you'll only bruise yourself." His voice was soft but firm. "I don't want to hurt you."

"Then let go…" She twisted to swing the large bag in her hand, but his other hand closed on the strap and jerked it. The bag dropped to the ground.

"Look at me," he said softly.

Rowan averted her eyes from his glowing orbs. "I need," she whispered under her breath and wracked her brain. The Powers That Be were usually very swift in answer to her needs, but she had to ask out loud before they would deliver. For some strange reason, that was how her magic worked.

He reeled her in by her sleeve. "It'll be better for you if you let me put you under hypnosis." His voice was deep and soothing.

Better for me? Rowan looked everywhere but at his face. *I'll just bet.* He was incredibly strong. Her boot-heels skidded unpleasantly on the cement walk. He released her sleeve, then captured her wrist with a motion that only took a split second. He pressed her hand over his heart.

He's warm? She felt a thump under her palm. *He has a heartbeat?*

"I can make it very pleasurable for you." The Germanic lilt to his words shimmered down her spine with the shadowy brush of dark velvet.

"No, thank you." *Jeeze, his voice is turning me on.* She bit her lip. *What the hell do I need? What will hold off a vampire? Oh, wait…*

"I need a holy item or a religious symbol." Rowan barely breathed the words, then felt a pinch at her neck. *A religious symbol…* She pulled her silver chain from under her coat. Her pentacle popped out and blazed like a miniature sun.

"Shit," he hissed. He flinched back, but didn't release her wrist. He growled and held up a hand to block the small blaze of light from his eyes. "Something that small isn't going to do you much good, but it is pissing me off. Get rid of it."

Wait a minute, I'm a high priestess; technically my whole body is sacred. Rowan pressed her free hand over her heart and lifted her eyes to the vampire. "My Lady," she whispered. There was a curious tingling and warm sensation in her blood. She watched the veins in her captured hand suddenly ignite with a tracery of blue-white light that brightened until it blazed from her hand.

"Shit, that hurts!" He released her and lunged away.

Light radiated from under her coat, enough to seemingly reverse shadows like a photograph negative. *Whoa, cool. I didn't know I could do this!* She smiled and picked up her bag. *Wow, this feels good, really good...* The parking lot was just beyond the graveyard, and he was standing in her path. Rowan took a step toward him and it was his turn to back away. Her coat and long hair floated out behind her, floating on the soft wind of power. She took another step, and then another.

He backed away from her. "What the Hell is that?" The light from her face and limbs was bright enough that he cast a shadow.

"I guess I forgot to tell you." She felt like she was walking on air, she could barely feel the ground. "I'm a practicing witch. That makes me clergy." *Of a sort...* Rowan's thoughts were getting decidedly light and floaty. She couldn't stop smiling. *Oops, can't keep this up long or I won't be able to drive.* She laughed softly. *No, really, officer, I'm high on my religion.*

The vampire was driven back by her radiance and frustration marked his face. "Damn it!" The vampire turned and fled, his long coat flying out like wings. With incredible speed, he was gone from sight.

"Thank you, my Lady," she whispered to her deity. The light faded from her skin. *Well, that is a handy trick to have. Fortuneteller three points, creatures of darkness, still at zero...* She took a step and almost stumbled. Her body felt heavy and off balance, like she had just climbed out of a swimming pool.

Placing her feet carefully, she continued past the graveyard to the parking lot. Slowly the feeling of heaviness wore off, but exhaustion quickly took its place. *Uh oh... I'm probably gonna have to pay big for this magical expenditure...*

The broad, well-lit parking lot was empty of cars except for hers. Rowan unlocked her back door of her black Saturn, and dropped her satchel on the floorboard. She closed the back door and the pentacle blazed to sudden life. Alarmed, she whirled around.

Rowan was shoved hard against the side of her car. She gasped. Her chain was grabbed and yanked painfully from her neck. Her pentacle went spinning off into the darkness like a shooting star.

The vampire's eyes gleamed Hell-yellow bright from only inches away. "You're not glowing anymore." A hand cupped under her chin, roughly tilting her head back and exposing her throat.

"Lady," she choked out and brought her hands up. Light blazed from her palms. Her arms bloomed with an inner explosion of spreading light until her entire body was suffused and glowing.

"Ow, shit," he spat, releasing her. He lunged away from her with an incredible leap. "Damn it, that hurts."

Rowan bared her teeth in a feral grin. "Get it through your thick, undead skull; I'm not on the menu." She coughed and rubbed at her throat. *I'm going to have a bruise, I think...*

"I've never met anyone who could hold off a vampire." He circled her just outside the circle of light "What the Hell are you?"

Rowan shrugged. "I told you, I'm a witch."

He sneered. "I've met witches before and they couldn't do anything like that." He waved his hand at her pulsing glow.

"I think it has to do with faith." Rowan tucked her hands under her arms. It was cold and she was not dressed for standing around in it. Her radiance felt good, but far from warm.

"Faith?" He gave her a disgusted look. "I've taken priests and they've never done anything like that, either."

"Don't know what to tell you." She frowned, working to keep her thoughts focused. The radiance was making her light-headed, only this time it was stronger. She could feel her thoughts trying to drift away. "So, are you ready to give up on me now? It's cold and I want to go home."

"Do you have a card?"

Rowan blinked at him. "What?" Her mind was definitely starting to drift. *Shit, I'm going to have to sit here until I can think straight enough to drive.*

"Can I contact you?"

She frowned. "What for?"

"I run across weird shit, like that sorcerer, every now and again. I can use a good source of accurate occult information." He shrugged. "Everyone at the club said that your readings were very reliable and that you knew your arcane shit." He raised a sarcastic brow. "Apparently, they're right."

"You were asking about me?" Rowan couldn't tell if she was offended or flattered.

"Sure." His smile was slow and utterly sexy. "Technically you were my first choice, but I couldn't get anywhere near you. You always had too many people around you."

Rowan made a tart face. "Just what I always wanted to be, first on the menu."

He frowned. "I like redheads, especially ones that look as good as you do in a corset." He was staring at her chest, and then he smiled.

Rowan felt her sex-drive sit up and take notice. *Brain to libido: I don't care how cute he is; he's a vampire. Get over it.*

"Seriously, will you let me contact you?" He took a step closer to the car. "You're the only fully functional witch I've ever met."

"Will you swear not to attack me again?"

He grinned. "Sure."

"Good." Rowan smiled right back. "I want you to spill some blood, then swear on it that you'll never seek to harm me."

"What?" he looked at her, dumbfounded.

"Do it." Rowan raised a brow. "Spill your own blood and I'll believe you."

"Fuck," he said softly.

"If you're going to get to the next town, you are running out of time." Rowan smiled and shrugged. "I'm perfectly okay with not giving a vampire my contact information, so if you want it, you'd better hurry up and make up your mind."

"Bitch," he said softly, then raised his hand to his mouth. He nipped a finger, then held up his hand. In the glow of her light the red of his blood sliding down his palm was very vivid. "What do you want me to swear?"

"That you will never seek to harm me." Rowan could feel her mind expanding within her skull. She was having a hard time concentrating. *Hell, I'm running out of time, too. I have to stop radiating light real soon.*

"I so swear." He raised a brow. "Will that do?"

"Say the words." A flicker of motion caught her eye. She could see movement in the graveyard behind the fence that bordered the parking lot. *Ghosts. I'm looking at ghosts. There's more to this radiance than I thought.*

She heard him growl and her eyes jerked back to his face. The blood was running down his upraised wrist. "Say it," she repeated.

"I swear never to seek to harm you," he bit out, then closed his hand in a fist. "There."

"Accepted." Her light winked out. She rocked on her feet and fell against the side of the car with exhaustion. Her eyes fluttered closed and she felt herself hit the nice, comfortable pavement.

* * * *

Rowan opened her eyes to find herself cradled in the vampire's arms, sprawled over his lap. He knelt on the tarmac with her head over his arm and her long hair spilling over them both. She blinked up at him. His eyes were no longer orbs of flame-lit copper but a normal, hazel brown. She could feel the cool brush of death and the subtle wrongness that marked him as a predator and a vampire, but she felt perfectly safe in his embrace. *I don't feel like I've been bitten...*

"You passed out." He frowned down at her. "What happened?"

"I can't hold the radiance for very long. It takes a lot out of me." Rowan suddenly grinned. "It makes me light-headed."

He gave her a disgusted look. "Bad pun." He shook his head, then casually stood straight up with her in his arms.

Rowan blinked as he set her on her feet. *Wow, he's incredibly strong. He lifted me like I was a doll.* Abruptly, he released her. Rowan staggered, grabbing for the side of her car for balance.

Suddenly, his mouth fell open. "Wait a minute, you mean that you would have eventually passed out?"

She shrugged and bit her lip. "Looks that way."

"Damn it, I can't believe I swore on my blood when all I had to do was wait." He looked at her with a frown. "You know, you don't even smell the same."

Her brows shot up. "I don't?"

He shook his head. "You no longer smell like food."

Rowan bit back a grin. *The oath worked! Hot shit!*

He leaned back against the side of her car with his arms crossed. "I don't believe this." He looked over at her with annoyance. "Damn it, you actually put a spell on me!"

Rowan couldn't stop smiling and dug for her car keys. "Hey, for the record, you spilled your own blood, so you put that spell on yourself." With shaking hands, she unlocked her car door. "I'm sure there are lots of other people you can bite."

"Right. Whatever," he said in complete disgust. "Piss! I don't believe I'm bound by a fucking blood oath."

She ducked to sit in her driver's seat then leaned over to dig in her Arte bag. Clumsily, she got back out of the car to thrust a small rectangle of paper into his cool palm. "Here's my card. You can email or call me."

"Great," he said without enthusiasm, then eyed her with speculation.

"What?"

With inhuman speed, he grabbed her by the shoulders and pressed his lips to hers. Startled, her mouth opened and his tongue surged in. He turned his head, angling his mouth to cover hers, then thoroughly and expertly kissed her with long, slow swipes of his tongue.

Without thought, she kissed him back, her tongue moving against his, exploring his mouth. He tasted of darkness and shadows, but it was surprisingly warm and wet. *He doesn't taste dead.* Her body clenched in sudden and voracious carnal response. *He's a very good kisser...* Rowan let out a small sound. Her hands fisted in his coat and her eyes fluttered closed. His arm closed around her waist, pulling her tightly against him.

She felt a small, sharp prick. She'd jabbed herself on one of his teeth. The taste of sweet copper bloomed. *Uh, oh.* She felt herself lifted from her feet and he sucked at the small burning wound on her tongue. He seemed to be getting warmer.

He broke the kiss and stared at her from barely an inch away. "Damn, I haven't fed this well in years." His eyes were pools of fire surrounded by thin rings of beaten copper. A tiny smear of blood escaped the corner of his mouth. He chased after it with his tongue.

I don't feel like part of my soul has been sucked out, or even dented. Rowan frowned. "It was only a scratch. You barely had any."

"Apparently your quintessence is supercharged. I only needed a little." He grinned, showing the sharp points of his teeth. "I won't need to feed again for a few days."

Rowan glared at him. "What the hell was that kiss for, anyway?"

"I swore not to harm you." He grinned. "I never said I wouldn't seduce you."

"What?" Her mouth fell open.

"I have a few hours before I have to go." He let her slide down his body, then pressed her back against the car.

She could feel the firm strength of his body and the rigid length of an impressive erection letting her know, in no uncertain terms, that he was more than interested in something other than food. His hips swiveled against hers with a slow, suggestive roll. Her panties became embarrassingly moist.

"I'll make it good, I promise." He licked his reddened lips and smiled.

"Oh, no, we will *so* not go there." She shoved against his chest. It did as much good as shoving against a rooted tree trunk. "Not with you!"

"Why not?" His smile drained away and his lip curled back, baring an over-long incisor. "I can practically taste how much you want me," he said with complete conviction.

Rowan winced. *Mother of us all, he's right. I want him so bad I'm shaking with it.* She took a deep breath, and it was a mistake. His scent was redolent of leather and sandalwood soap. He smelled warm and very masculine. Moisture pooled in low, hidden places. "Let me go. Please," she said very softly.

"Damn it..." He abruptly released her and turned away with both hands curled into fists up in the air.

She was forced to put a hand against her car to stand. Her knees were rubber. *I don't believe he actually let me go...* The night was suddenly a lot colder.

He turned toward her and was suddenly standing only inches away. "Admit it, witch, you want me as much as I want you."

Startled, Rowan backed hard into her car door. *Well, he is a vampire...* She blushed fiercely. If the legends had any truth in them, there was probably no way she could hide her body's physical reactions from his sharper senses. "Yeah, I feel the lust," she grudgingly admitted. "But that doesn't mean I am going to sleep with you."

"Why the Hell not?" He planted his fists on his hips and towered over her, glaring angrily.

Rowan swallowed. "Because I will absolutely not have anything to do with something that preys on humans."

He frowned. "I'm not 'a something', I'm a man."

"Okay, you're a man. You still prey on human beings," she

ground out.

"So, I'm a predator, what of it?"

Rowan looked at him in surprise. "You see nothing wrong with this?"

"It's not as if I kill them." His brow furrowed. "Look, there's a lot worse than me running around."

"Really?" Rowan cocked a brow up at him and tucked her chilled hands into her armpits. "You're the only true vampire I've encountered so far, and you admit to preying on people."

"Aren't you forgetting the sorcerer?" He tilted his head to the side sarcastically. "You know, the one that blew up the club? That was a lot nastier than I've ever thought of being."

"Really?" she said dryly.

"Really." He curled his lip. "Just so you know, that was the kind that didn't just kill people, it ate people, preferably while still kicking and screaming. I've run into them before."

"Yeah, you're right..." She nodded. "That was a nastier creature of darkness than you."

"Oh, gee, thanks... I think." He turned to face the empty parking lot and leaned back heavily against the car next to her.

She turned her head and frowned up at him. "I've still never run across anything like either of you before."

"Well, then count yourself lucky." He looked over at the graveyard at the far end of the parking lot. "I run into shit like that pretty regular."

"In that case, you're probably drawing them, so you definitely don't need to be in my town. I am not a strong enough witch to deal with things like that on a regular basis."

"Drawing them?" He turned his head to look at her. "How do you figure that?"

Rowan shrugged, "I don't know. *Like unto like*, maybe?"

You," he jabbed a finger at her, "are a snide little bitch."

"I'll take that as a compliment." She nodded then raised a brow. "Does this mean you'll leave me alone now?"

He rolled onto his side and leaned an elbow on the roof of her car. "How's about a good-bye kiss?" He smiled.

Rowan's heart lurched in her chest in reaction to his smile and her eyes focused on his lips. She swallowed hard and jerked her eyes from his mouth. "Don't you ever give up?"

"Only if I'm forced to." He straightened up. "Are you absolutely sure that you don't want to...uh, spend some quality time?"

Rowan pressed the fingers of one hand to her temples and pointed toward the graveyard with the other. "You need to go."

"Oh, all right." He sighed dramatically.

Rowan looked at him in surprise. *He's actually leaving?*

He flashed her a tight smile. "See you later." Between one moment and the next, he was gone.

"I certainly hope not," Rowan said softly and jerked open her car door. She hurriedly slid behind the wheel and locked the door with trembling fingers. *That was a really close call...* Rowan couldn't tell if she was shaking in reaction to her encounter with a blood-sucking vampire, the magical drain from the radiance she had been forced to pour forth, or the vampire's toe-curling kisses.

"Gods, I need a cigarette..." She reached over and dug out one of her black cigarettes and lit it with unsteady hands. *Let's be honest here, that was the best damned kiss I ever had.* She cringed at her pun. *Even if I did nick my tongue...* She froze where she sat. *Oh, Goddess, he drank my blood. I hope that didn't give him any kind of hold on me.*

It was over ten minutes before she was able to stop shaking enough to drive out of the parking lot.

* * * *

Rowan awoke on the edge of dawn burning with fever and frustrated carnal hunger. She could feel moisture on her inner thighs. She brushed her hand across her breasts. Her nipples were swollen and tight. *I should have expected this...*

Fortune-telling usually sharpened her sexual appetites, but the blatant use of magic to break the sorcerer's hold on the vampire, then the radiance she had generated to protect herself, had only aggravated her need for sexual release. *With the bar going up in flames and then dealing with the vampire, I didn't have a chance to pick up a guy to take to bed and take care of this.*

Sex and magic...

The story of her life. One was joined to the other in a never-ending circle-dance. The rush of sexual heat awakened her full magical power with her first mismanaged fumble in the backseat of a boy's beat-up car. Power blazed forth with his premature ejaculation and the world opened. Color had burst forth in the pit of night; the colors of thought, emotion and life itself.

In that instant, when her magic first uncurled, warm and alive within her, she discovered her would-be lover's greed for status amongst his teenaged peers. She saw and tasted his self-interested thoughts of burying himself between the thighs of a pretty untouched girl, a known virgin, and his intent to brag of the event that very night. He did not care for her; he only cared to make his own reputation as stud.

Indignant and humiliated, she called him to task for his intent. She also succeeded in terrifying him with her willingness to report to every girl in school of his inability to take her virginity because of his lack of control.

He had driven her home, furious with indignation and fear.

She had gone to school the next day, head held high and waited to hear what traveled on the high-school grapevine. She was pleased to hear nothing of the boy's conquest of her virginity; however, revenge remained his. For the first time, the word Witch was used in connection to her name. Virginity remained hers, into college. No one in school would go anywhere near a Witch.

She squeezed her thighs together to relieve the sensual ache, knowing that it wasn't going to help. She bit her lip and her fingers found the tender bud hidden in her feminine folds. Her fingers danced on her slippery flesh. Her body tightened and climax burned quickly. She sighed in repletion, but tension still shimmered through her body, signaling that she was far from satisfied. *Damn, this is probably going to take a while.*

She had learned the hard way that true Magic demanded sex in return, or more precisely, orgasm, to replenish. But orgasm, encouraged by her own hands, was not enough to feed the hungry beast that was her power. This lesson was learned with her triumphant conquest of the dormitory ghost in her first year of college.

The rush of ravenous sensual hunger caught her off-guard. Panting with need, she had stumbled back toward her lonely bed, only to encounter a professor walking the halls. She had stopped in a corner to dip her hands into her panties for a moment of relief when he saw her. The professor took swift advantage of the situation. And so her virginity was finally lost, with her skirt up around her waist, her panties around one ankle, against the dormitory wall with his hand muffling her moans. She wore the bite bruises on her breasts for a full week.

Then the other problem became manifest.

The professor, it seemed, was only able to gain an erection in her company. It took two whole weeks of careful avoidance for his pursuit to end. Her only consolation was that he had not been one of her instructors, so her grades had not suffered.

She had tried controlling her sexual appetite by not doing true magic, but there was always another ghost to dispel, another spell to break, an accident to prevent, another person in need of her skills as a fortune-teller... She had no idea how these people even found her. She didn't have a sign on her door, but the calls still came and usually in the middle of the night.

"A friend of a friend said you could help me," was how the calls began. "Help me," was the whip that drove her. Her magic was fueled by sex, but her abilities were triggered by need. She had tried refusing and discovered that her powers left her completely until she responded to their summons—their need.

She had refused once, and once had been enough. Utter magical blindness, the inability to feel the life coursing around her or sense what anyone's intentions were at a glance was a terrifying experience. She learned her lesson and didn't ever want to repeat it.

Because of her magic, the need for a lover was unavoidable. However, tonight there was no one but herself.

She rolled over onto her stomach, coming up on her knees. One hand fisted in the pillows, she strove to give her body what it wanted. Her fingers danced while the memory of the vampire's kiss and his strong body holding hers, burned in her mind. She panted, groaned and shuddered hard with yet another climax and collapsed among her blankets.

The hunger still raged.

"Damn it," she whimpered into her pillows. "I should have taken the vampire up on his offer."

❧ Four ❧

Correspondence

The email appeared on Rowan's computer on Monday.

I have a problem. A distant cousin has dropped in to
say hi.
Can you advise?
V^^V

Rowan sat at the kitchen table and frowned at her computer
screen. "That signature has to be from the vampire." She shook her
head. Only two days had passed and he had a problem already?
"Well, that was quick." There was a cell phone number after the
signature followed by the phrase; *Call anytime.* She turned around
and checked her kitchen clock. It was two in the afternoon on a
bright sunny day.

"Moron." Rowan picked up her cordless phone. *Let's see, what
kind of message can I leave and then do to avoid his return message
after sunset?* She smiled and dialed the number.

The phone rang twice. "Hello?" The voice was digitized.

Rowan's brows rose. "Hi, this is Rowan." She bit her lip. *Shit, he didn't give me his name. I don't know who to leave this message for!*

"Oh, hi. I didn't think you'd answer my email that fast."

Rowan blinked. "Is it actually you?" She checked the window. *Yep, it's still daylight.*

"Yeah, this is my cell phone."

Rowan frowned. "Aren't you supposed to sleep during the day?"

She heard a sound that might have been an undignified snort. "Nope, I just have to stay out of direct sunlight. I can even go out in daylight as long as I wear a coat, sunglasses and a hat."

"And a hundred proof sun-block?"

"Never leave home without it." He chuckled softly. "The miracles of modern science."

"Okay. Um, I don't know what to call you." She made a face at the wall. *Other than amazingly cute, blood-sucking parasite?* "Cute signature on your email, by the way."

"Glad you like the signature." He laughed. "And I'm Rick."

Vampire Rick? Rowan swallowed hard to keep from laughing out loud. "Well, Rick, what can I do for you?"

"I have a guest."

She nodded then realized that he couldn't see the gesture. "Your note said that he was a cousin?"

"You could say that."

"A cousin. You mean he's like you, he's a… "

"You don't need to say it." There was a pause. "He's very, very distantly related and from the old country."

"Old country?" She frowned.

"Yeah, old country. As in from Europe. I think he's Russian, Czarist Russian, not Soviet Russian."

"Okay." Rowan blinked at the wall. "And?" she pressed.

"And, I can't get rid of him," he said very softly.

"I see…" Rowan bit her lip and frowned. "Um, Rick, I really don't think any of the more traditional methods for getting rid of unwanted, um, cousins, are going to work for you." She had a sudden vision of Rick attempting to chase off another vampire by holding out a cross with oven mitts on. She bent over in her chair to muffle her sudden fit of nervous giggles.

"You don't say." His voice was very dry. "Are you laughing at me?"

"Uh, no." She coughed and wiped her eyes. "Of course not." She cleared her throat. "Um, how did you get, uh…I mean, how did your cousin find you?"

"Would you believe, I found him on my couch yesterday, when I got up?"

Rowan's brows rose. "Are you serious?"

"Deadly."

"Can't you just drive him off? You are supposed to be stronger, faster, etcetera, etcetera?"

"He's an older…cousin. A lots older cousin."

The frustration traveled over the phone. She could just imagine his handsome face frowning while he spoke through gritted teeth.

"How much older?"

"You know that mirror thing with us?"

"I think so…" She frowned. *Is he talking about the seriously traditional no-reflection thing? But, I thought I saw him reflected in the mirror over the bar?*

"Let's just say, that if I needed to check the closeness of a shave, I can actually do so. He can't."

"You shave?"

"Uh, no." She thought she heard a soft growl. "But the point is, if I wanted to, I could actually see what I'm doing." There was a pause. "He can't. There's not a trace of him, not even a shadow. Come to think of it, I don't think he casts a shadow either."

"Oh, weird…" Rowan got up from her chair. "Wait a minute, that doesn't make sense. Either you are there enough to have a reflection and a shadow, or you aren't. What the Hell is he? A ghost?"

"Well, for someone who isn't there and might be a ghost, he sure is taking up a lot of room on the couch in my TV room." Rick's voice was a harried whisper. "Any ideas?"

Rowan frowned. "So far, the only thing I can think of is a basic barrier spell. But, anything that might work on your um, cousin, might cause a problem for you too." She nibbled on her bottom lip. "I'm going to have to do some serious research on this one. Whatever I come up with will probably have to be made for you specifically."

"I figured as much." She could hear fingers tapping over the phone. Rick was a lot more agitated than he was letting on. "When can you come up here?"

Rowan's mouth fell open. "You want me to go there? To where you live?"

"You're the um, professional. I have no clue how to do this kind of thing."

"Look, I have no interest in learning secrets that might get me killed, such as where you live. I'll email you the, uh, recipe."

"I still have to get him out of the house before the uh, thing can be set, right?"

Rowan frowned. "Yeah, so?"

"Now do you see my problem? It's probably going to take your glow-in-the-dark routine to send this one packing. Then you can cook up your whatever it is to keep him out."

She made a sour face, knowing that he couldn't see it. Rowan absolutely did not want to go out there. He was cute, sexy and very interested; unfortunately she seemed to be just as drawn to him. Using her magic would generate an appetite for sex that would make her very vulnerable to his persuasion. She could already feel her body's simmering awareness. *I don't need to hop in the sack with a vampire.* She paced the kitchen fishing for an excuse. "You are just as much a threat to humanity as the other guy, how do you know I won't go up there and just fry both your asses?"

"Easy." She could almost hear his grin. "I'll meet you somewhere neutral, like a diner or something and have you do the same thing I did. We can go from there."

Rowan frowned. "Do what you did?"

"Yeah, you can swear not to harm me." Rick chuckled. "Exactly the same way I did."

"Forget it, I am not going." She angrily stood up, jerking her kitchen chair back. Rowan flinched. The sound of the scraping chair had traveled over the phone-line. *I need a cigarette...*

"You're supposed to be, um, one of the good guys, aren't you?" he said softly. "Isn't there some kind of rule that says you have to answer a call for help, especially in your particular, um, practice?"

Rowan flinched. "I thought you said you didn't know anything about this stuff?"

"I've been doing some reading."

*Some reading, he says...*Rowan swept her hand down her face. *What the Hell is he reading? I had to learn that lesson the hard way.* And she didn't want to repeat it. *Now I really need a cigarette...* She picked up her clove cigarettes and lighter from the table

"Well, isn't there?" he pressed. "Along with something about telling the truth to a direct question, sort of thing?"

Damn it all! Rowans marched the cell phone out onto her back porch. *I can't believe a vampire is pressuring me for help! This is so messed up...*

"I can hear you pacing and you haven't said no, so I'm assuming I'm right." He sounded insufferably pleased with himself.

Rowan stood in a warm patch of sunlight and gritted her teeth. "Since when does the good guy ride to the rescue of the bad guy?" She frowned fiercely, lit her black cigarette, then exhaled the fragrant smoke.

"How about when the bad guy is smart enough to ask?" He definitely sounded extremely pleased with himself.

"You suck," she said through clenched teeth.

"Why yes, I do." He actually chuckled. "There's a diner right around the corner from my house. I'll email you directions. Give me a day to expect you."

"You are gonna owe me big for this," she spat.

"I'll write you a check. When can I expect you?"

Rowan blinked at the tree. "You have a checking account?"

He sighed. "And a credit card, a cell phone and a computer, just like the rest of the world."

"Good, cause I expect a fat one for this little favor." She paced and her heels thumped on the wood floor of the porch. "Do you actually have a job?"

"I work in an office, just like every body else. As a matter of fact, I'm calling from my desk."

"Your desk?" Rowan had a sudden vision of her devastatingly handsome vampire in a business suit, toting a briefcase. She shook her head. *Too weird...*

He chuckled. "I told you, I just have to stay out of direct sunlight and most offices are fairly windowless. My personal office is windowless. I own a small company."

Rowan's mouth fell open. "You own a company?"

"I, um," he coughed. "I inherited it. My um, grandfather invested very wisely. It's a long story and I'm racking up a hefty bill on my cell phone here. Give me a day to expect you."

"How about next year?" she said sweetly.

"Very funny." Impatience marked his voice. "How about today? I live in Watertown."

"Not today, Watertown is about four hours down the highway, that means an eight-hour turn around drive and it's already after two. I do not want to make a four-hour drive after I've done spell-work, I'll pass out and wreck on the way home. I'm going to need to arrange for a place to sleep." Rowan rubbed the back of her neck in frustration. *I can't believe I'm actually going to do this...*

"Don't worry, I make sure you have a place to spend the night." Rick's fingers tapped impatiently again. "Day, please? Preferably this week?"

"I have to make arrangements with a friend to come in and check my cat. How about Friday afternoon?"

"It's Monday. I don't know if I can deal with um, my cousin for that long." He sighed. "He's been here since yesterday and I need to get some sleep. Wait a minute you have a cat? Isn't that a little cliché?"

"She's a gray tabby, not a black Persian, get over it. You haven't slept with him there? At all?"

"Let's put it this way," Rick whispered harshly. "I have yet to see him um, dine and don't like the way he watches me. I got a bad feeling that his appetite is even more refined than mine."

"More refined?" Rowan frowned. *Does this mean he drinks something other than blood?*

"I told you why I uh, drink as much as I do. It's real possible that he's in my living room because he can't get his um, full nutritional value from ordinary, um, sources."

"He feeds off of other, um, members of his own family? Isn't that against the rules somewhere?"

"I don't know for sure what he finds, um, appetizing, but from the way he's always watching me, I get the impression that Klaus doesn't exactly take the uh, 'no relatives' rule into account." He sighed and added softly. "Or any other rules for that matter."

Rowan grinned. "So, he thinks you're chock full of vitamins?"

"Keep laughing. Remember, I found you very appetizing and you're not that far away. If he gets me, as powerful as you are, you could be next on the menu."

Rowan felt a slight shiver. *And he wants me to go out of my way to meet him?*

Rick was tapping again. "How about tomorrow?"

"Uh, I can't leave tomorrow." *Gods, no! I do not want to deal with vampires tomorrow...* Rowan turned to look at the collection of magic tomes on her shelf. "I have to go to work, laundry to finish."

"Work? What else do you do, beside the, uh, hocus-pocus stuff?"

"The hocus-pocus stuff doesn't give me an income to live off of." She closed her eyes and sighed. *Not that my other job does either.* "I work in the branch library right by the courthouse."

"You're kidding?" She clearly heard him choke back a laugh. "You're a librarian?"

"I'm a research assistant, actually. I help locate resources for students and professors."

"A Witch who's a librarian..." He was sniggering, the wretch. "What time to you get out of work?

"Four, and I'll have to pack, too."

"Pack? For an overnight trip?"

She sighed. "Yes, pack. Quit your bitching. I expect you to at least take me out to dinner, and I'm a girl. How about Wednesday after work? I have Thursday and Friday off for the holiday."

"What are you doing home at two in the afternoon today?"

"If you must know, I called in, they owe me vacation time."

"Are you all right?" His voice had dropped to a whisper and he actually sounded concerned.

"Yeah, I'm fine, just tired." She winced. *I am not about to explain that I needed to catch up on sleep because I haven't had any all weekend from masturbating—with him as my sexual fantasy.* She took a deep breath. "How about Wednesday?"

"Wednesday's good, and I know a nice restaurant."

"A restaurant that's not a diner?"

"Yes, a restaurant that's not a diner. If you can take care of my cousin, that's the least I can do." She thought she could hear a soft chuckle. "I'll send you directions by email."

"I am so looking forward to this," she said very dryly.

"I can tell." She could also tell that he was grinning. "What's your cell phone number, in case you get lost?"

"I don't have one," she said with a small amount of satisfaction.

"You don't have a cell phone?"

Rowan made a face. "Hell no! I already get all kinds of phone calls from people that need one magical thing or another; I'm not about to carry a phone that lets them find me faster! If I get lost I'll find a payphone."

"Alright...see you Wednesday." The phone cut off.

Rowan lit another cigarette. "Terrific, I've been hired to ward a vampire's house from another vampire." She bit her lip. "I just hope I can keep my sexual appetite under control." She collapsed into one of the lawn chairs on her porch. "Maybe I should find a safer career? Like law enforcement."

❧ Five ❧

Assignation

A round five Wednesday evening, Rowan drove her Saturn down Watertown's main street. "Sam's Diner is supposed to be around here somewhere," Rowan muttered and stopped her black Saturn at the traffic light guarding the intersection of Commonwealth Avenue and Main. The drive had been long and dull. She yawned. *Thank all that's holy that I was able to get out at lunch rather than four, or I'd be asleep at the wheel.*

The darkening sky cast the small town into deep shadow and set off a cascade of oncoming streetlights. The slipping grasp of sunlight stained the sky with smears of indigo, violet and flame behind the winter-barren trees of the surrounding hills.

She glanced right, then left. Her brow furrowed. The gleam of silver and the glow of green peeked out behind a little strip mall on her far left. "Rick's email said to look for the green neon, so that has to be it." She drove through the light then darted over to the far left across traffic, pulling sharply into the small parking lot that surrounded the strip mall. She drove through the lot, headed for the far end and her Saturn thumped over a few low speed bumps.

A bullet-shaped diner of gleaming chrome glimmered under tall streetlights. It looked like it belonged on a nineteen-fifties movie set.

The building was completely outlined in glowing green neon and surrounded by well-groomed holly bushes. Silvered and reflective windows betrayed nothing of the interior. A huge round sign, also generously outlined in vivid green neon, sported a familiar Dr. Seuss character running with a plate in his hand. The marquee spelled out: Eat at Sam's.

Rowan smiled. "This has to be it." She stepped out of the Saturn and pulled on the black denim jacket that matched her jeans. The evening was growing chilly and her plain red T-shirt just wasn't warm enough. She fished her long red ponytail out from within her coat, then grabbed for her red velvet shoulder bag.

As she walked toward the chrome and glass doors, she spotted a midnight blue Dodge Viper parked by the door. "Looks like the vampire made it ahead of me." She shook her head with a small smile. He had mentioned it in his last email. "A vampire that drives a Dodge Viper..." She could feel nervousness mixing with a strange, physical excitement. As much as she was not looking forward to dealing with vampires, she was also honest enough to realize that she was pleased that Rick had wanted to see her.

The diner's interior was decorated with bright chrome and strong primary colors accenting a predominating neon green. Framed and poster-sized Dr. Seuss illustrations hung on the walls. Next to the register stood a beautifully restored Wurlitzer jukebox aglow with bubbling tubes and full of forty-five records from the nineteen-fifties. Elvis Presley was wailing away over the stereo system. The smell of burgers and fries made her stomach growl with hunger.

Rick was sitting in a booth by a broad, tinted window that overlooked his Dodge Viper. He looked up and spotting her, smiled and waved. Rowan smiled in return, then strode down the narrow aisle to his booth. The strong light of the diner showed the clean, sharp lines of his face to perfection. *Damn, I forgot just how cute he really was.*

Rick waved a hand toward the bench across from him. "Thank you for coming all the way out here. How was the drive?"

Rowan raised a brow. "Long, boring." She tossed her velvet bag on the seat opposite him and slid in. Her eyes were drawn to his hand. He was absently rubbing his elegant fingers in the condensation on the half-full glass of cola on the table in front of him. She took a breath to control the pounding in her heart and the slow coil arousal building in her core. *This was such a bad idea...*

A waitress in a frilly apron came up and offered Rowan a menu. She glanced at the vampire. *I'm hungry, but I don't know how he feels about food being eaten in front of him.* Rowan bit her lip. "Is it all right if I order something?"

Rick grinned. "Sure, order what you like." He turned to the waitress. "Just put it on my bill." The waitress nodded and took Rowan's order. In minutes, the waitress returned with her soda.

"Good service," Rowan said with a small smile, then sipped on her soda. "Thank you for dinner, I'm starved."

Rick nodded. "You're welcome, and the service is one of the reasons that I like this place."

Rowan almost choked on her soda. "You eat food?" It came out in a tight whisper.

Rick raised a sarcastic brow. "Yes, just not a whole lot of it."

Rowan bit her lip. "Sorry, I guess I have a lot to learn about, um, you."

He shrugged. "That's okay, I have a lot to learn about you, too." He leaned forward over the table and whispered. "For example, I still don't understand how you just started glowing like that."

Rowan shrugged and whispered back. "I told you before, it has to do with faith. It came on as a result of calling on my Goddess for protection, so it's obviously some kind of holy or blessed radiance."

"Faith?" He gave her a disgusted look. "I've seen a few crosses and other holy objects do that, but your whole body lit up."

Rowan rolled her eyes. "I'm a witch. Unlike the major monotheistic religions, my body represents my deity rather than a symbol, like a cross or a star."

He sneered. "So I'm supposed to be evil, while you're... What?

Good?"

She grinned. "Well, obviously there's something about you that She just doesn't like."

"Look," he jabbed an angry finger at her. "I don't buy into all that damned and evil souls crap," he whispered harshly. "I have gone out of my way not to kill to feed and I've seen ordinary humans do things I couldn't dream up on a bad heroin dose. I've never seen anything glow in front of ordinary psychos."

She rolled her eyes. "So, you're personally not as evil as your kind is rumored to be. I'm happy for you." She leaned back in her seat. "My radiance is probably just a simple matter of my magic being stronger than yours."

He raised a sarcastic brow. "What's magic got to do with it? I'm just a predator."

"Just a predator?" She laughed out loud. Curious diners looked over at them and Rowan choked her laughter down. She leaned across the table. "Hello," she whispered. "It takes magic to animate the dead, and you are an animated dead man. That makes you magical."

The waitress came back with Rowan's burger and fries. They both leaned back into their seats and dropped into silence. The waitress left and Rick leaned across the table.

"I am not dead," he whispered.

"Really?" Rowan raised a sarcastic brow and picked up her hamburger. "When was the last time you had a doctor's appointment?" She took a bite. It was cooked to perfection.

His brows rose then he smiled. "Last year."

Rowan nearly choked on her burger and swallowed hastily. "When were you...um, when did you become this way?"

His smile was smug. "Nineteen forty-three."

She sat back in the booth. "Damn." She whistled softly. "So, the eternal youth thing is actually true." She looked to one side then stared hard. "And the doctors see nothing odd about you?"

He shrugged. "I have an abnormally low temperature, but

according to them, everything is roughly in working order."

"Roughly?"

"They say I have some kind of long-winded, terminal illness." He grinned. "It's a rare blood disease, but not unheard of." He leaned closer. "It makes it real easy to set up a sudden death right before I change identities."

Rowan tilted her head curiously and swallowed. "How often do you have to do that? Change identities? Become somebody new all over again?"

He played with his cola. "I've had to do it twice now." He frowned. "I just arrange a public suicide, put a note in the papers about my cremation, then go into hiding. Ten years later I show up as a relative."

Rowan bit, chewed and swallowed. "Hence your grandfather's company."

He nodded. "Every once in a while I run across someone who recognizes my face, but they just assume it's a family resemblance." He shrugged.

Rowan smiled. "What, no vampire hunters out to get you?"

He smiled back. "Not yet." He threw out a hand. "So there, I'm not magical, just diseased, which doesn't account for your glow-in-the-dark routine."

Rowan pursed her lips. "Diseased? With a terminal illness that doesn't kill, but keeps you young and gives you an appetite for blood?" She raised a brow. "That sounds suspiciously like magic to me."

"Magic, huh..." He snorted. "So where does this 'your magic verses my magic' glow thing come in?"

"Simple, my magic is reacting negatively to yours." She chewed and swallowed. "I'm just stronger magically than you are, so it bothers you rather than me."

He made a wry face. "So, it's not me being damned and you being holy, it's that your magic doesn't like mine? Then where did all this traditional 'Damned verses Holy' stuff come from?"

"You admit to being a predator, but I bet not every, uh, predator, stopped at murder."

His expression went very neutral. "No, they didn't."

"Well, there you go." Rowan sipped at her soda. "Killing is taboo in just about any religion, that instantly labeled your kind damned. When the priests used holy or rather, magical objects that glowed, that just proved to the common people that your kind was evil." She shrugged. "Simple propaganda."

"So holy objects are actually magical?" He frowned. "Since when is religion magic?"

"Ritual is ritual, is ritual..." Rowan sighed. "Religion is the frame that basic magic works in. It's all centered on belief. Whether it's for magical gain or just for blessing something, you're involving some kind of deity in some way, shape or form. A religious ritual generates magic and a magical ritual still calls on deific powers, or gods, for help. Historically, it took a holy person to do magic, magicians were priests and priests were magicians. Realistically, magic and religion are basically the same thing, they're practically interchangeable."

"Right..." Rick looked doubtful.

"If it makes you feel any better, my magic works on non-magical people, too, or I wouldn't be able to do tarot readings." She made a sour face. "You wouldn't believe how many people ask me if they'll go to Hell for getting their fortune told."

He shook his head. "I still don't see how I can be magical."

She nodded then raised a brow. "Let's see, were you born this way or did somebody do something to make you this way?"

His mouth made a thin tight line. "It was offered, I accepted."

She looked at him in surprise. "You agreed to be made into a vampire?" Her voice was a very soft whisper.

He turned his head and shrugged. "It seemed like a good idea at the time."

Being made into a vampire was a good idea at the time? Rowan just stared at him. "Did you know what you were getting into?"

"Some." He stared out the window. "He explained a few things, I learned the rest."

She shook her head. "Okay... Whoever did it must have used some kind of ritual means to make you the way you are."

"He didn't do any kind of ritual anything." He looked back at her. "We exchanged blood. He drank mine, then I drank his."

"You shared blood." Rowan threw out her hand. "That was your ritual."

His chin went up. "How?"

"Look, it's a long explanation, do we really have the time for this?"

"I'll make time." He crossed his arms over his chest. "How is sharing blood a ritual? How does this make me magical instead of damned?"

Rowan sighed. She could feel his hunger to know rolling from his skin. *Well, come to think of it, if I were a vampire that didn't kill, I'd want to know that I wasn't some damned soul condemned to hell just for existing.* She nodded. "All right, but you're getting the short version." She looked up at him. "You know how you're actually drinking some of the essence or soul from someone when you feed?"

"Yeah..."

"The sharing of blood is the intermingling of souls. That's ritual. Any time you involve one soul in contact with another soul, you're doing ritual because you've involved a deific power."

His brow furrowed. "So every time I feed..."

"You are replenishing your magic." She sipped at her soda.

He tilted his head to one side. "I'm drawn to artists and musicians, they seem to, um, satisfy my needs better than the average person. Are they magical?"

"Anything that involves the soul is magical." She shrugged. "Art and music are conceived in the soul, so their creators are magical by default."

"Then I only needed a little from you, because as a Witch you generate even more magic than they do?"

"Uh, yeah." Rowan bit her lip. *I do not think I want him knowing that I have to feed my magic, too—with sex...*

He shook his head. "Okay, I get the soul thing, but I don't quite grasp where this deific power comes in."

She tapped her glass with a finger. "Even in basic Christianity, the soul is divine, a literal piece of God."

His brows rose, then he smiled. "So I'm not the soulless damned?"

"You have a soul or you wouldn't be moving around. In the simplest of terms, it's what animates your body." Rowan gave him a sour smile, then munched on a French fry. "But don't get your hopes up over the damned part. There are lots of things that stain the soul irrevocably, magically and non-magically. You must have done a few nasty things in your life or that sorcerer in the Goth club wouldn't have made straight for you."

Rick's fingers tapped absently on the tabletop. "Maybe he just didn't like the way I looked."

Rowan shook her head slowly and pushed her empty plate to the side of the table. "Demons eat the souls of the corrupt to feed their own corruption. The innocent have nothing for demons to feed off of. That sorcerer targeted you right away. He didn't even look at anyone else, so you were first on his menu."

"If a demon is already living in a corrupted soul, why does the sorcerer need to go after others?"

Rowan played with her straw. "To keep his demon under control, a sorcerer has to feed it enough to keep his own soul intact. If he does not feed his demon, the demon will consume the sorcerer, killing him." She smiled grimly. "As I said before, the sorcerer went straight for you, so you had to have something the demon thought was tasty."

He gave her a bitter smile. "You're just full of good news..."

"As I say to all my clients," Rowan raised her glass in a salute. "Don't ask unless you really want to know."

He frowned. "You're sure that I'm magical?"

Rowan smiled then sipped her soda. "Sorry, Rick, but you are one big hunk of magic walking around. Hell, I knew you were magical as soon as I saw you. I could feel it rolling off your skin, and so can anyone with the sensitivity to it, which includes demons and sorcerers."

He smiled suddenly. "You think I'm a hunk?"

It figures that he'd focus on that. Rowan rolled her eyes. "Don't push your luck."

Rick made a sour face. He pulled a twenty-dollar bill from his folding wallet, then dropped it on the restaurant bill. "Come on." He slid out of the booth.

"Where are we going?" She grabbed her bag and slid from her side of the booth.

"The parking lot." Rick marched up the diner's isle.

Rowan had to walk quickly to keep up with him. "The parking lot?"

"Yep." He held the restaurant door open for her. "You have a promise to make."

"Oh, yeah." Rowan walked through the doors sourly. *Damn it, I'd hoped he'd forgotten about that.*

He led her over to the bushes at the far edge of the diner's parking lot and just out of casual sight. "We might as well get it over with now, so I can take you to my house to meet Klaus."

"Is this really necessary?" The night air was very chilly and Rowan was glad that she had thought to grab her jacket.

Rick turned to face her with a grim smile. "Absolutely." He crossed his arms over his broad chest. "I'm ready when you are."

Rowan sighed, then reached into her red velvet shoulder bag. She pulled out her small, red leather Arte pouch and dug out a plastic bag. Carefully, she unsealed a silver-dipped horseshoe nail.

Rick looked at the nail curiously. "What's that for?"

Rowan smiled grimly. "My teeth are not as sharp as yours. I had a friend of mine who is a tattoo artist put this nail in his steamer to sanitize it." She stabbed the sharp nail into the ring finger of her right hand. "Ow…" she muttered softly. Bright scarlet welled and trickled across her finger.

He stared at her finger and the heart of Rick's eyes ignited with flame. "I would have nipped it for you."

Rowan raised her brow. "Thanks, but no thanks. Ready?"

He nodded once. "Yeah, do it."

Rowan stared at the blood dripping down her finger. "I swear to avoid bringing you deliberate harm." *If I'm lucky, I can get away with a small change in the words.* Rowan looked up at him. "Will that do?"

He tilted his head but he was frowning slightly. "It sounds about right."

Yes! She took a soft, calming breath. "Do you accept?"

His frown deepened. "Wait a minute."

"What?" Rowan concentrated on looking innocent. *Stay calm and don't panic...*

A tight smile twisted his lips. "I think I said something more like: I swear never to seek to harm you."

Rowan raised her brows and deliberately widened her eyes. "That's pretty much what I said."

"Nice try, but no cigar." He raised a brow. "Since when is cheating allowed by your faith?"

Rowan frowned stubbornly. "Who's cheating?"

He rocked back on his heels. "Come on, just use the same words that I did."

Rowan's jaw clenched stubbornly. "What for?"

He tilted his head to one side. "Because I asked you to, and you're supposed to be one of the good guys, remember?"

Rowan let out a small sound of frustration and glared at him. "You asked me to come here to rescue your ass. Remember?"

He nodded. "Oh, I know exactly why I had you come here." He smiled suggestively. "Just say it the way I did and get it over with." His smile broadened to show the tips of his long teeth. "You better hurry. The more you bleed, the hungrier I get."

"I swear never to seek to harm you," she bit out. "There." She clenched her hands and felt the stickiness of blood in her right palm.

"Accepted."

Rowan felt a shudder sweep through her body and the hair on her arms rose. Her balance shifted and she rocked on her feet. *Shit, I didn't expect it to take that much magic...*Desire burst within, instantly soaking her panties.

"What was that?" Rick frowned at her. "Are you all right?

"That was just my magic adjusting to the blood oath." Rowan blinked at the vampire in surprise. *Am I feeling concern coming from him?*

"So the oath took?" He sniffed the air between them. "You smell different," he said softly.

Rowan shrugged. "Yeah, it took." She dug into her red velvet shoulder bag, then pulled out a tissue. "What do you mean, different?"

He caught her wrist before she could wipe her palm. He drew her palm to his mouth. "Allow me." His eyes glowed brighter than the streetlight.

"Hey!" She fisted her hand and pulled back. He was unbelievably strong and absolutely unmovable. "Wait a minute, this was not part of the deal!" Rowan shoved a hand between them. His body was very solid.

"I'm not going to hurt you, take it easy." His flame-lit copper eyes bored into hers from only inches away. "Open your hand," he said softly and tugged her closer.

She felt a shimmer of something brush against her mind. Her palm opened. She blinked in surprise. *Did he just zap me with some kind of mind-power?*

He turned his head and his tongue swept her palm. His mouth was warm and wet against her skin. Rowan's body pulsed with hungry awareness and her mind abruptly closed shop for the winter. Moisture soaked through her panties and dampened her jeans. He slowly cleaned the scarlet smears from her hand.

His lips closed over the wounded finger and he turned his head. His burning eyes locked on hers. He sucked very gently, drawing fresh blood from the small wound. She felt a slight sting. He swallowed, and she watched his throat work. His lips slowly released her finger with a moist, sucking sound. He lowered his head and brushed his reddened lips against hers. Without thought, she opened her mouth to receive his kiss. His tongue swept in to taste her. He was flavored with a hint of bright copper. She was inundated by the scent of potent male with an undercurrent of rich earth.

Rowan felt her knees weaken from the sensual overload. His arms came around her waist to support her. He pulled her firmly against his surprisingly warm body. She felt a broad hand on her bottom pressing her into his hips and the rigid length of his arousal against her belly. He rocked against her and deepened the kiss, hungrily sucking on her tongue and plump lower lip. Rowan heard a pair of animal moans and realized that one of them was from her.

His arms lifted her effortlessly, from her feet. "You taste so damn good," he said against her mouth, "and you smell like sex." His smile reeked of satisfaction.

Rowan rapidly awakened from her sensual haze and blinked. "You can put me down now." Her voice was embarrassingly husky.

"And if I don't want to?" he asked softly. His eyes narrowed to slits like a cat's.

Rowan glared at him. "You didn't call me out here on false pretenses, did you?"

He sighed. "Unfortunately, no." He let her slide down his body. "Though you could easily talk me into it," he muttered.

"Get over it." Rowan stepped back on untrustworthy knees. *Goddess, that boy can kiss!* She wiped the tissue on her damp hand, then blinked. The wound was gone.

"Spoil-sport." Rick stepped back and made a wry face. "I suppose I better take you out to my house and get this over with."

Rowan pulled out her car keys. "I'll follow you."

He raised a brow and smiled. "I can drive us both in my Viper."

Rowan smiled grimly. "Not a chance, Fang Boy." Rowan strode past him, headed for her Saturn. *Not with the way my body is reacting...*

"Fang Boy?"

✎ Six ✐

Conjuration

owan followed Rick's midnight blue Viper off of the night black highway and into an elegant if elderly district. Whimsical black-iron streetlamps arched over the curving avenue and cast pools of warm amber light that illuminated broad, brick-paved sidewalks. Enormous oaks populated the entire neighborhood alongside charming, turn-of-the-century houses that were bordered by decorative stone, walls and cast-iron fences.

Rick's car turned off the avenue and onto a short blind drive. Tall, ornately worked gates of iron and brass swung open to admit both cars.

Rowan followed him onto a broad, brick-paved drive bordered by overhanging oaks. *Wow, posh neighborhood,* Rowan thought in amazement. *Business must be very good for the vampire.* She followed him into a tunnel of utter darkness cast by the huge trees. The drive curved to the left, abruptly opening up on a broad lawn. Rowan sat up behind the wheel. *That's a house?*

A huge ultra-modern building sat in the center of expanse, artistically lit with floodlights. At first glance, it looked to Rowan like a huge pile of windowed boxes precariously balanced on top of each other in multiple directions. The sharp-angled structure rose upward for four floors and extended across the well-groomed lawn. The building was trimmed with chrome rails and painted in stark shades of gray and black against bone white. Railed porches jutted out at corners and tall windows seemed scattered in random places. Rowan's gaze slid up to the breaking clouds above the house. A sliver of moon was showing directly above the house. She bit her lip and squinted at the moon. The whole curve was blood red. *That cannot be good*

Rowan followed Rick's car along the paved drive past the house then all the way around to the back. Rick stopped in front of a squat square and windowless building, painted to match the house. The doors rose upward and folded away to admit his car.

That's a garage? Rowan's brows rose wryly. *Can you say: functional?* She put her Saturn in gear to follow, then bit her lip. *On second thought, if I need to leave in a hurry, that automatic garage door could pose a problem.* She pulled up and parked along the side of the garage, turned off the engine and unfastened her seatbelt. Grabbing her red velvet shoulder bag, Rowan pulled the trunk-release, then slid out of her car. Closing her door with a thump, she walked around to the car's rear. She levered her unlocked trunk open, revealing her magical arts satchel.

A voice whispered in her ear. "Something wrong with the garage?"

"Shit!" Rowan jumped and whipped around. Rick was standing with bare inches between them. She could feel the warmth of his body.

He whispered. "Did I scare you?"

Her eyes dropped to his lips. They were barely inches away from hers. His lips bowed into a smile. She felt her breath hitch in reaction and the tender itch of her nipples tightening. Her rebellious body pulsed with damp warmth. She found herself frozen in place, focusing on the curve of his full lips. *He's way too cute when he smiles, and way, way too close...*

"Uh..." Rowan leaned away and struggled to focus her thoughts. *How the Hell am I going to survive staying this excited around him?*

She wiped her damp palms on her jeans. "Do you mind?" she bit out. "You're a little close."

Rick took an obliging step back and Rowan let out a relieved breath. *Wait a minute. Did he ask me a question? Oh, right. The garage.* "I parked out here because I can't open the garage myself."

His tilted his head slightly, the smile still on his lips. His eyes reflected the floodlights cast on the house and glowed like green-gold coins. "I can open it for you."

She raised her eyes to his in challenge. "And if you are somehow…incapacitated?" She tilted her head toward the house.

He glanced at the house and the eerie glow in his eyes disappeared. "Good point." Rick's face tightened into taut lines. "Speaking of incapacitated, if you need to get out, there's a box on the post of the property gates. Punch in thirteen-thirteen to open the gates."

Rowan blinked at him in surprise. "Thanks."

"Sure." He smiled wryly. "So, what do you think of the house I built?"

"You built it?"

He nodded. "Back in the forties when I first came to the 'States. I'm an architect."

Rowan looked at the sharp angles the defined his home. *It's ugly.* She bit her lip. "It's very modern," she offered.

He crossed his arms over his chest then snorted. "You hate it." He raised a brow, daring her to deny it.

Rowan looked at him helplessly, he was right, she did hate it. "Well, it's very different." She raised a brow. He looked doubtful, so she tried again. "It's um, very—angular."

He swiped a hand across his temple then shook his head. "Don't worry, I have yet to meet a single female that liked it on sight." He grinned broadly. "The interior is another whole story."

Rowan's mouth fell open. "You bring girls here? Isn't that kinda dangerous? What if your dinner dates remember where you um, took them?"

Rick laughed out loud. "I'm a well-known architect, a house designer; I have to throw the occasional house party for the clients. My dinner dates, as you put it, happen out of town." He shook his head and grinned. "I'll ask again once I get you inside."

Rowan found herself focusing on his mouth again. *Damn it—get a grip on yourself!* She took a deep, calming breath. *Oops, mistake to breathe in...* The scent of clean and potent male laced with an undertone of warm earth washed across her senses. Her belly clenched hungrily.

"By the way, how much time do you need to be ready to do your, um..." He wiggled his fingers. "What ever?"

Rowan jerked her eyes from his mouth back up to his eyes with a stab of shame. "Um, give me a minute to get a few things." She turned abruptly to rummage in her bag, looking for what she needed. *Me and my runaway libido,* she thought in chagrin. *Get your mind out of the gutter girl. I don't care if he's a great kisser; he's also a vampire.*

Taking a steadying breath, Rowan began pulling things from her satchel and making a small pile. There was a small, cloth bag of salt, a small box of colored chalks, a bottle of blessed water, a handful of incense, her ritual dagger, a fresh sprig of holly wrapped in thick cotton and a pair of white candles wrapped in silk

"How long will it take?" He watched curiously while she pulled item after item from the satchel.

"The casting? About an hour." She turned her head to glance at him. "Do you have a working fireplace?"

He nodded. "Yeah, there's one in just about every room."

"Is there one somewhere near the center of the house?" Her fingers busily sorted through the myriad cloth packets.

"There's one in the living room that opens onto the main dining room, too."

"Good. A fire in the center hearth will cut down on the time it takes me to, um, complete this." Rowan turned back to her items and stuffed small bags of her spell ingredients into her oversized red velvet bag. "How fast can you build a fire?"

"Damn fast."

"Excellent." She smiled grimly and tucked the last item in her bag. "Once we get inside, I'll need you to get a fire lit as fast as you can." She closed the trunk decisively then went over her bag's inventory. *I'm pretty sure that this is everything I need,* she thought. *Either I have it all or I can make do with what I have.* Taking a deep breath, she turned to face Rick. "Okay, let's go."

"All right." He nodded and Rowan could see the muscle in his cheek tense. He turned and strode across the grass, headed for the door on the back porch.

Rowan gripped her bag and trudged through the damp grass after him.

His long strides carried him to the top of the porch steps where he turned and waited for her. The top half of the whitewashed back door was windowed and showed nothing but darkness.

She climbed the steps to the door and he grabbed her wrist. She jumped and looked up at him. *He's so damn fast...* Tension threaded with sharp fear vibrated across her senses from his hold. Rowan stared up at the vampire. *Goddess, he's terrified. What the Hell is he putting me up against?*

"Rowan." His voice was soft and deadly serious. "I want you to promise me that you will take no chances. If things go bad, I want you to swear that you'll do whatever you need to, to get the Hell out and gone."

"What about you?" she asked softly.

He smiled grimly. "Thanks for the concern, but I'll survive." He jerked his head toward the house. "He wouldn't be here if he wasn't after something. I doubt he'll kill me until he gets whatever it is." His eyes narrowed and his grip tightened. "I mean it, promise me that if something happens, you'll get out, by whatever means necessary."

She nodded solemnly. "I promise."

He nodded grimly and pushed open the porch door. Light from the outside striped a heavy oak door that led into the house. He took two steps and she heard a door being unlocked, then opened. Rick disappeared into the shadows.

Rowan stood in the doorway, blinded by the deep blackness. There was the click of a switch and light flooded a broad kitchen gleaming with chrome. She gained the impression of white walls with smoked glass cabinets, and a large glass and chrome kitchen table. She stepped across the threshold into the house proper. An oppressive breeze of ominous power suddenly slithered across her skin and she gasped in alarm. Her body ignited and radiated with intense blue light. Her bound hair floated up around her shoulders on the wave of brightness. Rowan squinted against the blazing glare that filled the room. She turned to see Rick standing by the sink and well within her pool of light. He looked at her in astonishment, completely bathed in her light. He looked at his hands, rubbed his arm, grinned, then shrugged. *Oh, shit, the radiance isn't working on him.*

"What have you brought to this house?" someone whispered in a voice that echoed with age.

Rowan gained the impression of deep black forests and endless killing snow but saw no one.

"Just a friend," Rick said in a conversational tone of voice. He waved her to come in.

She bit her lip and took a step deeper into the house. *I hope I'm not about to get killed.*

Rick walked across the kitchen toward a doorway leading to a darkened hall. He turned and silently waved at her to follow.

She shouldered her bag and walked carefully across the black and white tiled kitchen floor. She stopped cold on the threshold. The hallway was black with menacing shadows.

The shimmer of dark power retreated sharply. "Make it leave," the voice whispered from further away. "Make it leave now." The voice was fading fast.

Rowan smiled grimly. *Hot damn, the radiance seems to be working just fine on the other vampire...*

"But she's my friend." Rick switched on a line of electric lamps in chrome sconces with amber globes, mounted on the wall very close to the ceiling. The warm amber glow illuminated a narrow hallway papered in vanilla white. The floor was a deep black, highly polished wood.

Rick beckoned her to follow him then turned down the hallway. "Why should I make her leave?"

Rowan walked cautiously through the heart of the house and her boot heels thumped on the wood floor. She followed him past a broad staircase with an elegantly curved marble banister.

Rick took a sudden left turn past the stairs into a bookshelf-lined and windowless study. There was a huge ultra-modern glass and chrome desk on an ornate carpet in the center.

Rowan stepped into the room and her heels clicked oddly. She looked down. *This floor looks like marble?*

Rick took a right and went up two steps into an enormous room. The walls were papered in bone white, with an ornate, deep-piled oriental rug in vivid jewel tones spread across the polished black floor. A brass and deep red velvet couch and a pair of matching squashy velvet chairs occupied corners of the room with small, fragile glass tables set with tiny, bubble-shaped lamps.

She found Rick kneeling before a round, almost egg-like white marble fireplace big enough to stand in. He held his hands out to the fireplace. There was a soft *whomp* and the wood laid in the iron grate burst into flame.

Rowan blinked. *Whoa, he wasn't kidding when he said he could light a fire fast.* She raised a brow at him. "Tell me again that you're not magical," she whispered.

He made a wry face and backed away from the hearth. "Gas fire with an electric starter."

"Sure, right." Rowan yanked off her jacket then dropped it and her bag in a chair sitting by the fire. She dug in her bag and pulled out her black-handled dagger and some small packets of herbs. The runes carved deeply into the hilt felt reassuringly rough against her palm. She narrowed her eyes and concentrated. The blade began to glow with blue-white light. With a flourish of the blade, she began her incantation.

"A *ved'ma*," said the echoing invisible presence.

Rowan glanced at Rick. "A what?"

Rick looked over at Rowan with a grim smile. "It's Russian for Witch," he said softly. "Yes." Rick said louder. "She is a witch."

Rowan felt rather than heard a scream of fury that abruptly dissipated. The oppressive power shredded and unraveled around her. The glow of her skin died down to barely a glimmer.

"I don't know how much time we have, but I think he's gone." Rick turned to Rowan. "It's now or never."

"Have a seat, I'm driving," Rowan said with a tight smile. She yanked the band from her bound hair and flung it on the floor. Her red-gold mane fell in thick waves to her hips. She toed off her shoes and stood barefoot in front of the round fireplace.

Rick dropped into one of the chairs by the fireplace. Rowan turned to face the huge fire. Carelessly, she tossed three small packets of herbs on the fire, bag and all. Thick, richly scented white smoke drifted from the hearth, then swelled and flowed across the high ceiling. She pointed her glowing dagger at the fire. In a strong, clear voice, she began chanting.

* * * *

Rick sat very still while Rowan continued to work her magic. Covertly, he glanced at his wristwatch. Twenty agonizingly long minutes had passed.

Abruptly the fire's flames turned a bright green. A bell sounded, but Rowan's hands held only her dagger. She turned away from the fire and flung her arms outward. Her eyes went solid, glowing green and her hair floated up on a wave of power. Her chanting voice suddenly swelled, echoing and vibrating as though she spoke in a vast, empty hall.

Rick sat up in his chair. *Okay, now I'm impressed.*

A wave of green light rippled from the fire in a broad ring and spread across the floor at knee level. The wave slid through Rowan's body as though it was made of mist, then shimmered through him. He shuddered, the hair on his body rising in reaction. The ring continued on and passed through the walls behind him as though they weren't there.

The fire suddenly went out as though smothered, leaving the room in deep shadow.

* * * *

"It is done," Rowan said and lowered her dagger. Exhaustion and nerves shivered through her. She took a harsh breath. "How about turning on some lights."

Rick stood up from the chair and flicked on a lamp. "I hope this works 'cause I can feel Klaus coming in fast."

"What?" Rowan turned to look at the vampire in shock. Her senses fanned out and she felt the approach of malevolence sliding past the border of her spell. "Something's wrong," she said through gritted teeth. "He shouldn't be able to cross the property line."

"I guess it didn't work," Rick said sourly.

"Damn it!" Rowan felt a gathering of force collect in the furthest corner of the room. There was a chittering vibration of laughter that was more of a feeling than a sound. Darkness pooled and stretched upward. She gasped softly and pointed her dagger at the menacing darkness. A shimmer of power slid across her skin and she erupted with dim light. *I must be tired. This isn't much of a glow.* The dagger began to glow with concentrated and brilliant blue fire. *On second thought...*

The chittering laughter intensified and the mass of darkness seemed to gather in on itself as though hunching over. She felt the sound suddenly die away as though to take a breath. Abruptly the darkness unfolded upward in the darkest corner of the room. It coalesced, then solidified. Suddenly, Rowan was staring at an over-tall and excruciatingly slender man. He was dressed in long, tattered robes that appeared to be made of semi-solid darkness rather than fabric. Long, dark hair began in a deep point on a high brow, parted over sharply elongated and pointed ears, then slid past broad, bony shoulders like dripping smoke.

The face turned into the light cast from Rowan's skin. Over-large eyes of solid crimson under crooked brows regarded her with menace over a bladed nose. The jaw was clean-shaven and slightly out of proportion. The man smiled impossibly wide, showing far too many teeth, all of them filed to sharp points.

"*Ved'ma,*" it whispered.

"Dear Lady," Rowan whispered in shock. A buzz, like an electrical charge, shivered through her arm then raced down into her dagger. The glow of her ceremonial dagger abruptly brightened, intensified and lengthened. *What the Hell?*

Rowan found herself pointing a blade of concentrated blue light that extended at least three feet from the dagger's tip, then stopped as though it had been cut off. Her brows rose in surprise. "Use the force, Luke," she quoted with grim humor.

Rick shifted closer to Rowan. "Rowan, this is Klaus. Klaus, this is my friend Rowan."

"Her light..." Klaus winced at her glare and turned his head. He raised a slender, clawed hand to shade his eyes. He stepped back into deeper shadow and stared at Rick. "She does not burn you?"

Rick shook his head. "It's a little bright, but no, I don't feel a thing."

"I smell..." Klaus raised his chin and took a deep breath. His nostrils flared, like a dog scenting the air. His white-less ruby eyes shifted to Rowan. "I smell spellwork." He shifted his gaze to Rick and his lips curled back, showing far too many serrated teeth. "Youngling..." Klaus's brows swooped down over his burning eyes. "What have you done?"

Rick opened his eyes very wide. "Who, me?"

Rowan's temper got the better of her. "It's a barrier to keep out intruders." Rick's hand dropped on her shoulder and squeezed in warning.

Klaus's brows winged upward. "I see." He nodded gravely then smiled sharply and fleetingly at Rick. "Perhaps there is wisdom in you after all."

Rick glanced at Rowan. She shrugged in reply.

Klaus regarded Rowan curiously. "So, this *ved'ma* is your woman?"

With lightning fast reflexes, Rick covered Rowan's mouth. "Yes, she's mine."

Rowan grabbed his wrist. She tugged at his arm but his hand was immovable. *What the Hell does he mean, I'm his woman?*

"I see." Klaus tilted his head to one side with another fleeting smile. "Very well then, I will leave you to your pleasures." He nodded, then stepped back and faded into shadow.

Rowan felt Klaus's presence dissipate completely from the room. Abruptly the glowing sword of light went out along with the shimmer under her skin. Rick released her mouth. She shot him a glare then exhaustion hammered her between the eyes. She pressed her fingers to her throbbing temples and barely reached the chair before she collapsed. She heard the dagger hit the rug.

"Hey, are you all right?"

Rowan opened her eyes and blinked. Rick was leaning over her, and she was propped up in the chair with her red velvet bag jammed uncomfortably in her back. "I'm okay." She struggled to dig her bag from her back and sit up. "Too much magic, I guess." Shimmering on the edge of her senses, she felt Klaus somewhere at the top of the house. "He's in the attic, I think," she said softly.

Rick looked up at the ceiling and choked out a harsh laugh. "There's a TV up in the loft at the highest point in the house. That's where he usually stays."

Rowan blinked. "He watches TV?" She leaned over, picked up her fallen dagger, then tucked it into the bag jammed in next to her.

Rick bit his lip and shrugged. "I don't think he's ever seen cable before."

She frowned at him furiously. "I'm your woman? Just what the Hell are you trying to prove?"

"Sorry, about that." Rick stared at her grimly. "I wanted him to know that you were off limits." He rolled his eyes ruefully. "It was the easiest way to get my point across." He stood up and offered her his hand. "Come on."

Rowan took his hand and used it to lever herself from the chair. "Where are we going?" She wavered on wobbly legs.

Rick grabbed her jacket and bag from the chair. "To put you to bed. It's late and I want to get some sleep."

❧ One ☙

Vault

Rowan followed Rick past the main staircase, then stopped right by the small table with the lamp in the dimly lit hall. Turning to the right, he faced the side of the staircase, then reached up and pressed something. Rowan heard a distinctive click. A hidden door painted and papered to blend into the wall, swung out into he hall. He flicked a switch and light filled a narrow stair that descended steeply under the main staircase.

Rowan's eyes widened. "You keep the guest room in the basement?"

He glanced back at her with a wry smile. "In your case, yes. It's a vault." He waved her into the alcove under the stairs. "Come on."

Rowan dug in her heels and eyed the narrow alcove with skepticism. "A vault? In your basement?"

"Yes, I have a vault in my basement." He sighed and rolled his eyes at her. "I had it put in when I built the house." He tapped his foot and jabbed a thumb at the tiny stair. "Will you come on?"

Rowan looked up at him. "You are not serious? You want me to sleep in a vault in your basement?"

"Yes, I'm putting you to bed in the vault." He sighed, then unceremoniously grabbed her elbow and pulled her into the small alcove, then shoved her toward the stairs.

"Hey!" Rowan grabbed the handrail to keep from skidding down the stairs. She turned to face him. "What do you think you're doing?"

He closed the door firmly behind them. "I already told you, I'm taking you down to the vault." Rick scrubbed at the back of his neck, then stepped past her and yawned. "It's where I sleep."

Rowan nearly tripped. "Where you sleep?"

"Are you going to repeat everything I say?" Rick started down the stairs carrying her bag and jacket then turned to look at her in annoyance. "Trust me, you are far safer in the vault with me. Come on."

Rowan turned to look at the door. "Safer?" There was no knob on this side. She couldn't see a way to open the door. "With you?"

Rick frowned. "I don't know how safe you'd be anywhere with Klaus in the house. He doesn't actually have to sleep, just stay out of direct sunlight, and he holds a corporeal form indifferently. There's not a single place in this house he can't get to you."

"So, I'd be no safer in the vault with you?"

He shrugged and bit back a smile. "We're better off together. If Klaus pops in for a snack, I can hold him off long enough for you to..." Rick wiggled his fingers. "Do something."

"Terrific," she said sourly.

He leaned against the banister to stare at her. "You're not going to be able to open the door from this side, so you may as well follow me. Unless of course you really want to spend the next few hours on the stairs?" He shrugged and started down. "By yourself."

Rowan made a face at the descending vampire's back. *Piss and firewater... I don't exactly have a choice here.* She grabbed the narrow banister, then followed the vampire down.

The stairs ended at a huge vault door that looked like it belonged more to a high security bank rather than to a bedroom. Rick pulled on a huge handle and the round door swung silently toward them.

"That door has to be at least three feet thick," Rowan remarked softly.

"It's four feet thick and tungsten alloy steel, layered with brass. The bedroom floor, walls and ceiling are just as thick as the door." Rick grinned. "A bomb could go off and we'll never know 'til we get up."

"Terrific," she said sourly.

Rick shoved the door open wide. "Welcome to my chambers."

Rowan stared at a huge room and her eyes opened wide. It had to be the full breadth of the house. Two rows of immense and smooth round columns of black-veined marble supported a twelve-foot ceiling. A vast bed set up on a broad, three-stair marble pedestal occupied the center of the room. The rounded art deco headboard and footboard were of solid black marble.

The distant walls were painted in deep red with black trim. Black velvet curtains draped to the floor, framing enormous, gilt-framed landscape paintings of dark, brooding mountains in place of windows. An antique art deco black lacquered armoire and matching mirrored dresser sat against the far wall near a white-painted door.

Rowan raised a brow. "Wow, this looks like a cross between a bordello and a mausoleum."

"Thank you, I think." The sarcasm was thick in his voice.

With a gentle push, Rowan was shoved into the room. Her feet sank into thick silver-gray carpet. Rowan glanced over her shoulder at the vampire. "Business must be good if you can afford all this."

"These are just a few things I've picked up on my travels." He pulled vault door closed. The lock engaged with a decisive clank. "There's a full bathroom through the far door."

"This is not what I had in mind for sleeping arrangements. I can go to a hotel…"

"No." He shook his head firmly then walked past her toward the bed. "I want you in here, with me."

She walked toward the imposing bed and glared at him. "What the Hell for?"

He glanced back at her with a sarcastic grin. "You mean beyond the obvious?" He dropped her satchel by the side of the stairs leading up to the bed.

Rowan flinched. *That was a stupid question.*

He chuckled then climbed the stairs. "Actually I have another reason beyond that." He flopped carelessly across the end of the mattress. "As far as I can tell, Klaus still hasn't fed and damn it, I don't want to wake up bled half dry and snuggled up next to him."

She stopped at the foot of the stairs and smiled sourly. "What? Am I your bodyguard now?"

"You know, that oath really came in handy." Rick abruptly rolled to one side and propped himself up on one elbow. "Your light doesn't bother me a bit now." He licked his full lips, then smiled suggestively.

"Just keep rubbing it in, Fang Boy." She gave him a nasty grin. "I can get creative if I have to."

His smile broadened, showing the points of his fangs. "I'm looking forward to it."

I'm going to ignore that. She raised a brow. "You know, I can ward a hotel room and most come with two beds."

"You can ward against daylight?" He raised a brow.

Rowan shook her head. "I'm not that good, but most have light-blocking curtains."

"That would be fine, except for one thing, when I do sleep, I have to be under ground level and I have yet to see a hotel that has rooms in the basement."

"You have to sleep underground?"

He shrugged. "It's a vampire thing "

"Look, Rick, I really don't want to share a bed with you." Rowan hugged her bag to her chest. *After all the magic I just used, when my sex drive kicks in it's going to be a whopper. Sharing a bed with the most beautiful man I've ever seen will be far too much to resist, vampire or not.*

He rolled his eyes. "It's my bed and I am not sleeping on the floor." He watched her face then pointed a finger at her. "And neither are you, so don't bother suggesting it. Klaus can come up through the floor. I've seen him do it."

"You are making this really hard on me."

He smiled. "Not yet, but getting there," he said very softly.

"What was that?" She looked at him suspiciously.

"Nothing..." He bit back his smile and shook his head. "Not a damned thing."

Rowan raised her brow at him. *Do I really want to know?* She thought a moment more. *No, I don't...* She looked at the vampire lounging on the bed. He was looking very smug about something. She shook her head then frowned, pacing back and forth across the thick carpet. "I'd ward this room against him, but I have no idea why the barrier spell around the house didn't work and it's active, I can feel it..." She stopped and rubbed her eyes tiredly with a hand. "He waltzed right in as though it wasn't there; like he'd been invited." Rowan looked over at the vampire with a sudden nasty suspicion. "Rick, did you tell him that he was welcome in your house?"

Rick abruptly slid off the opposite side of the bed and busied himself with pulling back the deep black brocade comforter. The sheets and pillows were a vibrant crimson. "I, um, told him it was okay to come talk to me."

"You told him that he could come talk to you?" Rowan's mouth fell open. "You issued an invitation?"

Rick turned to face her. "I didn't think he'd follow me home and I certainly didn't expect him to hang around."

An inarticulate sound of utter frustration burst from her lips. "Mother of us all, no wonder the damn spell didn't have any affect on him, it was designed for uninvited guests!" She turned away and wiped her hands down her face. "I don't believe this. A vampire that invites another vampire to come visit." She wheeled to face him with her hands on her hips. "Don't you know any of your own vampire lore?"

"What lore?" He frowned. "Most of that stuff is pure crap."

"Damn it, Rick!" She stomped her foot on the thick carpet. "Even the movies have it right when they tell you not to invite a vampire into your home!" She jabbed a finger at him. "You *should* be scared to sleep! Traditionally, as your guest, he has every right to dine under your roof."

"I just wanted to talk to him." Rick bit his lip.

Rowan threw up her hands. "What the Hell for?"

"I've never met another as old as he is." Rick turned his back to her and shrugged. "I want to know what changes are coming to me. I get older."

Rowan frowned. "That's it?"

He arranged some of the pillows. "And, uh, he told me that he might be my sire."

"Your sire?" Rowan tilted her head to the side. "I thought you knew your sire?"

Rick bit his lip and looked at her from the corner of his eye. "I wasn't exactly in the right frame of mind at the time to commit everything to memory."

She looked at him in confusion. "What do you mean; the right frame of mind?"

He gave her a vague shrug. "I was barely conscious the whole time." He busied himself with folding the blankets on the foot of the bed. "I was on the edge of starvation and I was dealing with blood-loss from a bullet in my shoulder when he um, changed me. After that, everything is kind of a big blur." He shook his head. "He never told me his name and I um, can't quite remember what he looks like, only that he was Russian, like Klaus."

"I see." Rowan shook her head. "So when Klaus said that he might be your sire, you believed him?"

"If I'd believed him, you wouldn't be here." Rick looked over and smiled grimly. "That's the other reason I wanted you here. You're the only reliable lie-detector I know."

"He's not your sire. He doesn't even feel like you."

"I guessed as much." He stared at the bed sourly.

Rowan bit her lip. "Look, I'm sorry." She walked toward the bed. *It must be hard not knowing where you came from.*

He shrugged carelessly and gave her a grim smile. "Truthfully, I'm relieved. Klaus for my sire is a very scary thought." He sat down on the folded blankets at the end of the bed. "So now what?"

She stopped at the stair on the side of the bed. "Now, I have to reprogram the spell." She pressed her fingers to her temple. Her head was still throbbing.

"That simple?"

She shook her head and climbed the steps. "Not that simple." She frowned thoughtfully and pressed her hands into the scarlet sheets on the thick mattress. "Klaus now knows that I spelled the house to repel unwanted guests, so he's probably guessed that he's not exactly welcome."

"Yeah, so?"

"So, he has to be off the property for me to key the barrier to him personally. I surprised him last time, so he left. He'll expect me to reset the barrier, and now he probably knows that the range of my radiance is limited. I may not be able to get him off the property far enough to key the barrier, or even out of the house."

"Oh…"

"'Oh' is right." She turned and sat on the side of the bed facing one of the gloomy paintings then yawned. She twisted around and looked dejectedly at the vampire. "What if I can't get him out?"

"I have a better idea." He slowly leaned across the bed toward her then rested on one elbow.

Rowan looked at him suspiciously. "What?"

He tugged the elastic from his hair. It fell in a silken, midnight cloak over his shoulder and spilled on the scarlet sheet. "I vote we sleep on it and worry about it tomorrow." He smiled and began unbuttoning his shirt with one hand. Pale skin and the lean muscle of his breast slid into view along with an erect masculine nipple.

Oh, shit… Rowan leapt off the bed as though it was on fire. "Um, then I better get to warding the room." She took a few hasty steps to her satchel, knelt and fumbled among the contents.

"That's interesting Death doesn't seem to bother you, but sex does."

Rowan dug around in her satchel and refused to say a word.

The sheets rustled on the bed. "You're ignoring me."

Rowan nodded. "Yes, I am."

"Come on, you can tell me. What is it about sex that scares you so much?"

Rowan turned around with her black handled dagger in her hand. "I'm not sleeping with you, so what does it matter?"

"Fine, okay, whatever I'll change the subject." Rick sat up to watch her and tilted his head to one side. "Will the ward you're working on now keep Klaus out?"

She glanced over her shoulder. "Oh, it'll work, but that's because I'm going to use an archaic seal."

"An archaic seal?"

Rowan gave him a small tight smile. "Let's put it this way: if you need anything, you better go get it now." She stood up with her black-handled dagger shoved in her belt, a small cloth bag of salt in one hand and five silver-dipped horseshoe nails in the other.

He pulled his unbuttoned shirt from his pants. "I think I have everything I need." Rick leisurely peeled the shirt from his shoulders. Muscle rippled in his arms.

Rowan couldn't help but stare at the defined planes of his broad chest and arms. Her eyes latched onto a jagged double scar, pale with age that started at his shoulder and curved down onto his upper chest. It looked like someone had taken two claws—or two fangs—and savaged him. She swallowed and tried to look away. "Are you sure you have everything?"

With a small smile, he reached for the belt on his jeans. "I sleep in the nude."

Rowan's mouth fell open. "I am *so* not sleeping in that bed if you're naked!"

"What?" He grinned and slid the belt from his pants. "Shy?" His hand went to the button on his pants.

Rowan turned her back to him. "I can sleep on the floor and ward myself against both of you—you can wake up with Klaus, for all I care."

"All right, already!" He chuckled and Rowan heard him step off the stairs. "I have some pajama bottoms in my dresser somewhere. You can go to the bathroom and change into your nightclothes. I'll change out here and you can ward the room after."

Rowan turned cautiously around. He was over by the dresser and rummaging through a drawer. She stared at the muscular line of his back and her mouth dried. *I'm going to share a bed with that? I must be insane.* She swallowed hard. "Um, I'll sleep in my clothes, thank you."

He turned around with a double handful of black silk. "The Hell you will. Not in my bed."

Rowan crossed her arms under her breasts. "My suitcase with my night clothes is still in my car."

He leaned back against the dresser and raised a brow. "If you want to sleep nude, I won't mind."

Rowan tossed her head, ponytail flying. "Oh, give me a break!"

He rolled his eyes and stalked toward her with a smile firmly on his lips. She stepped back and he lunged, grabbing her wrist in a blur of motion. "Here," he said sourly and shoved a handful of black silk into her palm.

"What's this?"

"It's the top of my pajama set. I'll wear the bottoms." He pushed her to the bathroom door. "Now quit being a pain in the ass, and go change."

Pushy bastard... Rowan flicked on the bathroom light and gawked. *Holy shit!* She closed the door behind her as an afterthought.

Everything was silver-flecked white marble and chrome. By the sink were tiny bars of luxury soap in a tasteful dish beside a silver comb and brush set and a small pile of neatly folded white face cloths. Huge fluffy white bath towels edged in silver sat on a small table nestled between a glassed in shower stall and the silver curtain that was pulled back to reveal the tub.

Damn, you could have an orgy in here. The bathtub was enormous, with three steps that led down into a marble basin large enough to hold four bodies comfortably. It was mounted with jets that were obviously meant for a spa. A small wicker basket holding at least a dozen different kinds of shampoos and not a few designer bubble baths perched on the edge of the tub.

Rowan put her dagger, salt and the loose nails on the counter by the sink, then sat on the edge of the tub. With a sigh, she peeled out of her clothes, folded her jeans and tucked her underwear discretely into her T-shirt. She unfolded the pajama top she'd been given. It was short-sleeved, but long and very soft. *Must be made of real silk.*

Rowan looked longingly at the shower stall and decided against it. Stark naked, she ran hot water in the sink, unfolded a washcloth, then unwrapped one of the small bars of soap. Hastily, she scrubbed her face and body, drying herself with a white towel.

She pulled on the black silk shirt. It fell to the top of her knees. Rowan looked at herself in the beveled mirror and bit her lip. *I look like an advertisement for a porno-movie.* Even though she had buttoned all the buttons the shirt had, the neck plunged deeply, showing the swell of her breasts and emphasizing her pale skin. A single button sat directly between her breasts. If she moved just wrong, she was going to pop out. *And all my safety pins are in my bag out in the other room.* She picked up the brush and dragged it through her long, tangled mane.

A knock sounded on the door, and Rowan jumped.

"Are you coming out of there? I need to use the uh, facility." Rick's voice was slightly muffled.

"Be out in a minute," she called. *A vampire that has to use the toilet?* She shook her head. *No, I don't want to think about it...* She put the brush down, then picked up her shoes, clothes, and spell ingredients. *Let's get this over with.* Clutching everything to her chest, she opened the door.

Rick was leaning against the wall right by the door. Rowan was rendered speechless. His body was all long, lean muscular lines and the black silk of his trousers rode very low on his hips.

"Nice of you to join me." His smile was pure decadence.

She swallowed, then slid past him. *This is such a bad idea.* The bathroom door closed behind him.

Rowan raced to the bed, shoving her clothes under the foot. She grabbed for her bag and went digging for a safety pin. She couldn't find one and hissed in frustration. She heard the sound of the toilet flushing, then heard water running in the sink. She was running out of time.

"Damn it! Where the Hell are my pins?" Rowan abruptly stabbed her finger on a straight pin. She yanked out her hand and sucked on her wounded finger. *Not what I had in mind...*The bathroom door opened. Rowan sighed in defeat, picked up her dagger, the bag of salt, and the horseshoe nails, then stood up and turned around.

Rick sauntered, all grace and power in motion, toward the huge four-poster. He climbed up on the bed and crawled on hands and knees across the mattress. With a sexy groan, he rolled over, stretching out across the scarlet sheets. "Are you ready to come to bed?" His smile was broad and flashed sharply pointed teeth.

"Uh..." Rowan felt a strong shiver of feminine awareness and a warm, moist hunger. *I should have stayed in the bathroom.* Rowan abruptly turned her back on the wanton display of pale masculine flesh and midnight hair. *Mother of Mercy, I need a cigarette.* She squeezed her hands. The silver horseshoe nails bit sharply into her palm, and she winced. *I have a spell to cast,* she reminded herself. *Might as well get to it.*

"Rowan?" The vampire called softly from the bed. "Are you coming to bed?"

She took a deep breath. "I have a ward to cast." She knelt and dug a Djarum clove cigarette from her bag and her lighter.

"Are you smoking?"

"It's for the spell." She lit the cigarette and gratefully sucked smoke. "I used cigarette smoke when I broke the demon's binding on you, remember?"

"Oh…"

Rowan opened her bag of salt. "Mother of us all," she whispered and began the casting. Lit cigarette smoking in one hand, she walked to the head of the bed. Studiously ignoring the vampire, she strode counter-clockwise in a broad circle around the bed, scattering grains of salt. The pungent, incense-scented smoke of her cigarette billowed after her.

She reached the head of the bed again, completing the circle, then turned and walked clockwise. She placed each of the silver horseshoe nails point outward, marking the points of a star with the last nail at head of the bed for the fifth and master point. She stepped within her marked circle, clapped her hands and blew smoke on the last nail. A soft breeze erupted and a line of blue light marked the circle, then disappeared.

"It is done," she said softly.

"Good," the vampire said softly. "Put that cigarette out and come to bed."

I guess I can't put this off any longer. Biting her lip, Rowan stabbed the cigarette out on her dagger, then knelt and tucked both the dagger and the half-burned cigarette under the bed with her clothes. She took a breath and climbed the steps.

She hesitated at the top, staring at the magnificent male spread across the sheets. *I am in so much trouble…*His skin was stark white and his hair midnight black against the scarlet silk. A warm curl of anticipation shivered through her, and she felt a powerful urge to stroke his skin to feel the muscles moving underneath.

He smiled. "Scared?" He shifted to make room under the black comforter, and muscle flexed invitingly.

Rowan felt a hot surge of bravado. "Of you?"

"Look…" He shook his head. "I'm blood-sworn not to harm you, so I'm not going to attack you." He patted the mattress. "Nothing is going to happen, I promise." He licked his lips and his eyes gleamed copper-bright with heat. "Not without your consent, anyway," he added very, very softly.

Rowan swallowed. *That's what I'm afraid of...*

He chuckled. "Just get in. We're both tired and I haven't slept for three days, so I'll probably pass out on you in a few minutes."

Rowan gathered the shreds of her courage and climbed up onto the mattress. She crawled under the blankets and dropped her head back on the pillows before her nerve gave out.

"There, that wasn't so bad," he said softly.

The lights began to dim, draping the room with thick, encroaching shadows. Rowan looked around in alarm.

"The lights are on remote control." He chuckled. "Don't worry, they won't go all the way dark. Even I can't see in full darkness." The lights dimmed until Rowan could barely make out the shape of the bed she lay in. She felt the mattress shift and turned her head. Rick's face was a deep shadow only inches away. She clutched the blankets with white knuckles. "What?" Her voice came out in an embarrassing squeak.

"How about a good-night kiss?" His voice was a seductive whisper.

Rowan's lungs squeezed in alarm even as her body clenched with moist, interested hunger. It took a few moments to get air back into her lungs. "How about... Not."

He chuckled. "Fine, go to sleep." He abruptly fell back on the mattress.

She blinked up at the darkness and felt her heart pounding in her throat. *I can't believe I'm in bed with a vampire...*

❧ Eight ❧

Hunger

Rowan jolted semi-awake from deep sleep with her heart pounding as though from a nightmare. She kept her eyes closed, groggy with sleep and unsure of what was disturbing her, but heard nothing. *I don't remember dreaming about anything scary...* She didn't recall dreaming at all. *Maybe this feeling will go away.* She yawned and snuggled face down into the pillows and deeper into the blankets. The scent of warm male on the sheets caught her attention. Something heavy shifted on the mattress. Her eyes snapped open.

The room was lit by a disturbingly familiar bright blue glow that seemed to be coming from below the bed. *What is that?* Confusion colored her thoughts, then she suddenly remembered. The house, the vampire she was sharing a bed with—and the other vampire. Her pulse leapt in her throat. *That's the ward!* The magical barrier around the bed was glowing, which meant that something had set it off. Or someone...

Rowan cautiously turned over onto her back. Rick was sitting up rigidly still and staring at the foot of the bed. She felt the hair all over her body rise. She sat up to see what he was looking at. *Oh shit, I just found my scary dream.*

Klaus was standing just outside the barrier. His elongated face was starkly lit by the glow of the warding spell. His eyes were glowing with flame and locked on Rick's.

"Uh, hello, Klaus." Rowan couldn't think of anything else to say. *I'm not glowing, so I must not be in danger. The ward must be holding.*

Klaus didn't even glance her way. "*Ved'ma,*" he hissed.

"Yeah, I'm a witch. We already went over that." Rowan stared from one vampire to the other. *What the Hell is going on?*

"Rickart Holt," Klaus said softly.

An oily smear of rank power slid repulsively across Rowan's nerves. *Damn it! His power is somehow getting through the barrier.*

Rick's head jerked up and his lips pulled back from his teeth with an expression of pain. A soft hiss escaped his lips.

Oh, shit... I'm not in danger, but Rick is. Rowan's heart tried to pound its way out of her chest in fright. "Klaus, what the Hell are you doing to him?"

Klaus curled his lip in a jagged smile but did not break eye contact with Rick. "Nothing, yet." Klaus lifted a clawed hand, palm up. "Come." It was a command.

Rick came up on his knees, and every muscle in his body was rigid with resistance. His hands were fisted at his sides

"Leave him alone." Rowan threw the covers back and got up on her knees. "Why don't you go back upstairs and watch TV?" She thought about reaching under the bed for her black-handled dagger, but if she brought it too close to the barrier, the magically charged steel would dispel the ward. Earlier her dagger's ethereal radiance had extended into a long-sword of light in Klaus's presence. She had no idea if the light-saber effect would dispel the ward as well. *Better not take that chance.*

"I hunger." A long thin tongue snaked out past pale lips.

"Well, you're not feeding off of us. Go find your dinner somewhere else." Rowan cringed. *I hope I just didn't get someone else killed...*

"I am forbidden to feed on humans." His voice was so soft, Rowan barely heard him.

Rowan's mouth fell open. *He's forbidden to feed on humans? Terrific. Now what?*

"I hunger," Klaus said again, then rushed toward the barrier in a blur of shadow. The barrier blazed up in a curtain of blue-white flame. Klaus recoiled back sharply from the blue-white wall of fire with a scream like nails scraping a blackboard.

Rowan threw an arm up to shade her eyes from the phosphorescent glare. *Ouch. I'll just bet that hurts.* She bit back a smile. *Witch two points, if I include chasing him off earlier, Klaus still at zero.*

He turned his blazing and angry gaze on Rowan and bared his serrated teeth. "I hunger." His voice was almost plaintive. He stepped to the side and began circling the parameter of the ward as a shark circles a boat.

"So, go find another vampire." Rowan watched the circling vampire while Rick remained frozen on his knees. *What kind of hold does Klaus have on Rick?*

"I have searched. There is only Rickart Holt."

Rowan crossed her arms over her chest defensively and shook her head. "Sorry, Rick is off the menu."

He stopped on Rick's side of the bed and focused hungrily on younger vampire. "I can make Rickart Holt come to me."

"Klaus, the barrier works both ways. If you can't break the barrier and you're older, you know that Rick can't either." Rowan swallowed. *And I can't let him try—it might kill him...*

Klaus smiled with a mouth never meant to open that wide. "You will drop the barrier to keep him from harm. This I know."

Rowan recoiled in shock. *How the Hell does he know that?*

"Rickart," the elder vampire called softly.

Rick's head slowly turned to face the elder vampire. His face was stretched in a snarl of dread.

Shit! Rowan crawled across the bed and came up on her knees in front of Rick. "Rick, snap out of it."

Klaus came as close to the barrier as he dared. "Rickart, come to me."

Rick gasped and strained, fighting the call, but he began to slide across the bed toward Klaus.

"You see? He will come." Klaus continued to smile. "Take down your spell or he will die by your magic."

Rowan bared her teeth. "If I take down the barrier, you'll kill him."

Klaus shook his head slowly. "I do not need so much. He will not die."

"I said no, and I mean no. You can't have him." She turned to face Rick. "Rick, you need to wake up." She snapped her fingers in front of his face.

Rick continued to move toward Klaus as though unaware of Rowan at his side.

"Oh, but I will have him and then I will feed." He chuckled with the sound of sand grinding stone. "Come, Rickart, I wait for you."

Rick reached the edge of the bed and slid one leg over the edge.

*Oh shit, oh shit, oh shit...*Rowan snatched at Rick's arm. His arm was hard like marble and slick with cold sweat under her fingers. She could feel his fear radiating from his skin. "Rick, stay."

He abruptly stopped with one leg over the side then turned his head and stared at her. His pupils were tiny contracted points in flat, copper coins.

Klaus let out an animal snarl. "Rickart," he snapped.

Rick slowly turned his head to face the elder vampire, but his eyes strained to keep her in view.

Rowan came up on her knees and placed her other hand on his tense shoulder. "No, Rick, look at me."

He turned to face Rowan.

Klaus made a harsh sound of frustration. "His lust for you is all that you have to hold him, *ved'ma.*"

She spared a quick glance toward Klaus. He seemed to be sniffing the air. *What is he up to now?*

Klaus smiled suddenly. "You have not shared your body or your blood." His chuckle was an ugly sound.

Rowan shot a glare at him. "He's had some of my blood."

"A few drops, how generous." Klaus snorted. "You have not taken him into your body."

Rowan flinched. "So, I haven't slept with him. So what?"

"So, you will lose. You have no true hold on him. I can feel that you do not wish to soil yourself with his body."

Rowan looked into Rick's face. Carnal heat seemed to be warring with painful resistance in his expression. "He's still looking at me, vampire."

"Rickart," the vampire growled. "You will come. Now."

Rick strained between the two of them. His head tilted toward the elder vampire, but his gaze stayed locked on Rowan.

Rowan could feel the tension in his body. "Rick, stay," she said softly.

Rick's head continued to turn toward the vampire with agonizing slowness.

"You see, *ved'ma?* You cannot hold him. Your reluctance to do what is necessary to make him yours will bring him to me."

Rowan bit her lip. She reached up and took Rick's face in her palms. "Rick, stay with me."

He turned to look at her.

Rowan's thoughts chased each other back and forth. *I don't want to make him mine... But I don't want him to get drained by Klaus, either.*

"Rickart Holt, you will obey," Klaus snarled.

Rick's head turned in her palms. She did the only thing she could think of. She leaned forward and pressed her lips to his. His pulse jumped under her fingers. His mouth opened under hers and she sucked in his breath. Painfully aware of his sharp teeth, she brushed her tongue delicately against his.

Abruptly, he leaned into her kiss, his tongue surging within to stroke hungrily against hers. He groaned into her mouth.

White heat flared up her spine in sensual awareness. Her belly clenched in violent arousal and her nipples tightened sharply. "Are you with me?" she whispered against his mouth and fought for control of her heated reactions.

"I am now," he whispered back. "I was dreaming and I couldn't wake up."

"Rickart," the vampire shouted.

Rick cringed at the command. "I didn't realize that he was this strong," he whispered softly against Rowan's lips. "Hold on to me."

"All right," she breathed and wrapped her arms around his neck. Her hard nipples brushed against his broad chest with devastating sensual pleasure. Softly, she kissed him again. His arms suddenly came up and wrapped around her, crushing her against his chest.

Klaus screamed sharply in frustration. From the corner of her eye, she watched Klaus suddenly strike the barrier with his fist. There was an electric crackle, then a hiss of pain. She felt a bolt of magical awareness from the barrier. She broke the kiss to look at the snarling vampire.

"No," Rick whispered in the softest of breaths. "Please, don't stop." His mouth sought hers and she let him take her lips. He pressed her mouth open, wide seeking deeper contact and stroked his tongue against hers with appetite.

She felt Rick shift his arms, then suddenly she was on her back against the mattress and under him. His chest pressed against her breasts with full weight of his body. Her hands splayed across the muscular breadth of his back. She could feel the rigid length of his profound erection pressing against her hip and her body jolted hard with alarming greed. *Oh, Goddess, what have I gotten myself into?* She shifted under his weight, uncomfortably aware that Klaus was just beyond the barrier, watching. Her provoked body didn't seem to care.

She felt his hands slide under her shirt to encounter naked, unprotected flesh and he froze. *Oh shit! I forgot I'm not wearing panties,* she thought in panic.

She felt his groan vibrate against her chest, then his hand closed on her naked buttock, pulling her tight against him. The only barrier between them was the thin silk of his trousers. He flexed his hips against hers, shoving his silk-trapped length against her stomach in suggestive promise.

Voluptuous tension coiled tightly and desire burned a trail up her spine, arching her back under him. A silk-clad leg insinuated itself between her bare thighs, spreading her open, making intimate and shocking contact. She drew a sharp breath. The rigid length of his erection shifted dangerously close to the open juncture of her thighs. Merciless desire uncoiled and blazed in a shockwave through her body. A soft moan escaped her lips. She couldn't stop her hips from rising, pressing up against him in uncontrolled lust.

His mouth moved from hers and slid down to her throat. His lips and tongue swirled, making wet circles. Delicious shivers wracked her body. She gasped for breath and barely felt his hand reaching between them. His fingers plucked at her silk shirt, then his palm closed on the bare skin of her breast. She went rigid in alarm and grabbed his wrist.

He lifted his head to look at her. His eyes were pools of liquid fire. "Let me," he said softly.

"But, I…" she began. His fingers closed on her nipple, bringing it to aching attention. A bolt of pleasure streaked straight to her core and she bit back a moan.

"Please." His eyes narrowed with determination. "I need this. I need you."

Abruptly his head dropped and his wet mouth closed on her breast. His tongue made damp circles, then he sucked. Ravenous and unreasoning appetite clawed in her belly. His teeth tugged gently on her tender nipple. Her back arched and she moaned her pleasure.

His hand slid down her side, between their bodies, and his palm slid across the soft skin of her inner thigh. Her body rocked in violent anticipation. His cool fingers brushed against intimate flesh.

"You're wet," he breathed.

Rowan turned her head and saw Klaus watching them avidly. Icy shock dashed her body and she went rigid. "Stop," she gasped. She grabbed Rick's shoulders and shoved. He grunted, but was unmovable while his fingers continued to explore her. She tilted her hips to escape his touch and he took the opportunity to slide a finger deep into her. Her body clenched avariciously around him and she whimpered.

"Rick, please," she gasped. "Please stop." His hand withdrew and she breathed a soft sigh of relief. She felt him shift above her and suddenly felt the heat of his erection pressing against her intimate flesh. He was about to take her right in front of Klaus.

"Damn it, no." Her voice broke. Embarrassment and fear fought with her body's violent hunger. His back arched and she felt him pressing to enter. She shoved against him, struggling to escape, then grabbed his hair and yanked. "You have to stop."

His head came up sharply. Hunger was etched on his features. "Why? You're more than ready for me." His voice was thick and hoarse with passion.

"I am not doing this with an audience," she shot back.

Rick stared at her, then turned sharply to see Klaus. He bared his long fangs. "Get the fuck out," he snapped.

Klaus snarled right back. "I will not." His tongue snaked out, wetting his thin lips. "You will take her now, or you will come to me. Choose."

Rick looked at Rowan with determination and fear. He licked his lips and shifted, pressing for entry.

"Rick, you can't do this," Rowan gasped and grabbed his shoulders. "Not in front of him." She dug her heels into the mattress and shoved to get out of range.

Rick abruptly grabbed her wrists and pinned them over her head. "I will not go to him," he said softly. "I have to do this."

"Rick, don't. I said no. If you try to take me, it'll be attempted rape and that's harm." A shimmer of light began to play under her skin.

Rick winced and abruptly released her, pulling away. "Bitch," he snapped out.

Rowan sat up and grabbed the edges of her shirt to cover her breasts.

"See?" Klaus hissed. "The *ved'ma* will not allow it, and resistance to me is futile." He smiled coldly. "Come, Rickart, and let me feed."

Rick's spine arched as though struck. "You son of a bitch," he said through clenched teeth.

"Wait..." Rowan rose up on her knees. "Rick..." He shot an accusing look at her and she flinched under the weight of his gaze. She darted a look at Klaus, then looked at Rick. "He said before that I had no power to hold you because I hadn't shared my body..." She bit her lip. "Or my blood."

Klaus lunged at the barrier and it flared. "Rickart, come now!"

Rick fell forward onto his hands and grabbed the sheets. His body shook with violent tension. "Rowan," he gasped. "What are you offering?" His fingers clenched in the sheets with the harsh sound of fabric ripping.

"Blood," she whispered. "You can drink my blood in front of him."

"No!" The shout from Klaus was deafening. Klaus pointed a finger at her. "Taking your blood is harm!"

"Not if I say it isn't," she snapped back. "And I know Rick won't kill me."

Rick held out his hand. "Hurry," he whispered. "Come to me."

Rowan scrambled toward him and took his hand. He yanked and she tumbled against him. One arm wrapped around her waist, pinning her against his kneeling body while fingers slid into her hair. She grabbed his shoulders for balance. Her head was pulled to the side, exposing her throat.

She watched from over Rick's shoulder. Klaus snarled something dire and completely unintelligible from the other side of the barrier.

"I don't have the time to make this pleasant," he whispered

against her ear. "For Hell's sake, don't fight me."

"Just do it," she gasped out, then felt his lips on the tender skin on the side of her neck. She felt his tongue seeking her pulse, the sharp scrape of long teeth. She shivered hard. All the hair on her body rose.

He bit. The ripping pain of his fangs burned twin lines of fire into her throat and she whimpered. She heard the distinct sound of swallowing.

Klaus let out a hideous, screaming spat of something that she couldn't understand, then shattered into rags of smoky shadow that dissipated instantly. The ring of blue fire went out as though smothered, drenching the room in darkness.

He's gone... Thank the Gods. Rowan's lids grew heavy and she let them fall.

* * * *

She dreamed of endless falling snow

She stood on the edge of an endless horizon of shadowed white barely visible through a curtain of falling snow. The heavy sky was a dimly glowing pall of iron gray. A long and insubstantial robe of blue-white swept to her bare feet. She knew it was bitterly cold, but felt nothing.

She turned, her long hair and the hem of her robe lifting in a wind she couldn't feel. Through the whispering snow, she saw a massive and twisted tree, winter-barren of leaves. The tortured trunk was stark black against the dim blaze of snow.

She moved toward the tree in vague curiosity, ghosting across the top of the snow. A forest of winter bare trees appeared through the falling snow, behind the one tree. The falling snow thinned. The sharp crags of snowy mountains appeared in the far distance all around.

Someone was sitting with their back to her, hunched down among the roots. The person shifted. It was a man, bareheaded and shuddering with cold.

He wore a long and tattered dark gray coat that was belted at the waist and smeared with ice. The ragged ends of his pitch-black hair brushed well past his coat's high collar. Tarnished silver glinted at the lapels. There was a filthy black stain on one shoulder and some kind of insignia on his sleeve.

She drifted closer. He used a black, metal stick to laboriously lever himself to his feet. Tall black boots rose to his knees, tall enough to be partially hidden by the hem of the long coat. The black belt had an empty pistol holster and a strap that crossed from his hip to loop over the opposite shoulder.

She stopped a dozen or so yards away. He was wearing a uniform that she thought she recognized, but couldn't actually place. From this close she could suddenly see that the stick was an odd-looking rifle. She caught the ripe scent of copper; the stain on his shoulder was blood. He turned to face her.

It was Rick.

* * * *

"Rowan? Hey, are you with me?"

Rowan's eyes fluttered open. Everything was a blur of muted color. *Gods, what the Hell hit me?* She took a deep breath and flinched. Her throat hurt. She blinked to clear her vision. Rick leaned over her, frowning. His eyes were a warm and ordinary hazel. She caught sight of the distant ceiling over his head. She was still in his bed and the lights were on.

"Can you hear me?" His voice was soft and a wrinkle creased his brow.

"Yeah." Her voice came out hoarse. "Cold…" She swallowed, and that hurt, too. She lifted a hand and he caught it. His hand was hot against hers.

"Don't touch. It's still healing." He gently tucked her hand under the thick comforter then dropped to lie against her side. "I'll get you warm." He pulled the comforter up over them both.

She struggled to sit up. "Is it morning?" Rick put a hand on her shoulder and casually held her down. Struggling seemed to hurt her throat, so she gave up.

"No, not even close." He leaned over and kissed her forehead. His lips were fevered against her cool brow. "I just wanted to be sure that you were okay before we went back to sleep."

Rowan turned her head to look at him and bit back a groan. Her brows dipped in confusion, then flew up. "You bit me."

He raised a brow. "You volunteered, remember?" He smiled grimly and propped his elbow on her pillow, his chin on one hand. "I just wanted to fuck you, but you had a problem with that."

Rowan made a face. "I'm not into public sex." She swallowed and flinched against the sharp pain in her neck. "I didn't think two holes would hurt this much."

He sucked in his bottom lip. "Um, it's a little more than just two holes. It'll only hurt for about another twenty minutes, then it'll be gone."

Rowan frowned. "More than just two holes? Aren't you guys supposed to be neater than that?"

Rick's lips twisted in a brief smile. "Put some fake fangs in, then bite down on something, and see what you get."

She thought about it. "Oh, you have a point," Rowan nodded, and regretted the motion immediately. She flinched.

"Two points, actually." He fussed with her pillows.

"Bad pun." She made a face and swatted at him with a hand. "The pillows are fine."

"See? You're feeling better already." He suppressed a smile. "Anyway, they'll be completely healed by the time you wake up."

"They will?"

"Yeah. There's something in my saliva, I think, that promotes fast healing. You might have a bruise, but the wounds themselves will be gone."

"You think your saliva heals?" The lights began to fade and his face disappeared into shadow. "You're not sure?"

"It's not something I had checked." He slipped an arm around her and draped his length warmly against her side.

She felt his leg slide over hers to hold her in place against him. The silk of his pajama bottoms rubbed suggestively against her skin. *This is so far past my comfort zone...* She stiffened in his arms. "Um, aren't you a little close?" She felt his chuckle and realized that his mouth was resting near her collarbone.

"Right now you need to stay warm, so get over it and go to sleep."

"Hey, I don't want to get munched in the night." She shifted to move away and his arm held her firmly against him.

"You don't have to worry about another bite, I've had plenty. You're pretty damn potent, I'm kinda buzzing."

"You're buzzing? As in drunk on my blood?" She moved to make room for herself and somehow ended up getting entangled more securely against him with the blankets.

"Something like that," he mumbled and snuggled closer.

"What am I? A hundred proof?"

"Are you always this chatty before you sleep?"

"I'm not used to sleeping with someone else."

"Good." His voice was barely audible.

"What?"

"Just go to sleep."

She heard him yawn and immediately yawned in response. *Terrific, I'm being cuddled by a vampire.* His skin was almost hot and felt more than good. She bit back another yawn that made her throat ache. *That has to be from all the blood he drank from me.* Lethargy swamped her and his stolen warmth soaked into her.

❧ Nine ❧

Invocation

The thud of a slow heart thumped against her ear. Rowan awoke with her cheek pressed snugly against a warm, broad chest and froze in alarm. *What the Hell? Where am I?* She blinked, but couldn't see a thing in the stygian darkness. The scent of warm, familiar skin filled her nose. Memory struck heavily. The drive to Watertown, the cubist's dream house… *Oh, yeah I'm in bed with Rick…* The rest of her memories came flooding back. Klaus, the kiss, the bite… She swallowed. *At least my throat stopped hurting…*

Her throat felt fine, but her shoulder ached where she had slept on her side, with her arm tucked under the pillow. Her other arm was thrown carelessly across his waist. Somehow, she had wrapped herself around him, snuggling into his warmth. *I must have been in a really deep sleep.*

Cautiously, she retrieved her arms and shifted onto her back. *No blue glow from the barrier, so Klaus isn't anywhere around… I suppose that's good, but I can't see a damned thing.* She blinked again, but darkness blinded her utterly.

Rick shifted, groaned, then rolled and flung an arm across her waist. From the angle of his draping arm, she guessed that he was lying on his stomach. Gently she moved his arm. He abruptly tightened his grip around her waist, then curled up onto his side against her, trapping one of her arms under his body. She felt his hand move up her arm to her shoulder. His arm stretched alongside her head, then his broad palm burrowed into her hair, cupping her.

"Where do you think you're going?" His voice was husky with sleep and very close to her ear.

"Um, can we get up now?" She writhed to get her other arm free of his weight. It was like trying to move a downed tree.

"Yeah... In a minute."

She felt his breath, then his lips on her throat, then his tongue, creating tiny shivers of delight. He nipped on the tender skin of her throat, then his wet tongue feathered down to her collarbone. Her skin tingled and warmed from his heated mouth. A honey-thick trail of desire blazed straight down into to her core. *I need to get out of this bed before I do something I'm going to regret...*

She turned her head away and his fingers curled in her hair, holding her firmly against his open mouth and clever tongue. "Hey..." She grabbed hold of his wrist with her free hand and worked to ease her head away from his mouth. "Wait a minute, I thought you said you weren't going to munch on me."

He released her hair and carefully twisted his wrist from her grasp. "Don't want blood."

Abruptly, the fingers of his hand closed on her wrist, gently pressing her captured hand to the pillow above her head. His lips brushed her collarbone. She felt the wet rasp of his tongue.

"Uh, Rick, then what are you after?" She wiggled her captured fingers, then shifted away from his mouth. *Please let me get out of this bed before my sex drive takes over,* she thought desperately. *After all that magic last night, it's going to be a doozy...*

His response was a sleepy chuckle. He rolled slightly, pressing closer with his legs tangled in hers. His mouth slid down into the plunging neckline of her shirt. The buttons suddenly gaped loosely.

"Uh, Rick?"

The silk of his long mane slid across her exposed breasts. Her nipples tightened to swollen points of fire. His tongue brushed between the curves of her breasts, then skimmed lower.

Hunger stirred deep within and she bit back a moan. *Uh oh...*

"Guess what I want." A muscular leg insinuated itself between hers. "I'll even give you a clue." His knee slid up between her thighs into brief intimate contact.

Her knees compulsively closed around his muscular thigh to stop him, but succeeded in only bringing him into closer. His hip pressed against her hip. The heat of a very rigid erection nudged boldly against her. All the unfulfilled passion from before came rushing back in a torrent of liquid heat. Rowan drew a shuddering breath. *Shit, there goes my libido into overdrive.*

"Don't say no," he breathed. He released her wrist and a warm hand closed on the fullness of her breast.

Her nipple was a bright, angry point under his palm. She fought to keep from arching upward under his caress like a cat that craved petting. Her body quivered with hungry tension and it wanted what he was offering, goaded by the magic she had expended. *I have to stop this. I do not need to become involved with a vampire...* "Rick, I..."

"Say yes," she heard him whisper. His fingers closed around the erect nipple, piercing her with a stab of pleasure. "There is no one watching now."

A hot, wet mouth closed on her other breast. Delicious tension speared from her captured nipples straight down into her melting core. She let out a sharp, gasping breath. Her hands found his head and her fingers tangled in the silk of his hair, holding him to her breast. Teeth tugged gently, then lips seized and sucked. Her back arched helplessly upward and a moan escaped her lips.

She felt the mattress shift under her. He pulled his mouth from her breast with an audible and wet sound, and his hair slid through her fingers. He rose up on his knees in the dark, lifting away the blanket. The air was cool on her fevered skin.

His lips touched, traced the inner curve of her breasts, then traveled lower, making a wet trail down toward her belly. His hair swept the fullness of her breasts, then slid down. She felt his weight settle between her legs with his knees spread between her thighs, holding her open wide.

"Say yes, Rowan." His whispered words came from somewhere near her belly. His hands closed powerfully on her thighs, raising her knees and pushing her further open. "Say yes, now." Breath stirred the fine curls at the opening to her body.

She took a startled breath. His mouth brushed lightly against the tender flesh of her feminine folds, then his tongue stroked. She gasped. His tongue dove deeply. Heat flared up her spine. She choked with the intense sensations of his mouth engaged in the most intimate of kisses. Her heels dug into the mattress and her hips rose into him.

The wet sound of lapping was loud in the utter darkness. She jolted with every tiny stroke of his rapidly moving tongue. Brutal pleasure built and burned white hot. Helplessly she bucked against his mouth and a scream caught itself in her throat.

He pulled away and she collapsed against the mattress, trembling and gasping with unfulfilled need. The mattress shifted and she felt him move up her body. She could hear his labored breath. He stopped and held himself balanced on his palms, poised above her. The light increased until she could see his face, carved with deep shadows.

"Let me give you pleasure," he said softly. The bright gleam of impassioned hunger smoldered in his eyes. "Let me give you what you need."

She stared up at him, vibrating and ravenous to the core. Her shirt was spread open around her, revealing her pale vulnerable flesh, and her nipples swollen hard with excitement. His silk bottoms were gone and his rampant flesh arched between them, swollen and tipped in moisture.

She bit her lip. "I..." *Too late, too late,* her thoughts chased through her mind. *Too late to stop now.*

"Say yes, Rowan." Concentration hardened his stark features and his eyes gleamed a vibrant copper tinged with molten gold. His lips were full, wine-red and moist. He licked them. "Right now."

As though in a dream, she lifted her hands and cupped his face. "Yes."

He fell to his elbows with a heavy sigh. His mouth captured hers in a searing, possessive kiss and his arm slid under her to lift her against his fevered body. She felt his hand between their bodies, then the bold firmness of his heated flesh seeking the entrance to her moist warmth. He flexed, his back and hips arching, and pressed within.

She arched up into his possession and gloved him in the snug, damp heat of her eager body. They both groaned and his breath stole hers. Her heels hooked over his thighs and she shuddered, her heart pounding against his in their tight embrace.

He flexed above her, pulling back and thrusting with a groan that vibrated through her, then again, and again, taking her with slow deliberation. She writhed under him, her nails digging into his back. His pace quickened with her urging.

Climax built swiftly in a murderous upsurge of pleasure. She felt her body tremble on the excruciating edge, then felt an echoing shimmer that felt like less like orgasm and more like magic. Confused, she resisted, holding herself back from the fall into ecstasy.

"You are about to come," he said in her ear in a voice thick with passion. "Let it go, I'll catch you."

She gasped with wavering resistance. "I can't."

"You can." He thrust, hard.

Rowan fell over the blazing edge, shattering in an explosion of rapture, and screamed.

Rick gasped. "Oh, shit…" Abruptly, he climaxed with a moaning cry, flexing within and filling her body with his essence.

Magic sparked and blazed in a wildfire of stunning power. A second wave of glittering delight rampaged through them both. They shouted in unison and shuddered violently, tight in each other's embrace, inundated with stunning glory. A blazing ring of violet light flared to brilliance around the bed. The wave of pleasure passed and they collapsed, in panting repletion. The brilliant light died down to a soft glow, but remained a vivid violet.

Rowan opened her eyes and sighed. Tiny tremors wracked her limbs, but her violent appetite for sex seemed to have been satisfied. Rick was a limp, heavy weight across her damp chest. *Well, this is the first time my body is content with only one orgasm... Gods, but what an orgasm...*

Rick rolled onto his back with a gasping sigh, then glanced to the side. "Hey, the circle is active."

Rowan frowned, staring at the violet glow. "It's the wrong color..."

He turned to her, his eyes blazing violet like a black light. "Rowan, your eyes..." There was shock in Rick's voice. "Your eyes are glowing the same color as the barrier," he said softly.

Rowan swallowed. "So are yours."

He frowned. "What the Hell just happened?"

"I think, our magic somehow combined."

"What?"

"That's what it looks like to me." Rowan shrugged and bit her lip. "Your magic is normally red, my personal power is blue. Blue and red make purple or violet. It makes sense if you think about it."

Rick rolled his glowing eyes and gave her a lop-sided grin. "Is this gonna happen every time?"

"Uh..." Rowan raised her brows. *I suppose this is where I tell him I'm not going to do this again...*

Rick frowned. "Don't give me that."

"Give you what?"

"The look that says we won't be doing this again."

Rowan frowned. "What? Are you telepathic, too?"

He ignored the question and rolled on top of her. "I got news for you, that was the best damn orgasm I've had in a long time." His smile was grim and feral. "Purple glow or no purple glow, you're stuck with me now."

Rowan bared her teeth. "No still means no, Fang Boy."

He kissed the top of her head. "You already said yes. You can't take it back now."

Rowan opened her mouth to argue and he covered it with his, filling her mouth with his tongue in a possessive kiss. He moved against her. He was still hard, leaving no doubt as to his intentions. Her body warmed with languid interest and she moaned into his mouth.

He abruptly released her lips. "See?" He grinned. "You still want me."

"You are a raging pain in my ass," she said succinctly.

He grinned. "Honey, if you really want kinky, I can be kinky…" He dropped his head to kiss her breast, then captured a nipple.

His lips kindled a curl of warmth and she felt her nipples stir, rising to points. *Better stop this now before my body decides to take this further than I want to go…Again.* She grabbed a handful of black hair and yanked his head up. "Can we get up now?"

He sighed dramatically. "I suppose…" He rolled off of her and sat up, gloriously nude. She watched him reach for the remote control for the lights. They came up to full brightness in a matter of moments.

Rowan blinked in the brightness. "Oh, my gods…" she squeaked. Smears of bright scarlet stained her thighs and darkened the red sheets below her.

"What?" Rick turned around on the bed to look at her.

"It's blood." Rowan swallowed. "A lot of blood."

Rick bit his lip. "I was going to tell you about that…"

"What did you do to me?"

"It's not you, it's um, my, ah…" He gave her an uncomfortable look. "It's my cum."

"Your what?" Her words ended with an embarrassed squeak. She swallowed, completely unable to tear her eyes from the darkened smears.

He shrugged. "I'm a vampire, remember? So, my uh, semen is

blood-based."

"Blood-based?"

"Well yeah." He rolled his eyes. "Vampires reproduce by infecting others, not by um, making them pregnant."

"I figured that." She frowned. "But, I thought it was a matter of drinking it from you, as in: from your veins?"

Rick's cheeks became amazingly pink. "Let's just say that there are short-cuts to the process." He held up a hand. "Don't ask any more questions because that's all I'm going to say about it." He looked away, then slid off the bed completely nude.

"Is this why your sheets are red, to hide the blood?"

"Yeah," he said off-handedly.

Rowan bit her lip. All of a sudden she wanted to take the question back. She didn't want to think about how many women might have lain on these sheets before her. *I have no right to be jealous; sex does not mean 'relationship'.* She flinched inwardly. *What the Hell am I thinking? I do not want a relationship with an immortal being...*

He stepped past the softly glowing violet ring of the barrier before Rowan could call him back. She blinked. He hadn't even noticed it. "Well, that's odd," she said softly.

"What now?" he called over his shoulder while rummaging in the drawers of one of his dressers.

Rowan sat up and pulled the sides of the shirt closed. "You shouldn't have been able to cross that barrier." He turned to look at her. Her eyes fell to his upwardly curving shaft that rose from a nest of dark curls. A small throb of sexual hunger churned in her belly. She swallowed. *Oops, I guess my body is not completely satisfied...*

Frowning, he strode back toward the bed with a red shirt thrown over his shoulder and a pair of jeans in his hands. He crossed the barrier and shrugged. "I don't feel a thing." He tossed the clothes on the end of the bed and held out his hands. "Come on."

"Where are we going?" She took his hands and he hauled her off the bed. She stood and she was forced to hang onto his arm. Her legs felt too weak to support her. *I will not look down...*

Rick's brows shot up. "Having problems walking?"

Rowan glared at him, but continued to hold his arm while her knees shook.

He grinned shamelessly. "It was that good, huh?"

Rowan shot him a withering look. "Yeah, it was that good. Feel better now?"

"Hell, yeah." His grin broadened to show the points of his fangs. He abruptly leaned over and scooped her into his arms like a child.

She threw her arms around his neck in surprise. "Hey, where are you taking me?"

"To shower." He strode for the bathroom.

She leaned back to look in his face. "I can shower by myself, you know."

He shoved the bathroom door open with his foot, then quirked a brow at her. "It'll be more fun this way."

"I can imagine," she said dryly. Her thoughts drifted shamelessly downward...

He stopped by the glass shower stall. "Oh, can you?" He grinned and shifted her in his arms until he held her, belly to belly. Her legs dangled and he cupped her ass in his palms. Slowly, he let her slide down his body. Her feet landed on the fluffy bathmat on the floor.

Still wrapped in his arms, Rowan caught herself peeking at his still-erect shaft. "Haven't you had enough?"

"Of you?" He rubbed suggestively against her belly then dropped a quick kiss on her forehead. "Never. And from your hard nipples, neither have you." He stepped away and pulled a pair of fluffy towels from the cabinet then set them on the sink's counter.

Embarrassed, she crossed her arms over her chest. "Why don't you let me take a shower while you go get my suitcases from the car, so I can change into clean clothes after?"

He turned to grin at her. "What if I like you naked?"

Rowan raised a brow. "Around Klaus?"

Rick grimaced. "Good point."

Rowan smiled sweetly. "The car keys are in my red velvet

shoulder bag under the foot of the bed."

His fingers closed on her shoulders. "I don't want to leave you alone."

Rowan made a face. "I'm safer from him than you are, remember?"

"Don't remind me…"

"Lucky for you it's daytime, so Klaus should be holed up in a dark corner somewhere." She patted his hand. "Go fetch my suitcases like a good little vampire while I clean up, then you can take me to breakfast."

"Got a better idea…" Rick pulled the glass shower door open and turned on the shower. "It'll be faster if we shower together. I'll make mine quick, then leave you to finish while I get your stuff." Steam fogged the glass. "

"That's okay, I'll wait while you shower."

"Chicken?"

Rowan crossed her arms. *Yes…* She gave him a stern look. "I have work to do. House-cleaning, remember?"

He rolled his eyes. "There you go, reminding me again." He slanted a narrowed glance at her. "I don't think we're going to be able to drive him out of the house while the sun is still up, so technically we have until sunset."

"Take your shower, will you?" Rowan stomped her foot. "I'm all sticky and I want to get cleaned up."

"Fine, whatever…" The shower door closed. "Coward." Water splashed on the inside of the glass and the sweet scent of shampoo filled the moist, humid air.

Rowan sighed in relief. *That was close. It wouldn't take much to wake my sex drive again A bit more magic and I would have pinned him against the shower wall.*

Long minutes passed before Rick slid the door open and reached for the towel Rowan held out for him. She darted into the shower and firmly closed the glass door in his face. She stood under the pounding water and promptly moaned with the delicious warmth.

"Hey..." The door slid open a few inches. "Don't get started on anything interesting without me."

Rowan flung water at him. "Go get my clothes!"

The door thumped closed. "Yes, oh mistress," Rick intoned in a deep voice.

Rowan heard the bathroom door open then close. "Gods, that man." She sighed, then cringed. *Oh Goddess, I just fucked a vampire...*

ஒ Ten ஒ

Thirst

R owan stepped out of the shower more wrung out than when she went in. *Exhaustion must be catching up with me...* She grabbed for a nearby towel. *At least my libido seems to be back under some control.*

Wrapped in a huge towel, Rowan stepped out of the bathroom. With delight, she saw that her suitcases were sitting at the foot of the bed unopened. Rick was sitting on the bed in a scarlet T-shirt and black jeans, reading a newspaper. The loose pages were scattered all over the bed. Rowan blinked and walked closer. *A vampire that reads the Wall Street Journal?* She shook her head.

Rick looked up from his paper. "I was beginning to think that you planned on staying in there." He folded up the newspaper with a crunching rustle and laid it to one side.

"I thought about it." Rowan grinned wryly. "Thanks for getting my suitcases."

"That reminds me, what the Hell have you got in that one?" he gestured toward the larger of the two. "It was heavy even for me. I don't know how you got it in your car."

Rowan frowned. "It's not that heavy, but it does have a bunch of my magic books in it." She felt a smile creep onto her face. "Maybe they just don't like you."

He frowned ferociously. "Bullshit."

Rowan shrugged and grabbed the handle of the larger suitcase. She lifted it from the floor using both hands and groaned. "You're right, it is a little heavy."

His mouth fell open. "How the Hell did you do that? I know I'm a hell of a lot stronger than you and I think it's heavy."

Rowan set the case down. "Oh, that's right...I forgot! Witchcraft." She bit back a smug smile. "I have an anti-theft spell on it. It's supposed to make the suitcase too heavy to lift."

"You forgot," he said with heavy sarcasm.

"Actually, yeah." She knelt and opened the smaller of the two. Gripping the towel around her with one hand, she dug out a fresh pair of black jeans and a black T-shirt emblazoned with 'Don't make me get my winged monkeys' in broad, white letters.

"I put the spell on the suitcase ages ago." She shrugged. "I'm so used to it that I don't feel it anymore." She tossed clean underwear and fresh socks on the pile, then gathered her stuff in one hand and stood up to see Rick watching her with interest.

"Red satin panties and a matching bra, I like it." He flopped on his stomach across the bed and propped up his chin with both hands.

She frowned. "Do you mind?"

"What?" He smiled and fluttered his lashes.

She growled and headed for the bathroom.

"Where do you think you're going?" The bathroom door shut with a hard slam.

"Did you do that?" She turned to glare at the smug vampire.

He raised a brow. "And if I did?"

"What? Are you telekinetic or something?"

"Actually, yes, somewhat." His smile was sharp, and pointed. "I guess I forgot." He shrugged. "It kinda comes and goes. It seems to be working pretty good today." He raised a brow. "I must be eating right."

Rowan firmly decided to let that last comment pass. "I was going to dress in the bathroom."

"Oh, give it a break, will you?" He rolled his eyes. "I've seen everything already. Dress here, I can feel Klaus moving around in the house."

"Whatever..." Rowan bit out in defeat and tossed the clothes on the bed. Fuming, she grabbed her underwear and turned her back to him. She tucked the towel as securely as she could, then leaned with her butt against the mattress. Balancing precariously, she struggled into her panties. She felt the bed shift.

Rick chuckled directly behind her. "Here, let me give you a hand with that."

Rowan's head jerked up sharply only to feel the towel grabbed and tugged off. "Hey!"

"I suggest you quit worrying about me and hurry," his voice was soft. "Klaus is coming down."

"Shit," she hissed. She jerked the bra on, fastened it in the front, then turned toward the bed, reaching for her T-shirt. Rick was leaning over the side with the shirt dangling from his fingers. His grinning mouth was barely an inch away. She snatched it from his hand and tugged over her head.

He held out her jeans, but his eyes were on the vault door. "Hurry."

Rowan stepped into her black jeans and tucked her shirt in quickly. She felt the shimmer of unearthly power. She buttoned and zipped as fast as she could, then turned, barefoot with her socks in hand. A pool of shadow was coalescing by the door.

Klaus formed in the corner of the room by the closed vault door, frowning and staring directly at Rowan. "I will ask you not drive me from this house, *ved'ma*." He folded his hands into his tattered robe and sniffed.

"What?" Rowan glanced at an equally surprised Rick.

"Look, Klaus, I'd like to keep you as a guest..." Rick threw a bewildered shrug at Rowan and slid off the bed. "But I can't have you, um feeding on me."

Klaus looked away. "I do not need so much. A glass will do."

Rick tilted his head to the side. "Only a glass?"

Rowan's mouth fell open and she looked wide-eyed, at Rick. "You can't be serious?"

Rick grabbed Rowan's arm and leveled a sharp look down at her. *What now?* She raised her brows in question.

Be still! Rick's voice was as clear as a shout.

She flinched then realized that though she had heard him, his lips had not moved. *He's telepathic, too?* Rowan thought to herself in alarm. *Shit, what's next?*

Rick nodded at her. *Yeah, I'm telepathic with anyone I drink from.* He shrugged. *It's a vampire thing.*

Rowan felt the hair on her neck stand up. *How telepathic and is this permanent?* Mother of Heaven, she did not want him poking around in her mind.

You have to actually form a sentence clearly and kinda shout it at me, for me to hear it. He smiled grimly. *But then, you tend to shout mentally anyway. I can normally pick up the drift but not always the exact phrase when you're pissed—even without the blood sharing.*

Terrific, she thought back at him with a sour smile. *Just what I always wanted, a man that knows my mind.* She frowned. *Wait a minute, are you saying that I'm normally loud enough for you to hear?*

Hey, this isn't perfect; it works just like any normal conversation. He shook his head and rolled his eyes. *Just 'cause I can understand what you say in your thoughts does not mean that I can figure out what the hell you mean—and no, I can't hear precisely what you're saying without the blood-share, but you're loud enough for me to figure out that you're usually bitching.* He grinned broadly. *And every guy I know likes a screamer.*

Rowan's mouth opened on a retort.

Klaus interrupted them with a cough. "If you are through with your private conversation?"

Rowan jerked around to look at the ragged vampire. *Goddess, I forgot all about him. Can he hear us?*

I didn't, and no, he can't, but he can tell when we're talking. Rick turned to Klaus and his smile bled away. "Were you saying that you'll take blood from a glass?"

Klaus dipped his head. "If that is all you will offer your guest." He kept his chin down and looked at them from under his brows.

Rowan stepped forward. "Why shouldn't we just make you leave?"

Rick squeezed Rowan's arm and pulled her back. *Will you keep quiet?*

Klaus leveled his crimson gaze at Rowan. "I have need of Rickart. There is no one else, unless you wish to provide?"

"Keep her out of this." Rick's European accent became pronounced with his temper. "I might be willing to part with a glass or two—if you will swear not to take what I'm not willing to give?"

Rick, are you insane? Rowan jerked on her arm. If he squeezed any tighter, she was going to have bruises.

Klaus inclined his head with a small smile. "That would be acceptable."

Rick jabbed a finger at him. "Look, I don't want to play the part of blood-donor indefinitely "

Klaus gave an indifferent shrug. "I have no plans to remain long."

Rowan projected strongly to Rick. *Make him bleed and swear.*

I know, I know. Rick winced. *And there's no need to scream it! I can hear you just fine.* Rick narrowed his gaze at the elder vampire. "All right, Klaus, I want you show me some blood, then swear that you won't take more blood from me than what I'm willing to give you."

Klaus frowned, his brows dipping low. His lip curled. "And if I do not?"

Rick smiled grimly. "Then I let Rowan do her thing, and you can go find your dinner elsewhere."

Klaus snarled, bearing his jagged teeth and lunged at them. The circle around the bed flared a vibrant violet. Klaus jerked to a halt with a hiss, throwing an arm over his eyes.

Rowan felt a shimmer in her magic, swiftly followed by a sensual throb deep and low. A warm flush came over her skin. "Oh, shit," she said softly. *I'm reacting to the barrier,* she thought to herself softly.

Rick stepped forward, yanking Rowan behind him. "I mean it, Klaus. Swear on your blood or I'll have Rowan send you packing "

Klaus backed away and the blazing ring dropped to a shimmer. He lowered his arm and turned his shoulder to them stiffly. "Very well. I will bleed for you and swear."

Rick nodded. "Good." He crossed his arms over his chest. "Do it right here and I'll go upstairs and find you a glass."

Klaus raised his wrist to his mouth and stared at Rick. There was a flash of sharp teeth and dark blood began welling in a thick, syrupy rivulet down his arm. It began dripping, then streaming onto the floor and soaking into the carpet. A pool quickly formed on the floor.

"That's an awful lot of blood," Rowan said softly.

Rick's eyes widened. "Shit, Klaus, you didn't need to shed that much! A few drops will do."

Klaus shrugged and watched his blood pooling on the carpet. "It is my nature, as I do not have veins."

He doesn't have veins? Rowan moved a few steps toward the bleeding vampire. "What's to keep you from bleeding to death?"

Rick jerked her to a halt. *Don't cross the barrier,* he projected.

Rowan suddenly realized how close she was to the glimmering ring and stepped back. She looked at the wounded vampire and saw him watching her.

Klaus raised his brows. "Would you care if I were destroyed, *ved'ma?*"

Rowan bit her lip. "I don't want anybody to die."

Rick shook his head. "Just hurry up and swear that you won't take any more blood than I'm willing to give, then we'll bind that wound and get you fed."

Klaus's head came up. "Are you both concerned with my existence?"

"Well, yeah." Rick gave him a sour smile. "You're staining my carpet."

Klaus frowned. The bloodstain on the carpet continued to spread.

"Damn it, Klaus!" Rick waved a hand at the pooling blood. "Just swear!"

Klaus rolled his eyes the sighed. "I swear not to take more blood than I am given."

"Like this, Klaus." Rick growled. "You swear that you won't take any more blood than I am willing to give."

"So be it." The elder vampire looked away from them. "I swear that I will not take any more blood than you are willing to give."

"Accepted." Rick let out a heavy sigh of relief. There was a feeling of released pressure throughout the room.

Klaus gave a small shudder and his face showed surprise. He abruptly collapsed straight down like a marionette with its strings cut. He lay in his own blood in a tumbled heap of crooked limbs.

"Fuck!" Rick lunged across the barrier toward Klaus.

"Oh, shit!" Rowan whirled and grabbed a pillow, jerking the case off. She turned and hurried toward Klaus. Rick was kneeling and using his hands to staunch the flow of blood from the elder vampire's wrist. Her bare feet sank into the bloody carpet. *Eww, gross!* She held out the crimson pillowcase. "Here, use this to bind it."

"Not my pillowcase, those are silk." He rolled his eyes. "There's a first aid kit under the bathroom sink."

"In that case, let me hold his wound while you go get it." She tossed the pillowcase aside.

Rick stared up at her in surprise.

Rowan looked down at him. "What? You're faster."

"Nice of you to notice," Rick said dryly. "Don't let him bleed dry on my carpet and don't go all glowing and burn him."

"As long as he stays out, he'll be fine." She dropped to her knees with a moist squelch on the wet carpet and made a face. *What a mess* Leaning close to Rick, she reached for Klaus and he let go. Rowan closed her hands around the jagged tear in the Klaus's wrist. His blood welled quickly and tried to ooze past her fingers. She shifted to cover the wound with her palm and gripped tightly. The vampire's arm was solid, like wood, and his skin papery to the touch. She could feel the hum of otherworldly darkness thrum across her senses. *Oh, yeah, this is so not a human being*

She sat back on her heels, cradling his arm in her lap and felt the slimy wetness that told her that his blood was seeping through her pants. *Now I have to change my jeans. I hope Rick has a washing machine.*

Rick was suddenly at her side with a white metal case and a dark hand-towel. She looked up at him in some surprise; she hadn't noticed when he'd left. "Shit, you're fast."

Rick flashed her a wry grin. "Good to know you think I'm useful. Use this to wipe your hands." He tossed the towel into her lap, then jerked the kit open. Quickly, he dug out some stick-on sutures, a handful of sterile pads, gauze and surgical tape.

Rowan released Klaus's wrist and blood poured past her hand. "This is pretty bad. Do you think he needs stitches?" She wiped her hands on the towel, but the blood proved difficult to get off. It was as thick as glue.

"I hope not."

"He looks like a jumbled doll." Rowan tilted her head to one side, trying to make sense of all the angles that represented the fallen vampire. "That position can't be comfortable." Klaus's arms and legs appeared to be all tangled up with his head sitting perched atop the pile. No human could achieve that kind of a collapse unless every bone in their body was broken at the joint.

"Who gives a shit whether or not he's comfortable? He's the bad-guy in this little soap opera, remember?"

Rowan raised brow at him. "And you're not?"

Rick gave her a cheeky grin. "Oh, hell no, I'm the hero."

Rowan rolled her eyes. "You wish…"

In less than a minute, Rick had the wound taped closed and tightly bound. "Looks like I got the bleeding stopped."

She handed him the towel. "Good, because he looks like he lost a gallon on your carpet." Rowan bit her lip and looked up at Rick. "Now what?"

Rick wiped at his palms. "Now I go get a glass from the kitchen." He sighed and shook his head. "He's going to need to put back all the blood he lost." He worked to get the blood off his hands and frowned at the towel. "I hope this shit comes out in the wash," he mumbled.

Rowan's brows shot up. "You can't afford to give him this much."

"Let's hope he doesn't need this much, I usually don't." He rose to his feet in a smooth motion that looked like he'd been pulled with strings.

Rowan suddenly realized how careful Rick had been to use slow and human motions around her. *I guess I forgot that he's as inhuman as Klaus.*

Rick raised a brow at her. "I'm not nearly as bad as Klaus. I won't bleed to death from a scratch."

Shit... She cringed. *I forgot that he could read my thoughts, too.*

"Not all of your thoughts." He grinned. "Just most of them."

Rowan frowned. "Was that supposed to make me feel better?"

Rick sighed and held out his hand. "Come on. I want you to go back inside the barrier and stay there 'til I get back."

"But—"

"No 'buts'." Rick shook his head. "He's oath-bound, so he won't bleed me, but he hasn't sworn not to bleed you."

Rowan took his hand and stood up then frowned. "I can protect myself."

"Just do it." He shook his head. "Look, it'll make me feel better about leaving you alone with him."

Rowan threw up her hands. "All right! Just be quick, I want to get back in the shower—this stuff is all over me."

"I intend to." Rick smiled grimly. "I want 'in the shower' too." He pointed at the bed.

Rowan sighed and walked back over the barrier. She needed to get some clean clothes out anyway. She pulled at her T-shirt and noticed dark smears. *How the hell did I get blood on my shirt?*

"And stay there!" Rick called out.

Rowan turned, but he was gone already. "Pushy bastard," she growled, then knelt to dig her suitcase out from under the bed. *Damn good thing I packed a few changes of clothes, but I didn't think I was going to need to change before breakfast.* She pulled the suitcase out and lifted the lid.

"So, *ved'ma...*"

Rowan turned so fast she nearly fell.

Klaus slowly drew himself straight upward, like a toy on a string. His skin was very gray, almost blue and tight against his skull. Only his crimson eyes held color.

"How are you feeling, Klaus?" *He looks awful...*

Klaus regarded her with a puzzled frown. "Why did you not try to destroy me?" His voice was not much more than a whisper.

Rowan slid her suitcase around so she could rummage without losing sight of the vampire. "Just have a seat, Klaus. Rick has gone to get you a glass for your, um, dinner."

His lip curled with a sneer. "Rickart was gone long enough for you to burn me to oblivion with your witchcraft." He tottered toward the circle. "Why did you not?" Violet began to glow in a soft ring around the bed.

"Whoa! Stop right there." Rowan put out a hand and slowly rose to her feet. "The barrier is still active, don't hurt yourself." Rowan nibbled on her lower lip. The low sensual throb in her belly was growing more pronounced. *Shit, if he keeps activating the barrier and triggering my magic, I'm going to have to sneak off to masturbate or I'm going to end up sleeping with the vampire... Again.*

Klaus frowned at the circle's glowing edge, then pinned her with a glare. "Tell me, *ved'ma!*" He raised a fist and the barrier began to rise.

"All right! Just don't hit the ring!" *I'm already soaking my panties as it is!* She took a deep breath. "It's like this; you can't hurt me and you're sworn not to feed off of Rick, so you're not a danger to either of us. Okay?"

Klaus's brows rose. He took a step back from the glowing barrier then tilted his head to the side thoughtfully and frowned. Abruptly, he collapsed straight down into a vaguely sitting position.

Rowan stared in surprise. "Are you all right?" She moved to the edge of the circle and stopped. *What the Hell is taking Rick so long?*

Klaus shook his head slowly. "You, I do not understand." He flung up his hand and waved it at her. The bandage was a stark white against his gray skin. "I am your soul's enemy and yet, you rush to save me from harm." He waved his hand towards the stairs, then drew his wrist close and poked at the bandage with a finger. "And he binds my wound to keep me from..." He barked out a laugh then a twisted and sour smile curled his lips. "Bleeding to death."

"It's part of being one of the 'good guys', we're supposed to save people if we can." Rowan rolled her eyes. "Why? Do you want to die?"

"I cannot die." Klaus curled a lip, showing his long teeth. "I am not alive."

Rowan snorted. "For a dead guy you're awfully mobile." She knelt to dig through her suitcase. "And a pain in the ass," she muttered.

He leveled a venomous glare at Rowan. "You, *ved'ma*, stink of this 'goodness'..." He jabbed a finger at her. "And yet you have allowed one of the damned—a vampire— to drink of you."

"Yeah, so? It wasn't all that bad." She swallowed with the vivid memory. *Yeah, well, the bite wasn't that great either.*

Klaus bared his serrated teeth. "You have also defiled yourself with his body; the very air reeks of your pleasures." His voice was a low rumbling.

Rowan flinched and her cheeks grew warm. "Well, I wouldn't call it defiling exactly." She felt something moving in her thoughts.

That's good to know. Rick's mind-voice was clear, but it sounded a little hollow and very German.

Rowan looked up at the ceiling. "What the Hell is taking you so long?"

I'm on the phone.

"On the phone?"

Yeah, it's Thursday. Remember? I have a business to run.

"I'm happy for you, but you have a guest waiting, remember?" Rowan glanced at Klaus, still hunched into something resembling a seated position.

Keep him busy.

"What?" Rowan stomped her foot then grimaced. *Gods, that's nasty.* Her foot was covered in blood and sticking to the carpet. "Are you insane?" She pointed at the ceiling. "You can call them back. Klaus is about to pass out from starvation down here."

I'm hanging up; I'll be there in less than a minute.

"You'd better be," she snapped.

Rick was suddenly at the doorway tall, dark, devastatingly cute and grinning. "Or what?" He twirled a glass in his hand.

Rowan jabbed a finger his way. "I can still make you hurt, Fang Boy."

Rick waggled his brows. "Do you promise?"

"I give you my word, but first things first." Rowan waved a hand at Klaus who was watching the exchange with interest.

Rick turned to look at the elder vampire and frowned. "Right." He pulled a small and wickedly curved dagger from his belt. "You don't look so good, Klaus." He glanced at Rowan. "Come over here and give me a hand with this."

Rowan walked over with a grim smile. "Do I get to slice you open?"

Rick smiled sourly. "No, you get to hold the glass." He held out a clear tumbler. "Hold it right here."

Rowan took the glass and held it close to his wrist. "Why do you get to have all the fun?"

"'Cause I'm the bad guy, and you're the good guy; that means I get to do all the blood-letting." He tilted his wrist sideways to the floor, then positioned the dagger at a spot on his wrist. "Hold it close, it's going to fill fast and don't spill, I've got enough blood on the carpet."

"I thought you wanted to be the hero?" She batted her eyelashes at him.

He looked at her. "Have I told you that you're a sarcastic bitch?"

Rowan raised a brow at him. "Yes, you have. Do you want to do this by yourself?"

He took a deep breath and huffed it out. "Just hold the glass steady."

"Alright already, let's see the color of your blood."

Rick frowned, then jerked the dagger at his wrist. Red flowed thick and fast.

"Mother of us all!" The glass filled quickly in her hand and got heavy fast. It seemed almost hot. "Do all you vampires bleed like faucets?"

"Looks that way," he mumbled. "Don't lose any!" He jerked his wrist away and licked the wound. It closed almost immediately.

Rowan frowned.

Rick shot her a quelling look. *I can hear that thought forming in your head—I was not about to lick Klaus, so stop thinking about it.*

Rowan bit back a smile. *You're homophobic!*

Rick snorted and took the glass. *Actually, I'm not.* He gave her a sour look. *I just didn't want to get my mouth near Klaus's blood.* Rick turned and handed Klaus the glass.

Klaus came up from the floor and snatched it from Rick's hand. He downed the whole thing so fast, Rowan barely saw him tip the glass. Klaus licked his lips, then studied Rick with a frown.

"What?" Rick asked uneasily.

Klaus shot a glance at Rowan then looked steadily at Rick. "I taste her power."

Rick frowned. "Well, yeah, you saw me take her blood last night."

"I do not taste yours." Klaus raised a brow. "If I had known, I would not have sought you out."

Rick took a small step back. "Known what?"

Klaus wiped a hand across his mouth "That you are not fully vampire."

"What?" both Rowan and Rick said together.

"I merely thought you young." Klaus tilted his head slightly to the side while staring at Rick. "You still live."

Rick frowned. "Yeah? So?"

Klaus pursed his lips. "Your sire must have been very old and very strong to have passed enough vitality that I did not realize this. You are close, but not truly vampire."

Rowan looked at Rick then Klaus. "Is this bad?"

Klaus sighed. "He is not strong enough to sustain me."

Rowan bit her lip. "Then you'll leave?"

Klaus's eyes moved from one to the other. "No."

"No?" Rick and Rowan said together.

"If he's not what you need, then why do you want to stay?" Rowan stomped her foot on the soft carpet.

Klaus shook his head slowly. "It is now too late for that."

In exasperation, she focused on the ancient vampire, trying to guess what he was up to. Abruptly, the hair on her neck started to rise and her balance started to slide a little to the right. *Oh, shit!* It was a sensation she recognized from being a fortune-teller for so many years. She was experiencing the weight of an irrevocable decision shifting possibilities from *'might be'* into *'will be'*. Klaus was planning to do something that was going to change the road to the future, irrevocably; she was literally, feeling it coming.

Abruptly, Klaus shattered into shredded darkness. The glass fell to the floor.

"I hate it when he does that." Rick knelt to collect the glass.

Rowan looked up at the ceiling. "Rick, he's up to something."

"Yeah, I know." He jerked his head toward the bed. "Come on, we both need a shower."

Rowan followed Rick toward the bathroom. "Rick, I have a really bad feeling about this."

"Yeah, me too."

❧ Eleven ❧

Satiation

With his back to her, Rick dragged his shirt over his head, then tossed it into the bathroom sink. "Throw all your stuff in the sink. I'll toss the lot in the wash after we get out."

"Sure." Rowan found her eyes traveling the play of muscle across his back. She blinked. On the back of his shoulder, near the collarbone, was a round white scar the size of a silver dollar. It was directly opposite the twin gouge scars on his breast.

There was a jingle of a belt buckle and Rowan's eyes dipped lower. Rick's hands gripped his waistband and he pulled the wet and clinging jeans down his flanks. His firm ass appeared and Rowan had to remember to breathe. Her body gave an interested lurch and she felt her temperature rise. Her body's hunger was awakening.

Rick jerked his jeans down. Long, dark red smears painted his muscular thighs. He stopped and turned to look at her.

"What are you waiting for? Get undressed, you're dripping on my floor."

Rowan swallowed and wrenched her eyes away from the view. "I can wait."

"It'll be faster if we shower together." Rick pulled off his pants and tossed them in the sink. "Come on, get that shit off."

Rowan sighed and turned her back. She yanked off her T-shirt, tossed it in the sink, then fought with her wet jeans. She found her eyes sneaking glances at Rick in the mirror. Completely and deliciously nude, he put one foot in the shower, bent over and turned on the water. She swallowed. *Watching him is not doing me any good,* she told herself softly, then finally succeeded in yanking off her jeans and panties.

His head came out and turned to look at her with a raised brow. "You ready?"

Rowan gathered the shreds of her dignity. "We don't have to shower together."

"Yes, we do." He smiled and held out his hand. "Scared?"

"Of you?" Rowan swallowed. Reactionary moisture was sliding down her thighs. *Yes...*

"Just get in. I'll be quick." He smiled. "I promise." He grabbed her wrist and pulled.

Rowan was jerked under the hot water. "Hey!" Rowan stepped back against the wall, blinking the water from her eyes.

"Come here." He turned with a sponge in his hands and reached for her.

She flinched back.

"Take it easy, it's just a sponge with soap." The water glistened on Rick's skin and his wet hair lay like ink across his shoulders. His hand closed on her shoulder. "Hasn't anyone ever bathed you before?"

"Uh, no."

"Good." With strong, downward strokes, he covered her shoulders and breasts in masses of foam.

Rowan's nipples tingled with the attention. She bit her lip. "I can wash myself..."

"This shit is hard to get off, so it'll probably take both of us to get it all and I like touching you." He swirled the sponge across her belly. The foam gathered and dripped down her legs. He knelt and shoved the sponge between her thighs to wash her intimately.

Rowan bit back a gasp.

"Admit it, you're enjoying it." His smile was all male and his mouth was only inches from her belly.

She shuddered and leaned back against the wall while her knees shook. *Don't remind me...*

"You used magic," he said softly. "Didn't you? Every time that barrier flared from Klaus, that was you, wasn't it?"

Rowan bit her lip and nodded.

"Turn around and spread your legs."

"What?"

Rick stood up and took her shoulders, turning her gently but firmly. "Just do it, so I can wash your backside. You sat in it, remember?"

"Oh..." Rowan turned around and placed her palms on the cool tile.

"Much better," he said softly.

The sponge swirled down her back, then concentrated on her buttocks and thighs. Abruptly one of his hands covered hers, trapping it against the wall and she felt his chest pressing against her back. His breath was warm in her ear.

"Have I told you what a sweet ass you have?"

"What?" Rowan jerked. She felt his soap-slippery fingers slide down the seam of her backside to brush her intimately. "Hey!" She moved away and his arm slid around her waist to hold her in position.

"Why is it that whenever things get interesting, you always run away?" His hand imprisoned her palm against the wall and the fingers of his other hand slid down and parted the outer lips of her intimate flesh. He pressed firmly against her back, holding her buttocks tight against his heavy arousal. His teeth nipped at her ear.

"What do you think you're doing?" A finger stroked her and a bolt of pleasure stabbed, inducing carnal heat that roared through her. She bit back a hungry moan.

"What does it feel like?" His fingers moved, lightly, quickly, touching, rubbing and encouraging.

Pleasure built with swift and crushing force. She gasped and bucked under his dancing fingers.

"That's my hot little girl." He chuckled in her ear. "You used quite a bit of power last night and then today, too. I know that you need sex to recharge your magic…"

Rowan froze. *Mother of us all, when did he figure that out?*

"First thing this morning." His fingers slowed. "As soon as you climaxed, I felt you drawing from me and recharging."

Son of a bitch, she thought.

"No big deal." His voice rasped against the tender skin behind her ear. "I suspected that using your magic made you hot, I smelled it on you last night right after you set the barrier, but you seemed to shut that right down." His lips and teeth nibbled lightly on her throat. "Then I smelled the lust rolling off you when the barrier flared last night, then again when Klaus charged it this morning." His fingers slowed even more. "It made me really fucking hard," he said very softly. "I wanted to bury myself in you right there on the floor."

His potent words and resonating voice simmered like warm syrup, pooling low and deep. She could feel her body's excitement wetting his hand and her thighs. "I can't…" She took a panting breath. "I can't help it." The razor edge of climax threatened and Rowan came up on her toes in anxious anticipation.

He stopped, pulling his hand away. "Going somewhere without me?"

She moaned in frustration and dropped to her heels. Her knees trembled and his hands steadied her against the shower wall. She bit her lip and burned with hollow and grasping hunger. "I can put off sex for a while, but sooner or later…" Restlessly, she shifted her backside against his delicious heat.

"Oh, I know. Sooner or later, it catches up to you and you have to fuck." He took a deep shuddering breath. "And I have just what you need, what we both need, right here." The heated brand of his shaft pressed down until it slid between her thighs and rubbed against her tender flesh.

Her feet jerked further apart all by themselves and she arched, rubbing wantonly against him until he was pressing hard against her body's entrance.

He stopped, poised on her threshold. His arm released her then his palms covered both of her hands, pressing them against the cool tile. "It's your turn." His voice deepened and grew husky. "It's your turn to fuck me."

Rowan took a harsh breath and writhed with an appetite that pulsed in time with her heart. "That's not fair..."

"I think it's perfectly fair." He shifted, rubbing invitingly against her warm, slippery and engorged sex. He stopped with the blunt tip of his shaft nosing at her body's moist entrance. "If you want it, you're going to have to take it," he said hoarsely.

She froze in trembling indecision while ravenous need clenched within her. Hot water pounded his back and slithered down hers. She felt moisture spreading and her body opening to receive. A soft tremulous sound escaped her lips.

"You need this as much as I want to give it," he whispered. "Take me, sweetheart, take what you need... What we both need."

With a small shudder of submission to her desire, she pressed back against him.

He grunted and slid into her body. "Oh, God, yes," he hissed and held perfectly still.

She lifted a foot and writhed to take him deeper until her buttocks pressed back against his hips. She stopped and took a breath.

He let out a harsh breath. "Now, do me, Kitten."

She arched her back, easing his rigid length out, then flexed to slide him back in. He leaned in and his lips touched the corner of her mouth. She turned and opened her mouth to kiss him. He groaned and his arm encircled her waist. She shoved back against him and he thrust slowly; too slowly.

Rowan mewled in impatience, broke the kiss and shoved hard

against the wall, pushing in earnest. "More," she gasped out. Her hips twisted as she sought to get him deeper, but his height and the angle was not allowing for enough speed or a deep enough stroke to satisfy, only to torment. Frustrated and impatient in her hunger, she slid out from under him.

"Hey," he said, catching her around the waist.

She turned in his arms, grabbed his hair and pulled him down to press her open mouth to his in a kiss. "Get down on the floor," she husked into his mouth.

He pulled away. "What?"

"The floor," she pushed at his shoulder. "Get on the floor."

His arms wrapped around her and he took her down with him. They hit the floor and she gasped. The shower poured over her shoulders. He crawled back, with her straddling him until his face was out of the spray and he sat back propped up against the wall. He shook the water from his face and grinned. "You want floor? We got floor."

Without ceremony, she grasped his shaft in one hand and dropped down onto him hard, taking him whole. He gasped and his back arched under her. He slid in her slick channel, impossibly deep, brutally rigid and utterly satisfying. "Yes," she sighed. "Better."

"Fuck, Rowan." He lifted his head and stared at her with his eyes ignited to flame-lit copper. "Give a guy some warning."

Her eyes narrowed in the spray, she came up on her knees, splaying her hands on his shoulders. "You want me to fuck you? Then I'll fuck you." Her voice came out low and harsh.

His lips curled in a feral grin. "I think I like this aggressive side of you." His hands came up to cup her breasts, then pulled at her swollen nipples.

She stayed poised on her knees with his fingers deliciously tormenting her excited flesh, and then she dropped, impaling herself on his length.

His head fell back, baring his long teeth in a throaty moan. "God, yes..." His hand cupped the back of her neck and pulled, angling her breast into his mouth sucking hard.

She felt a delicious pulse of intense pleasure race from her breast to her core and moaned. She rose, leaning forward and squeezing his length with her inner muscles, then twisted her hips, tilted her pelvis back and slammed back down.

He gasped and shoved upward, hard. "That's it, that's perfect and God help me, Kitten, don't stop."

She lunged, back and forth, with unrelenting force, riding him harder than she would normally dare, gathering speed and momentum. His hand found her ass and pulled her in time with his upward thrusts, helping to speed her to satisfaction.

"Yes," she gasped out. This was what she needed. This was what she had always needed and never knew she was missing; a lover that could satisfy her rapacious demands without holding back. A deep rolling wave of brutal urgency built with vicious speed.

His arms lock around her. "Rowan," he panted, "I'm going to cum." He moaned. "Any second."

"Good," she said harshly and felt the muscles of her body tighten, clenching. Climax crested with ruthless tension. Straining against her rigid body, she grabbed the back of his neck and pulled his mouth up onto hers. Her breath stopped for a long moment, then frenzied rapture took her and she bucked, moaning her impassioned ecstasy into his mouth. An electric frisson of power shivered at the base of her spine.

His moan joined hers and mouths locked together, he rolled her under him, pulling her leg up over him, thrusting violently once, twice and then he came. She felt the vibration of him within her and the wash of hot liquid coursing from his body, filling hers.

Power flared hot and electric, scenting the air with lust and ozone. A second rapture of pure arcane power crashed, washing through them, and they howled.

* * * *

Rowan blinked the water from her eyes. Rick was a heavy weight on top of her. "I am so gonna hurt after that one."

His chuckle vibrated through her. "You're not the only one," he said into her neck. He lifted up onto his hands, still locked within her body. "Think we'll live?" His grin was broad and his eyes were a brilliant violet. He raised a brow. "Your eyes are purple again."

She smiled. "So are yours." She sighed, feeling warm, light-headed and wholly satiated.

"I guess that answers that question." He shook the water from his hair.

She flinched against the droplets from his flying hair. "What question?"

He grinned down at her. "Whether or not the two of us will always generate a purple glow when we have sex." He rose up off of her. "That is going to complicate things if we do this anywhere out doors."

"You are not planning to do this outside?" Rowan rolled up on her knees and groaned. Her body felt like it had been beaten.

"Sure, why not?" Rick leaned his palms against the wall under the showerhead then stuck his head under the water. He shook his head, spraying water from his long dark hair then turned to stare at her. His eyes gleamed with violet flame. "Kitten, I will do you any time and any place you'll let me into that tight body of yours—purple glow or no purple glow."

Rowan leaned a palm against the wall to climb to her feet. Her knees were shaking. "Do me? I am not a sex toy!"

Rick barked out a laugh. "Maybe you're not, but I sure felt like one less than a minute ago." He turned and grinned at her through the falling water.

Rowan grabbed the sponge and raised a brow at him. "Is that a complaint?"

He shook his head. "Hell no, I love the idea of being your sex toy." He grinned, then suddenly dove for her.

She yelped and dropped the sponge.

He caught her in a bear hug, then lifted her from the floor, holding her tight against his chest. "Kitten, any time you want to use me for sex, I am your willing toy." He dropped a quick kiss on her lips.

"Terrific, I'm happy for you." She shook the water from her eyes.

"Speaking of sex toys…" His eyes narrowed and his arms tightened around her. "I expect to be your only toy."

Rowan bit her lip. "I'm not exactly dating anyone "

"Not exactly?" His lips curved in a predatory smile.

She shook her head and sighed. "I broke up with my last boyfriend the night I met you."

"Good." He nodded sharply then arched a brow. "Let me guess, he couldn't handle it."

She gave him a sour smile. "He said that I was using him." She bit her lip. *Do I really want to mention the rest?*

Rick tilted his head to the side. "You get aroused every time you do magic, so it wouldn't take long for somebody to figure out that you use sex to recharge."

Rowan nodded. "That's about it."

"Okay, now what's the rest?"

Rowan swallowed. "The rest?" Her voice ended in a squeak.

"Yeah, cough it up. Most guys would love to be used for sex, I know I do." He waggled his brows. "So what's the problem?"

Rowan felt her cheeks getting warm. "Well, I sort of, feed off of them when they cum."

"Yeah, I figured that one out," Rick said dryly. "So what's the problem?"

"So they, uh…" She swallowed hard. "So they uh, can't um, do it without me."

Rick frowned. "You're saying that they can't get it up with anyone but you?"

Rowan nodded and looked away. "After about a week of not sleeping with me, their sex-drive comes back, but, uh…"

"Sounds to me like they'd only find out if they tried it with somebody else." His voice was soft. "So they try to sleep with somebody else, can't get it up, then come running back to you pissed, is that it?"

Rowan turned and looked into his eyes. She nodded.

Rick shrugged. "I still don't get what the problem is."

Rowan let out an exasperated breath. "I was taking all of their sex-drive."

Rick raised a sarcastic brow. "But, they had no problems 'getting it up' for you?"

"Um, no problems there." Rowan bit her lip and blushed. "But, the only person they could uh, perform with was me."

Rick raised a sarcastic brow. "I think you're missing the point here."

She frowned. "What?"

He loosed a hand and tapped her nose lightly with a finger. "They were cheating on you. If they hadn't tried to sleep with anyone else, they would have been fine, right?"

"Well, yeah…"

He shrugged. "Since I have no plans to sleep with anyone else, I'm good."

Rowan sighed. "There is just no arguing with you, is there?" A smile tugged at her lips.

"Nope." He grinned. "So when are you going to do some magic so I can be your sex toy again?"

"Can you put me down now? I want to finish my shower, I'm getting all wrinkly from being in all this water." She lifted her chin then stuck out her bottom lip. "And I haven't washed my hair yet."

"So much for afterglow." He rolled his eyes, then stared intently. "Kiss first, then you can go."

Rowan stared into his half-heated eyes. "A kiss?"

He nodded, and focused on her lips.

"Okay." She leaned forward and touched her mouth to his. He opened under her and his tongue stroked her in a gentle caress. His lips were so soft and his tongue so warm… Her fingers slid into his wet hair and a soft groan was her reward. She broke the kiss and stared into his serious copper gaze, uncertain as to what she was feeling right at that moment. Her heart thudded and ached in a way she wasn't sure she wanted to think about. "Um, can I go now?"

He let her slide down his shower-slick body. "Spoil-sport."

Rowan rolled her eyes. "Haven't you had enough?"

Rick chuckled, then handed her the shampoo. "You already know the answer to that one."

* * * *

Rowan put a hand up to balance the white towel wrapped around her hair and crouched down at the foot of the bed. She opened her suitcase, then pulled out a new set of underwear, a fresh pair of black jeans and her second-favorite black T-shirt. Emblazoned across the front in bold red type was: 'Don't piss me off, I'm running out of places to hide the bodies.'

"Hurry up and get dressed, and I'll get us some breakfast."

His voice came from the other side of the bed. She could hear him pulling out drawers. "You cook?"

"Yeah, I cook, a little. I make a mean pot of coffee, too."

"Coffee sounds heavenly." Rowan stood up then leaned against the bed to step into her pink satin panties. The bra was another front-closing push-up, like the red satin, now sitting in the bathroom sink. *What was I thinking, packing all my good lingerie?* She heard a drawer close on the other side of the huge room. She stepped into her jeans and tugged them upward.

"Pink satin, I like it." His voice was soft, and right behind her.

Rowan turned sharply with her jeans halfway up her thighs and nearly fell over. Rick was lounging across the bed in just a pair of jeans. "Will you cut that out?"

He blinked. "What?"

She shook her head and dragged her jeans up. "And you complain about Klaus popping in and out. At least you know by his aura when he's coming." She yanked on her T-shirt, tucked it in, then sat down to put on her socks and shoes.

He gave a low chuckle. "Kitten, the neighbors two blocks away know when you're coming."

"Oh!" Rowan rounded on him, mouth open for a scathing retort. He reached out, lightning quick and covered her lips with his. His mouth angled and his tongue swept in to take possession with leisurely strokes. Rowan felt a slow liquid interest stirring.

Rick released her mouth. "You were saying?"

Rowan blinked. "What?" For the life of her she couldn't remember what she was going to say.

"Good." He nodded. "You ready to get out of here and see the rest of my house?"

"Am I ever!" She turned and closed her suitcase. "Especially if you're going to bribe me with coffee."

"I can do that." Rick rolled off of the bed, wrestled into a plain black T-shirt, then padded barefoot across the carpet toward the vault door.

Rowan grabbed her red velvet shoulder bag and followed him. Her eyes locked on the dark stain on the pale gray carpet. "Are you going to be able to get that up?"

"I certainly hope so." Rick opened the vault door. "The worst part is that I have to do it myself." He waved her through. "Can't get my cleaning service to do it, they'll tell the cops that I murdered somebody."

ɞ Twelve ଢ

Nourishment

After completing a full tour of the huge monstrosity that Rick called a house, Rowan followed Rick from the hall into the kitchen. The tour had been pretty damn impressive. All the rooms were huge with broad windows in unexpected places, frequent changes in hallway direction and sudden changes in levels. Every floor seemed to have more than one level. The furniture was very modern in metal, glass and velvet and built for comfort with spare lines yet graceful curves.

The kitchen was huge, airy, and ultra-modern like the rest of the house; with stainless steel fixtures, white marble counters and smoked-glass cabinets. The broad room was a little dark, even though there were a lot of windows. During the tour, Rowan had noticed that the whole house had been a little dark in spite of the many picture windows. Some kind of purple coating had tinted the window glass in every room. *Must be to keep out the sun.* She bit her lip. *Well, he is a vampire...*

Rick sniffed. "Great, the coffee's done." He strode toward the sink. "Go have a seat, I'll get some mugs." Rick opened a glass cabinet over the sink and pulled out a pair of plain white coffee cups, then walked over to the counter and fiddled with the coffee maker.

"Don't mind if I do." Rowan pulled a chrome, back-curved kitchen chair out from under the clear glass kitchen table. She slumped into the chair and groaned. "My poor feet. That tour took longer than I thought. Your place is huge."

With the full mugs balanced in his hands, Rick came to the table. "So what do you think of my house now?" With his foot he pulled a kitchen chair out, parked the mugs on the table, then sat with a long sigh of his own.

Rowan put some thick cream and a spoonful of sugar into her coffee. "How about 'wow'?"

"Wow is good, I like wow." He leaned across the table toward her with an eager smile. "Go on, tell me more."

More? Rowan smiled. *Well I did kinda insult his house when I got here.* She blew on the coffee. "Let's see I really liked the way the whole house is one surprise after another, like a huge puzzle box. I never knew what I was going to see next. It'll take forever to figure out how to get through it all without getting lost."

"That's nice." Rick raised a brow, and sipped at his coffee. "And?"

Rowan choked back a laugh. "And, all the chrome and glass furniture looks like it belongs in a futuristic space movie." Rowan sipped her coffee and sighed. "Mmm, good coffee."

"Columbian dark, my favorite." Rick nodded with a satisfied smile on his face, then got up from the table and began rummaging under the cabinets. "Hard to believe I brought a lot of that from Germany back in 1945." He pulled out a stainless steel frying pan, opened an overhead cabinet and took down some spice containers. "By the way, how do you like your eggs?"

"Eggs? Over easy." Rowan blinked. "You brought this stuff over in 1945? I didn't think they had anything like that until the sixties."

"Trust me, these were all done in the forties. The style got popular in the sixties." Rick turned to look at her and shrugged.

"But if you got it in the forties, where did it come from?"

"I went to school at the Bauhaus, a university for architectural design." He walked over to the fridge, opened it, then pulled out a handful of eggs, a plastic envelope of bacon and a small loaf of bread. "This house was designed on their model."

"So that's why you went into designing houses, you went to college for it."

"When the college was the first of it's kind." Rick cracked eggs into the pan. The sound of sizzling food filled the kitchen. He sidestepped to the fridge and took out a butter-dish. "Not something I can share with just anybody."

"And the super-modern paintings and metal sculptures?"

Rick nodded. "Bauhaus as well." He pulled a spatula from a drawer. "Most of the pieces in my house are originals from old schoolmates, or reproductions from their work."

"They painted at a design university?"

"Absolutely, and sculpted, too." Rick nodded. "I studied architecture, but the Bauhaus also taught art along with furniture design. They combined art with engineering and craftsmanship: form equals function. The style was very radical back then."

Rowan heard the distinct sound of a toaster being depressed.

"The Bauhaus was more of a combined arts school." Rick opened a cabinet and pulled out a pair of plain white plates. "The idea was to encourage the individual artisans and craftsmen to work together and combine their skills." Deftly, he scooped eggs and bacon onto each plate, then dropped the emptied pan on a cold burner with a clang.

"The school," he continued, "was trying to elevate the status of crafts like chairs, lamps teapots etc., to the same level as the fine arts, like painting and sculpting." The toaster sprang. He reached for the toast and dropped two pieces on each plate. Balancing the two plates in one hand, full of eggs, bacon and toast, he turned and dragged open a drawer to pull out flatware.

Rowan frowned, puzzled. "But the furniture all looks so familiar. I think I've even seen some of this stuff before."

"Like I said, the Bauhaus style got popular. These days, just about everything that's known as modern, like the tubular steel framed chair you're sitting in now, adjustable reading lamps and ordinary drywall are only some of the things that came from designs innovated at the Bauhaus." Forks and knives in one hand and plates in the other, he came to the table, placed a plate in front of Rowan, then sat.

Rowan pulled a napkin from the holder in the table's center. "I had no idea all this stuff, stuff I see all the time, came from your school."

"A lot of people don't." He handed her a fork. "Eat."

For some minutes, the sound of forks scraping against plates was loud in the kitchen.

Rowan pushed back her empty plate. "That was great."

"Glad you liked it." Rick picked up the dirty dishes from the table, put them in the sink and ran water over them. "More coffee?"

"Gods yes, that stuff is heavenly."

Rick carried the coffee pot over to the table and refilled her cup. "Here you go, service with a smirk!"

Rowan let out a short laugh. "By the way, do you know where Klaus is?"

Rick tilted his head at the ceiling then studied the floor. "I can feel him, but it's spread out and thin. I think he's deep under the house in the ground, somewhere, possibly sleeping."

"Good, then while he's not paying attention…" Rowan twisted in her chair to get to her shoulder bag that hung on the back of her chair. "Let's find out what he's up to." She dug in the bag and pulled out a small cloth-wrapped bundle.

"Huh?" Rick frowned. "What's that?"

"My tarot cards." She pulled the red cloth from the oversized deck.

Rick frowned then sat down at the table. "Tarot cards?"

Rowan shuffled her cards. "You know, for fortune-telling?"

"You're going to tell Klaus's fortune?" He rolled his eyes. "Let me guess, he's going to meet someone short, red-headed and feisty."

"Laugh it up, Fang Boy. The cards told me that you were a vampire and what the sorcerer that attacked you in the club was planning." A card slipped through her fingers and landed, face down on the Formica counter top. Rowan deftly flipped it over; it was the Eight of Cups, meaning search.

"Well, according to the cards, Klaus is definitely here for a reason. He's looking for something." She shifted the card and discovered another card sticking to it, the Emperor, also known as the Entrepreneur. "Uh, I think he was sent."

Rick frowned from across the table. "Sent?"

Rowan frowned at the card. "Looks like someone is holding him at the end of a very long leash."

Rick's brow furrowed. "How could anyone hold him? He's so old that he's more of a ghost than a physical being, he barely holds a human shape."

Rowan nodded. "So I noticed." She gave him a tight smile. "Just from looking at him you can tell he's having problems remembering what he once looked like."

He shrugged. "I still show up in a mirror—he doesn't. It's hard to hold on to a form when you can't even see what you look like."

"Oh, gee, something for you to look forward to?"

Rick grimaced. "Can the sarcasm for five minutes, will you?"

"Whatever." Rowan sighed. "My guess is that he's being held with sorcery. It's the only thing that would have any effect on him." She raised a brow at the vampire. "I just hope, for your sake, that his owner didn't send him to find new employees."

"Or make them," Rick said through clenched teeth.

Rowan nodded. "Scary thought."

"Here's a scarier one..." He stared into his coffee cup. "I'm not strong enough to stop him. Even if I could catch him off guard and actually succeed in staking him out for the morning sun, he'll just discorporate through whatever I bind him with."

"I'm barely strong enough to get him out of your house. I'm definitely not a strong enough witch to bind him magically."

Rick gave her a serious look. "We may be in real trouble if he decides that we're too much trouble to leave alive."

She raised a brow at him. "What's this *we* stuff, *Kemo-sabe?* I'm getting the hell out of Dodge first chance I get." Rowan shuffled the cards and three fell out. "You know, I never ran across any of this stuff at home. Since I met you, I've met a demon-infested sorcerer and another vampire. Gee, I can't wait to see what's next."

"Come to think of it, this is a bit much, even for me." Rick made a sour face. "I do run across the occasional weird shit, a ghost here, a magician there..." He waved his hand about. "But not in the same year, never mind the same week." Rick's fingers tapped absently on the glass tabletop. "If this keeps up, I may need to get the hell out of Dodge too, so don't be surprised if I'm in your passenger seat."

Rowan flipped the cards on the table, the Hermit, the Magician, the Eight of Cups She raised her brows and looked over at the vampire. "Well, I know what Klaus is looking for." She gathered up the cards and two more cards flipped out and fluttered to the floor.

"Good. What?"

"A runaway sorcerer." Rowan leaned over and picked up the fallen cards. The High Priestess, also known as the Witch and the Devil, also known as the Vampire... She slid them back in her deck and bit her lip. *The witch and the vampire... Shit.*

The vampire sat back in his chair. "As long as he wasn't looking for either you or me. "

Rowan pressed her fingers to her temples. "That was the good news. The bad news is that we've been added to his agenda."

"Shit." The vampire turned in his seat and sipped his coffee.

"That's what I was thinking," she said sourly. "I'm guessing that when I kept him out with the barrier around the bed last night, I must have impressed him." She gathered her cards and another two cards slid to the tabletop. The Eight of Wands, meaning communication, and the Emperor again. She winced. "According to the cards, he's in communication with his master. Apparently Klaus wasn't the only one impressed."

He turned to look at her. "Are you sure?"

"I could be wrong..." She gave him a tight smile. "But that hasn't happened in a really long time."

Rick frowned grimly. "I don't how. He can barely use the TV, never mind the telephone."

"It's got to be part of the magic being used to bind him." Rowan shook her head. "Who ever has him on a leash has to be one hell of a magician."

Rick made a fist. "Can you tell who it is? Are they nearby?"

"I don't know." Rowan shook her head. "I've tried asking who he's working for, and I keep flipping the Emperor card. The Emperor normally indicates a Master of business, so I'm taking it to mean that it's one person, but they are rich, powerful and very likely organized. Beyond that, I get nothing else. I can't tell if his owner is in town or half a world away. It feels like I'm being blocked."

"This is not good news." Rick's fingers thumped. "Klaus is a problem, but an organization that can leash a creature like him is a nightmare."

"Tell me about it. The gods only know who else he has on staff." Rowan wrapped her cards neatly in fabric. "You may be forced to leave town for a while. I can take off and just go home. He can't get to me, night or day, especially on my home turf. I have it hexed twenty ways to Sunday. You, on the other hand, should probably get as far away as possible, then stay out of range. What do you say we just get in my car and go, right now?"

He looked at her sourly. "Direct sunlight equals really bad sunburn, remember?"

"Yes." She held up a finger and grinned. "But, you can still wear your coat, hat and sunglasses for the drive. Worse comes to worse, you can ride in the trunk."

Rick grinned. "I'll stay at your house."

Rowan snorted. "We don't know how long Klaus will hang around. It could be a month."

"So? With my laptop, I can stay in touch with my office by using the Internet."

She sighed. "So, I have two jobs and a life, you know." She shook her head. "Your best option would be an airport. I vote a flight to the other side of the country. If your Visa's in order, you can go to Canada. That should be far enough away. It'd take him days just to follow you."

"Canada?" He frowned. "That's a bit further than I want to go."

Rowan lowered her brows. "You don't really have a choice, you have to put enough physical distance between yourself and Klaus that he loses your trail. If I drive you to the airport in my town during the day, it'll give you a four hour lead and it's an international, so you're good for just about anywhere."

"Sounds great." Rick smiled thinly at her. "Just one problem."

"What?"

Rick put his elbow on the table then propped his chin on his hand. "Right now, it's after eleven in the morning and the drive takes four hours. If the car was already packed and we left now, sunset would still catch us at five." Rick shook his head. "The damned airport security checks take so long these days, that he'll stop me before I get on the plane."

Rowan frowned. "So? He still has to wait 'til sunset and we'll be four hours ahead of him."

"That's not long enough for either of us to escape." The fingers of his other hand thumped on the glass tabletop. "He can follow me anywhere I go and he flies."

She bit her lip. "He flies?"

"Yep, and really fast. It would take him maybe an hour to catch up to me." He picked up his mug and swallowed a gulp of coffee. "I have no idea how he flies, because he's damned solid while he does it. I've seen him carry shit."

"Wait a minute, how's he going to track us? The car doesn't leave a trail."

"He drank my blood, remember? He can follow me that way."

She tilted her head to one side. "Yeah, but out of a glass "

Rick stared at the floor. "That has nothing to do with it. It's the blood itself, not the process, that makes the link." Rick's worried at his lower lip. "He'll chase after me before he makes an attempt on you, so I can wait 'til dawn tomorrow, then just take off on my own "

"No." Rowan shook her head. "Absolutely not. He'll catch you, and I am not leaving you to that monster."

He grinned. "So you do care."

"Don't push your luck." Rowan rewrapped her cards. "We can leave at dawn tomorrow, that ought to be enough time. Maybe we can add a distraction, then take off while he's busy."

Rick frowned. "What kind of a distraction?"

Rowan looked out the window thoughtfully. "I can probably find his missing sorcerer. I'll leave him the location and we can take off while he goes to play tag with him."

"We find who he's looking for?" Rick frowned. "We help Klaus?"

Rowan raised a brow at him. "Can you think of a better distraction?"

He frowned. "It's not looking that way. All right, how do we find this sorcerer?"

She tucked her cards into her belt pouch. "I can use a pendulum and a map to find the sorcerer, but the trick will be to get enough distance between Klaus and us to make a clean escape."

He nodded. "Sounds like a plan." Rick leaned back in his chair. "In the meantime, I'll get online and get a plane ticket. He can barely use the TV remote, never mind figure out what I'm doing on the computer."

"Speaking of TV remotes..." Rowan sat back in her chair. "I still can't get over the fact that Klaus was watching soap operas when we walked through the TV room upstairs."

Rick snorted. "Soaps? That's nothing. I caught him watching Babe-Watch the night before you got here. The way his mouth was hanging open, I don't think he's ever seen it before."

"Babe-Watch?" Rowan groaned.

Rick grinned. "I thought he was going to have a heart-attack when a pair of girls in bikinis ran across the TV screen and then the camera zoomed in on their boobs."

Rowan snorted then grinned. "Considering that you have one of those wall-sized TVs that gives 'Bigger than Life' a whole new meaning, I'm not surprised."

Rick nodded. "I was convinced that he was going to make a grab for the screen."

Rowan sipped at her coffee. "You know you can get a ticket at the airport."

Rick shook his head. "It's easier to do it online. I have to arrange flights, and do some interesting time juggling so I don't end up flying in a window seat during daylight hours." Rick leaned across the table to capture her hand. "Come with me."

"What for?" She tugged on her hand but his hold was iron firm. "You can contact me by email and you have my home phone number."

His fingers tightened and he frowned. "I don't want to lose you."

"You don't have me to lose."

He leaned across the table toward her and his eyes ignited with flame. "I don't?"

She glared at him. "You like being used to feed my magic?"

"It's not doing me any harm and the sex is hot." His smile was grim and determined. "I already told you I'd be your sex-toy any time you wanted. Besides, I feed from you, too, so it's even."

"Let me go."

"Why should I?"

"Because, you're starting to cut off my circulation." She wiggled her fingers.

He bit out something harsh in German and released her hand. Glaring at her, he picked up his coffee cup.

She pulled her knees up onto the chair, folding in on herself. "Anyway, you can't afford to become too attached to me." She turned her head away.

"Why not?" His fingernails dug into the coffee cup with unconscious strength. There was a crunch. The cup crumbled in his hand, spilling coffee on the floor. "Shit." Rick got up and tossed the remains of his cup in the trashcan by the back door. At the sink he grabbed a rag, then knelt to clean the spilled coffee and glass shards from the floor. He looked up from the floor. "Look, it's pretty damn rare that I have a lover that knows what I am," he said harshly. "Never mind one with a sexual appetite that matches mine. Do you think I'm about to give that up?"

"You live forever, I don't." She said softly. She fixed a cool and level look at him. "Remember?"

"That…" His lip curled and his fangs flashed briefly. "Can be fixed." He got up from the floor.

"No." She shook her head firmly then pointed her finger at him. "That—is not an option."

He frowned. "What's wrong with living forever?"

"As a witch, I already live forever." She smiled grimly. "Reincarnation comes with the package and I don't have to change my diet."

"Reincarnation, huh?" He crossed his arms across his chest. "And how many memories do you retain from each life?

She flinched. "I remember enough."

"Oh, really?" His eyes narrowed. "As a vampire you keep them all, crystal clear. Will you remember me?"

Rowan bit her lip. "I am not giving up my abilities to become something like Klaus."

"Vampires have powers, too," he said in a soft whisper. "And I am nothing like Klaus."

"But eventually, you will be," she said very, very softly.

He put up a hand. "We'll argue about our relationship later." He turned and dumped the rag in the sink. "Before you find a good enough excuse to really leave me," he added in barely a whisper. "What kind of stuff do you need to find this damned sorcerer for Klaus?"

Rowan sighed. "I have a pendulum in my big, brown suitcase and I'll need a map of the local area."

"Stay here, I'll go get them." He headed for the doorway and his eyes flashed flame. "Don't go anywhere." He strode from the kitchen.

Rick pressed the catch, opening the door to the vault under the staircase. "Damn it, Rowan," he muttered under his breath. "I am not losing the only person in my life who hasn't freaked out on me, and the only person that I don't have to pretend to be human with." In a blur of speed fueled by anger, Rick descended into the vault. On bare feet, he crossed the carpet to the bed. "Sooner or later I'm going to beat some sense into that ass of hers…"

The larger brown, leather suitcase lay flat on its side at the foot of the bed, where Rowan had left it. He grasped the handle of the suitcase and whirled, only to be jerked to a halt when it resisted being moved. The suitcase weighed a ton, literally.

"Shit." He ground his teeth. "I forgot about her damned spell!" Groaning, he lifted it, one-handed from the floor. "Damn it, she could have at least pulled the spell until she left." One step at a time, he walked the bespelled case toward the stairs, then stopped.

Something wasn't right. Eyes narrowed in concentration, he opened his senses. *I don't feel anything unusual* He looked up at the ceiling. Klaus was still buried somewhere on the grounds and Rowan was sitting in the kitchen. He looked around the room. All the paintings and the furniture was in place, the bed was still made and the floor His eyes opened wide. *The floor!*

Klaus's blood was gone from the carpet.

A warning chill shivered through Rick. "Shit," he hissed. Grabbing the case awkwardly with both hands, he walked faster. *Damn it, this thing is heavy.* He sucked in a breath. *Next time she gets her own suitcase.*

Hauling the case up the stairs with both hands was a pain in the ass but he made it to the top. He dropped the case in the hall, then turned and pushed the door under the stairs closed. Rick felt a fleeting shimmer of impending malevolence. *Klaus?* He turned.

Darkness exploded upward from the floor under his feet, cascading high over top of him. He shouted, his hands shot out and instinctively dark claws lanced from his fingertips. The darkness spilled down onto him, drowning him in impenetrable stygian black. He raked at the shadows around him and it parted like smoke.

Hands abruptly closed on his throat, cutting off his breath. He gasped and grabbed wrists that felt like they were made of steel. His claws slid against an unbreakable surface. Suddenly a pair of familiar crimson eyes appeared in the boiling blackness only inches away.

"Klaus, what are you doing?" he gasped out with the small amount of air he had left.

The hands tightened. "Sleep."

A fist of dark power closed around his mind and Rick knew no more.

* * * *

Rowan reached across the table and picked up the coffee pot still on the table. She went to pour coffee into her mug and paused. Her head lifted. *Something isn't right...*

She focused on Rick and got the distinct impression that he was climbing the stairs with her suitcase and he was pissed about something. *Oops, I think I left the spell on the suitcase.* She smiled and put cream in her coffee. *That puppy has got to be heavy, I bet that's what he's bitching about.*

She lifted the mug to her lips and felt the wave of darkness that meant Klaus was close by. Her head shot up. She heard a shout. Rowan scrambled out of the chair and dashed into the hall.

Klaus filled the narrow hall with his pooling shadows and had Rick by the throat.

"Klaus, no!" She ran for the two vampires and her radiance blazed to life.

Klaus exploded into tatters of shadow and disappeared, taking Rick with him.

"Shit!" Rowan focused her mind, desperately searching for Rick or the concentrated violence that was Klaus. She felt them both well above her head. "The TV room…" She lunged for the stairs.

* * * *

"Awaken."

Rick coughed then sucked air into his bruised throat. His eyes snapped open. *What the fuck?* He was sprawled face down on a hardwood floor. His head snapped up. He was in the TV room at the top of the house, between the leather couch sitting in the middle of the room, and the wall. He could see the door just past the end of the couch. He lunged up onto his feet.

A fist closed viciously in his long hair at the base of his neck, jerking his head back. "Ow, shit!" He could feel the solid, heavy darkness that was Klaus directly behind him. He reached around with clawed fingers and his hands closed on a wrist, but his sharp nails found no purchase. The hand in his hair twisted tighter. He winced. "Klaus! What the fuck, are you doing?"

"I need to strengthen your blood."

"What?" Rick felt Klaus's clawed hand grab his shoulder. He was shoved down hard. He landed on his knees with a heavy thud. "Fuck, Klaus!" If he had been human, his knees would have been broken. He tucked his chin and attempted to stand. "Cut this shit out!"

"Stay down."

"What the Hell are you talking about?" The clawed fingers dug through the fabric of his shirt and into his shoulder, forcibly keeping him down on his knees.

"Hold still. This will be over soon." He knelt at Rick's back.

Rick's head was suddenly jerked back, baring his throat. Rick could see Klaus's carved profile only inches from his cheek. Rick bared his teeth and hissed. "I am *so* going to kick your ass for this!"

Klaus's brows rose then he chuckled. "So fierce, but so young."

Rick's head was pulled painfully back until it rested against Klaus's right shoulder. He winced again. The rich smell of cool and rotted earth rose from Klaus's body. "You're sworn not to take my blood, you son of a bitch!"

"So it would seem." Klaus nodded. "However, you are here to take mine."

"What?" Rick watched from the corner of his eye. Klaus shook back his long ragged sleeve, baring his emaciated left forearm. Rick's eyes widened and his blood turned to ice. "Oh, Hell, no! I am not drinking vampire blood!" He twisted sharply and felt his hair tearing free. He got his feet under him to rise.

Klaus growled and released Rick's hair. Rick lunged to his feet. Klaus's arms snapped out in a blur of speed. He grabbed Rick's right wrist in one hand, pulling Rick's arm back and twisting the wrist viciously.

Rick felt the bones of his wrist near the snapping point from Klaus's strength and jerked to a halt. "Damn it!"

Klaus yanked the wrist up sharply then pressed a palm against Rick's elbow for leverage. He pulled, twisting and locking Rick's entire right arm straight out behind his back.

Rick was forced back down onto his knees with his head bowed to the floor to keep his arm from dislocating at the shoulder. He couldn't move, his shoulder would go or his arm would snap.

Klaus bent over him to snarl in his ear. "You forget—I hunt vampires older and more powerful than you."

"Goddamn you, Klaus, let me go!" He could feel a sweat from fear forming along his spine.

"Be done with this foolishness." He twisted Rick's arm a fraction more. "Do not make me harm you needlessly."

Rick felt his arm trying to tear from the socket. A small sound of pain escaped his lips. He shook his head "I can't let you do this, Klaus I won't drink your blood."

"You can not stop me," Klaus said softly. He twisted Rick's arm a fraction more and dislocated the arm with a wet pop.

Rick shouted with the sudden and brutal wave of pain. He felt his sight dissolve into blackness from the shock and collapsed.

Kneeling, Klaus released Rick's now useless arm. Wrapping his arm around Rick's chest, he lifted the stunned, younger vampire, propping Rick against his right shoulder. Rick moaned, then sluggishly tried to pull away. Lightning fast, Klaus released his embrace to wrap his right hand around Rick's throat, holding him against his shoulder.

Rick grabbed for the hand around his throat with the fingers of his one working hand and scrabbled for purchase.

Klaus clenched his fingers tightly, cutting off Rick's air. "You have no choice. Be still," he said in the younger vampire's ear.

Rick tried to breathe past Klaus's fingers around his windpipe and choked. "Not drinking..." He wheezed for air. "Your blood."

Klaus eyes slid to focus on the struggling, younger vampire and he raised his left arm to his serrated mouth. He bit. The ancient vampire's blood flowed thick and black. Klaus shoved his wounded arm against Rick's mouth.

Rick threw out his hand to stop the descending arm, but the elder vampire was too strong to resist. The open wound came in contact with his mouth. He came up on his knees and fought to turn his head away with his lips tightly closed. Klaus's blood smeared across his mouth and dripped from his chin.

Klaus shifted his hand from Rick's throat and grabbed his jaw. "You will drink." Klaus' fingers dug into the muscles in Rick's jaw.

The pain from Klaus's fingers was excruciating. Rick moaned. Klaus pressed harder, nearly dislocating his jaw. His mouth popped open. Klaus shoved his wounded arm tight against Rick's sharp teeth while other his arm pinned Rick against the older vampire's body. Blood filled Rick's mouth. Thick, sweet as honey and potent as expensive whiskey. He spat.

Klaus pressed his arm tighter, tilting Rick's head back. "You will drink."

Blood flowed in a heavy stream down Rick's throat and into his airway. He choked. He was forced to swallow or drown. He swallowed. The blood hit his stomach and churned. The raw power of Klaus's blood caused warm waves to race from his stomach into his veins. He felt himself losing control of his body from the potency. *I'm getting drunk...* He could feel drowsiness flooding through him. *I am drunk...* Rick couldn't stop himself from swallowing again.

The younger vampire's body became limp as the old blood infiltrated his body. Klaus released Rick's chin and wrapped a supporting arm around Rick's back, holding him upright against his shoulder like a child. Rick swallowed again. His eyes were dilated wide and clearly out of focus. He was barely conscious. Abruptly, Klaus pulled his arm away and Rick sighed. Blood, thick as syrup, ran down his chin. His shirt was black with it.

Klaus swiped his tongue across the gash on his arm. It closed instantly. "Now, young vampire, let us see how you react to a fresh dose of what made you Vampire." He pushed Rick onto the floor, shoving him face down. He frowned at the odd angle of Rick's shoulder. Coming up on one knee, Klaus grasped the arm he'd dislocated. With brutal efficiency, he popped the joint back in place.

Rick cried out hoarsely, then moaned. Slowly he curled up on his side with his good arm wrapped around his stomach. His body shuddered. Rick gasped and his eyes opened wide. He flopped onto his back and his body suddenly jerked taut. His heels thumped on the floor and his back bowed up sharply.

Klaus's brows rose. "A fast reaction. Very good." Klaus rose to his feet, leaving Rick laid out on the floor. "If he holds my blood down, all will be well." He walked around to the front of the couch and sat. His head tilted to the side and his eyes narrowed in concentration. "Now, *ved'ma,* you may find us."

The TV hissed as it switched on by itself.

* * * *

A shout echoed in the upstairs halls.

"Son of a bitch, I know they're up here." Rowan ran through the maze of joining halls on the top floor and panted. Her feet thumped on the carpeted floor. Rick's fear and desperation was clawing at the back of her mind, adding to her own growing panic. "Where the fuck is the TV room?" She could feel that Rick was nearby but she couldn't focus on his exact location.

A sharp pain in her side stopped her cold in the middle of an empty hall that ended with a window before it took a sharp right turn back to the stairs. She put a hand on the wall and leaned over, gulping for breath. Her heart was hammering in her chest. "Damn it, Rick, where the Hell are you?" This was the third time she'd stopped in this particular hallway looking for the door to the TV room, but she still couldn't find it.

She slowly stood upright and frowned. There was a door on her left. *Wait a minute, I passed through this hall three times and that door wasn't there...* She heard the sound of a TV switching on then a breathy moan. She took the three steps to the door. It opened with a push. Klaus was lounging in the center of the couch watching TV.

She didn't see Rick. Panicked, she looked around the room, then saw bare feet sticking out from behind the couch, near the wall. *Don't be dead, you idiot vampire... Please, Rick, don't be dead...* Suddenly his feet kicked out and he shook hard as though having a seizure. "Shit! Rick?" She dashed around the edge of the couch.

Klaus flung out a long arm. "Do not go near him, he is not in control of himself just yet."

Rowan stopped short. She did not want him touching her. She glanced at the old vampire. Though his arm was out, he continued to stare at the TV. She looked back at Rick. He had stopped shaking and sprawled limp on his back with his eyes wide open. His face was pale as milk. Some kind of thick black liquid was oozing from his mouth and covered the front of his shirt. *My Gods, what's wrong with him?* Rowan felt anger mixed with fear boiling in her gut. "What did you do to him?" She balled her fists. "You're sworn not to bleed him "

"I have taken nothing. Your spell still holds." Casually, he pulled back his arm then picked up the remote control and changed the channel. "He has drunk of my blood."

"What?" She looked at the elder vampire. "Your blood, but why?"

"As he was, he could not provide for me. By sunset he will be stronger than before and fit sustenance."

Rick gasped and began shuddering and writhing on the floor. He rolled to his side and started retching. A small amount of thick black bile spattered out of his mouth and onto the floor. He groaned and curled up with his arms over his stomach.

"Son of a bitch!" Rowan took a step closer.

Klaus flung his arm out again, stopping her. "Do not go near him. He will kill you accidentally with his strength."

"It looks like it's killing him!"

Klaus turned red eyes on her. "It is."

"Shit!" She ducked around his arm and came to a sharp painful stop. Klaus had grabbed a handful of her long hair. "Let go."

"Do not concern yourself. There is nothing you can do. He survives with a heartbeat or he survives as a full vampire without one, but he will still survive."

Rowan turned to look at him. "Let me go, or I will fry you where you sit." She felt the shimmer of power begin to dance under her skin.

Klaus abruptly released her. "That would be unwise." He shook his hand as though it had been burned. "My blood is coursing through his body. If you use your magic on me, you will destroy him, too."

Rowan stomped her foot in frustration. *The son of a bitch is probably right. If I throw enough light to get rid of him, I may hurt Rick.* She took a deep breath to calm herself. Concentrating, she eased up on her power. Light still shimmered under her skin but she forcibly kept it from breaking free.

Klaus picked up the TV remote and changed the channel again. "Go downstairs and occupy yourself. You will see him at sunset."

"I don't want to leave him." *Not with you...* Rowan grit her teeth. *I should have fried your ass this morning, you sack of shit vampire.*

Klaus chuckled. "I will ensure that he does no harm to himself."

Who said anything about Rick harming himself? She took a breath and stubbornly stayed where she was.

Klaus looked over at her with a frown. "Do you intend to stand there all day? Is there nothing else you can do to occupy yourself?"

Rowan looked over at Rick. *This sucks and it's my fault. Rick went downstairs to get my suitcase so I could help this monster.* She winced. *I should have never left him alone.* She nibbled on her lower lip. *I really don't want to leave him. Even if I could get past Klaus, I'm not strong enough to carry Rick downstairs, and damn it, I can't think of anything I can do here.* She thought about her witchcraft books sitting in the brown suitcase downstairs. *I can always work out the spell to keep the son-of-a bitch out of Rick's house.*

Rowan turned on her heel and headed for the door. Abruptly she stopped in the doorway and looked back. "By the way, just so you know, he was getting my suitcase so I could find your damned sorcerer for you."

Klaus came off the couch a boiling, black fury. Wreathed in arcane darkness, he stepped toward her. "How did you know?" His voice echoed as though he filled the room.

Rowan's light broke free of her skin and shimmered around her. He stopped cold at the edge of her light and she cocked a brow at him. "I'm a witch, a *ved'ma,* remember? I used my tarot cards to get a few questions answered."

Klaus bared his serrated teeth. "And what else did you discover?"

Rowan smiled and propped a hand on her hip. "That someone else is holding your leash."

"You little fool!" He turned sharply to look at Rick on the floor.

Rowan frowned at the older vampire. *What the hell is going on with him?*

Klaus turned back to stare at Rowan. "And?"

Rowan shook her head. "Nothing else, I couldn't get a straight answer past the point that they are powerful and organized."

Klaus studied her. "Do not look closer. It would mean your death."

Rowan blinked. *What the Hell is that supposed to mean? I thought he wanted me dead anyway?* She shook her head then waved a hand toward Rick. "So, do you want me to find your sorcerer or not?"

"Go." He pointed at the door. "At sunset we will discuss this further."

Rowan rolled her eyes. "Fine, whatever…" She turned and walked out the door. It slammed closed behind her. She turned to look at it and discovered that it was gone. She put out a hand, but felt no trace of the door. "How the fuck is he doing that?" She sighed then headed for the stairs.

❧ Thirteen ❧

Hunt

The silence of the huge house was deafening.

Rowan hunched over the kitchen table reading and flipped her long red braid from her shoulder to her back. Her gold, wire-framed glasses threatened to slip from her nose. Several large tomes were lying open and covered the entire surface of the table. A plate with a half-eaten sandwich rested atop one of the open books.

She pushed her glasses back up with two fingers of her right hand and picked up her cigarette from the ashtray. Her thoughts tumbled with incantations and ingredients. She was not going to think about Rick and the vampire upstairs.

Her eyes scanned the page crammed with tiny print. Absently she lifted her mug of lukewarm coffee with her left hand. She frowned at the complicated design on the page. She laid down her cigarette and picked up her pen to scribble yet another notation in her notebook. She was not going to think about whether or not Rick was still breathing.

Rowan looked around for her small notebook and discovered it jammed under her right elbow. The coffee mug finally made it to her lips and she drank the dregs while writing the exotic incantation in her notebook. She was determined keep her mind on her work and not think about what she was going to do if Rick wasn't. She scrunched her eyes closed. *Stop thinking, damn it!*

She set down her empty mug on the glass tabletop with a sharp bang. "Coffee, I need coffee." She looked over at the coffee pot and made a face. It was the second pot she had emptied and time to brew yet another. *Gods, I'm going to slosh when I walk from all this coffee...* She straightened in the chair with a groan, put out her cigarette, then got up to make more coffee.

Darkness moved against the back of Rowan's mind. She stopped with the bag of coffee beans in one hand and the grinder in the other. She glanced at the windows over the sink and finally noticed that night had fallen. She had to put the grinder down; her hand was shaking too badly to hold it.

"Make coffee," she muttered. "He'll want some." She took a breath. *If he is still human enough to drink it*

Rowan felt the darkness shifting at the back of her thoughts and worked silently. Listening with all her might for a sound on the stairs. The coffee maker began snorting and filling. The scent of fresh coffee filled the room.

"Good God! Open the back door, will you? The whole downstairs smells like cigarettes."

Rowan turned sharply. Rick was leaning against the kitchen doorway. His face was almost colorless and his eyes had dark circles, but he was smiling.

She swallowed hard, backed slowly to the kitchen door and opened it. She couldn't stop looking at him. His long black hair was wet and slicked back into a neat tail. He had changed clothes, but he was still barefoot. *He must have showered.*

"Is that coffee brewing?" He raised a brow. "I didn't know you wore glasses."

Rowan nodded. "I do when I read the Grimoires. The print in the older books is really tiny, and yes, it's coffee." She pulled the glasses from her nose and folded them closed.

He held out his hand. "Come here."

Rowan walked over to him more quickly than she had intended. He took the glasses from her fingers, then pressed her hand to his chest. *He's still warm.* She felt a thump under her palm. *A heartbeat?* She looked up at him.

"Yes, Kitten, I still live." His smile was thin and tired.

"Thank the Mother." Before she knew what she was going to do, she wrapped her arms around his waist and was squeezing him with everything she had. She buried her face in his shirt and took a deep breath smelling soap, clean cotton and male. *He still smells like Rick.* She felt his arms close around her squeeze back with breathless strength. She blinked. *I am not crying,* she told herself. *Not over an idiot vampire.*

"Yes, he still lives. Pity." Klaus coalesced from black shadow into solid existence, leaning against the counter by the coffee machine.

Rowan yanked out of Rick's arms to stand between the two vampires. She leveled two fingers at the old vampire and electric blue witch-fire blazed around her hand. "Don't you *ever* do that again!" She hadn't intended to shout, it just came out that way.

"Hey, what's with the hand?" Rick asked softly.

"I've been doing some reading," Rowan said through clenched teeth. "I mean it, Klaus. Don't you ever, go near him again."

Klaus blinked. He looked at Rick from under his brows. "I think your *ved'ma* is trying to protect you."

"Then I wouldn't piss her off if I were you," Rick said quietly. "In the meantime, Rowan, can I have some of that coffee?"

"Yeah, sure." Rowan lowered her hand and flexed her fingers; they felt a little numb. She hadn't expected the radiance to be quite so concentrated. Purposely she walked toward the coffee machine, glowering at Klaus, daring him to stand in her way.

Klaus bit back a smile, threw up his hands and moved to the counter on the other side of the sink, by the back door.

Rowan dug a mug from the cabinet, then poured a cup of the fresh brew. She shot Klaus a vicious look as she passed him. Rick put her glasses carefully down on an open book, then with shaking hands took the cup in both hands. He lifted the coffee mug to his lips.

"How do you feel?" Rowan asked quietly.

"Like shit." Rick leveled a black look at the ragged vampire leaning against the kitchen counter.

"You will feel better as the night progresses." Klaus propped his hands on the counter behind him, then hopped up on the counter and sat with his ankles crossed. It was such an odd motion that both Rick and Rowan blinked.

Klaus raised a brow at Rick, and Rowan felt a shift in the back of her mind. *Are they talking to each other?* She frowned.

Rick sighed and went to sit in Rowan's abandoned chair. "Rowan, can you get me a glass, please? They're over the sink."

A glass? Rowan looked at Rick wide-eyed. "You're not going to..." She didn't want to say it out loud: feed Klaus.

"Yes, I am," he said tiredly. He looked away. "Please, just get it."

Rowan walked over to the cabinet over the sink and retrieved a glass. She returned to Rick's side and saw that his small knife was already in his hand. She didn't bother to ask if he needed help, just held the glass steady. He sliced his wrist open. His blood was darker and thicker than she remembered. It was also cooler.

Rick licked his wrist to close the wound, then gently took her hand and pulled her around to stand behind him. With his free hand, he shoved a few of her books, making a cleared spot on the far end of table. He took the glass from her and put it down in the cleared spot.

Klaus came off the counter in a blur of shadow and drained the glass. He set it back down on the table and it clinked. He smiled. "Much better."

That son of a bitch! Rowan felt her temper rise and her magic begin to shimmer under her skin. Rick hissed in pain and came out of the chair. Rowan gasped in shock and dampened her magic. She reached for him, but he instinctively pulled his hands out of reach. "Rick, I'm sorry!" Rowan turned to glare at Klaus.

Klaus raised a brow at her. "He's more mine than yours now, *ved'ma*. It will take time before he can withstand your magic again."

"Rowan, it's okay…" Rick gingerly lowered his hands and touched her shoulders. "I wasn't expecting it either."

She turned to look up at him and felt his fingers close more firmly. "I'm sorry," she whispered.

"It's okay," he whispered again, then pulled her against him, wrapping his arms loosely around her shoulders. He dropped his chin on the top of her head.

"Now what do we do?" she said softly.

"Now," said Klaus, "you may tell me how you intend to find my prey."

* * * *

An hour later, perched on the edge of the chair, Rowan's knees were starting to ache from sitting hunched over the road map that was spread across the kitchen table. Her books were piled on the floor by the wall. *I just know I'm going to have a bruise on my elbow from holding the pendulum in this position for so long.*

Rowan frowned in concentration. The pendulum started swinging in increasingly smaller circles. "I think I got him."

Rick peered over her shoulder at the tiny scrawl that marked the streets. "Where is he?"

Rowan looked at Rick's face. He was a warm and vibrant presence at her back. *Klaus was right; he is definitely better.* Rick had gained color and energy in the last hour. He was still pale, but the dark circles under his eyes had disappeared and he seemed to be more his normal self. She looked back down at the map and the circling pendulum. "Looks like I have it narrowed down to somewhere in the middle of this street.

"I think I know where that is." Rick frowned. "Wait a minute, that's the ritzy district. What the Hell is a sorcerer doing in that neighborhood?"

The tiny button at the end of her silver chain swung in swiftly tightening circles. Rowan felt a shimmer of rancid power race up her arm. "Quick, put your finger on the spot."

Rick jabbed a finger onto the map. "What's the matter?"

Rowan gasped, jerking the pendulum away to sit back in her chair. "Damn, that was really starting to hurt." She shook her hand and wiggled her fingers. "There's a nasty ward around the place he's in." She looked up at Rick then over to the elder vampire sitting on the counter. "I think he felt me looking, so he knows somebody found him. Be prepared for a fight."

Klaus smiled, his mouth spreading wider than any normal human jaw would allow, showing teeth a shark would have been proud of. "No matter. He cannot escape me." He dropped from the counter, almost floating to the floor. "You." He jabbed an overlong finger at Rick. "Take me there."

"Sure." Rick picked up the black, flared long coat he had tossed over the chair. "I can drive us there in ten minutes." He pulled his car keys from a pocket and they jangled.

Klaus sniffed. "You may drive, I will follow." His lip curled up in a sneer. "I do not trust these cars."

"Fine, follow me, whatever..." Rick rolled his eyes at Klaus, then raised a brow at Rowan. "Stay here and out of trouble."

"Trouble? Who me?" Rowan gave Rick a tight smile. *While Klaus is busy playing catch with his sorcerer, I can get our suitcases packed into my car for the run to the airport.*

"I have need of you, *ved'ma.*" Klaus waved a clawed hand at Rowan. "You can ride in the car."

Rowan set her jaw stubbornly. "What for? I'm not strong enough to break the barrier spell he's in."

Klaus smiled and it was far from human. "But you are strong enough to hold his attention."

Rowan shook her head. "Look, I found the thing for you. As far as I'm concerned, I've done you enough favors. Go get him yourself."

Klaus stared at Rowan. "Are you afraid?

"Hell, yes!" Rowan took a step back. "Whatever he is, he's nasty. I know I can't take on something like that, I'm not stupid!"

Klaus shrugged. "Rickart and I will handle this one, you need only..."

"Rowan stays here." Rick's voice came out through clenched teeth.

Klaus leveled a crimson glare at Rick. He pointed an overlong finger at Rowan. "Her power will be irresistible to one such as he."

Rick abruptly stepped between Rowan and Klaus. "I said Rowan stays here!"

She shook her head. "My soul isn't corrupt enough to interest a demon anyway. I haven't killed anybody."

"This is not a demon." Klaus abruptly stepped away. "It is a very old, very lonely creature from a world that no longer exists."

Rick frowned. "What the Hell is this thing?"

Klaus glanced at Rick with annoyance then stared at Rowan. "The creature hides behind a wall of magic that I cannot pass, but he did not cast it. He is using a sorcerer that is little more than an animated corpse. The temptation to replace that one with a living *ved'ma* as strong as she will bring him from his lair."

"You are not using her as bait for that thing." Rick shook his head. "She's too fragile to take on this kind of hunt."

Klaus glowered from where he stood by the kitchen door. "This will be fruitless without her."

"Fragile?" Rowan said through gritted teeth. "I'm not that bad!"

Rick turned to frown at her. "Would you prefer the word *mortal?* As in: *easily killed?*"

Rowan felt her cheeks grow warm. "Hey, I held off two vampires." She crossed her arms. "I'm not completely helpless."

Rick turned and took her shoulders. "Only because neither of us thought to use a gun. Why? Do you want to go?"

Rowan raised her hands. "Oh, Hell no! I'm just protesting the fragile stuff."

"Good." He tilted her chin up and dropped a quick kiss on her lips. "You can argue with me about being fragile when we get back."

Rowan smiled thinly. "Count on it."

Rick nodded then pulled his cell phone from his pocket and checked to see that the battery was fully charged. He glanced up. "You still have my cell phone number, right?"

Rowan blinked. "Yes, actually. It's in my small pouch." She pressed her hand against a small red bag on her left hip, tied to her belt.

"Good. There's a phone right here in the kitchen." He pointed to cordless phone mounted on the wall by the doorway to the hall. "Call me if you need anything."

Rowan nodded. "No problem."

"That is an excellent idea," said Klaus.

They both turned to look at the ragged vampire.

"Take this as well." Klaus held out a thick black string about as long as Rowan's hand.

Rick frowned. "What is it?"

Klaus dropped the string on the kitchen table. "It is a thread from my robe." He looked at Rowan from under lowered brows. "Use it to call me if you have need."

Rowan blinked in surprise. "All right." She stepped over to the kitchen table and picked up the string. It may have looked like a string, but it felt like a strand of tightly coiled and vibrating otherworldly darkness. She hastily put it back on the table. *What ever that really is, it stopped being thread a long time ago.*

Rick tilted his head to the side. "With a piece of thread?"

Rowan made a sour face. "It's a direct connection to his spirit. I can use it to call him magically." *Wait a second; Klaus actually gave me a literal piece of himself for me to call him with?*

Rick frowned. "Oh..." He turned to the elder vampire. "So what the hell are you taking me into?"

Klaus raised a brow at Rick. "It is nothing that you have not dealt with before. You will see." Klaus actually smiled. Abruptly his form shattered into smoke that dissipated in seconds.

"I hate it when he does that," Rick snapped.

I await you outside...

Rowan looked at Rick. "Did you hear that?"

Rick's brows shot up. "Shit, you heard it, too?"

"Is that bad?"

He frowned down at her. "As far. I know, only a vampire's victim should be able to hear a vampire's thoughts."

Rowan bit her lip. "But the only vampire that's bitten me is you."

"Yeah, but he's been drinking my blood, remember?" His frown deepened. "Anyway, pack your shit in your car as soon as I'm gone. I want us both out of here as fast as we can arrange it. Don't bother with my stuff. I can buy more on the way."

Rowan nodded. "You got it. Get back here as quick as you can."

Rick grinned. "Count on it." He waked to the open the back door.

"Rick?" Rowan called out.

Rick turned in the doorway with the doorknob in his hand. "Yeah?"

Her hands fisted at her sides. "Don't get yourself killed."

Rick gave her a tight grin. "I'll try not to." He closed the door quietly behind him.

❧ Ƒourteen ↶

Sory

Kneeling on the kitchen floor, Rowan shoved her books back into the brown case. She placed the last notebook on top. Her eyes caught sight of a tiny corner of off-white paper sticking out between the suitcase's lid and the interior satin lining. She frowned and pulled out the small piece of neatly folded parchment. Opening the paper, she sighed at the colorful diagram drawn on it.

"Let's make this a little easier on Rick, just in case we have to actually run." She tore the small parchment in half and felt a tiny shiver as her spell broke.

"One anti-theft spell, down the tubes." She plucked a small piece of folded parchment from beside her knee. "Insert 'feather-weight' spell here," she said softly, then tucked the folded paper where the anti-theft spell had been. She slammed the lid down and fastened it closed.

She stood and lifted the suitcase experimentally. "Well, it's not exactly light as a feather, but it's light enough to carry with one hand." She towed the huge suitcase on its back-wheels to the back door where her other, smaller suitcase sat waiting. She checked the fastenings on both suitcases. "Good thing I found that 'feather-weight' spell in the books this afternoon, or I never would have gotten that puppy up the stairs, wheels or no wheels." A suitcase in each hand, Rowan headed out the back door to her car.

Rowan unlocked the trunk to her Saturn, then lifted the larger case. It wasn't exactly heavy, but it was awkward to maneuver. She shoved it in as deep as it could go and grabbed for the other suitcase. She lifted the suitcase up until it teetered on the edge of the car's trunk.

Rowan heard a loud ringing bong. She looked up. "What the hell was that?" Something in the base of her skull flared white-hot as though she'd been struck. Rowan gasped. The world turned green around the edges of her vision and seemed to tilt. She grabbed for the edge of the car's trunk to keep upright. The suitcase hit the ground.

The bong came again. Pain flared viciously in the back of her skull and she whimpered. The green flare became very pronounced. The world tilted harder and she fell, landing on her suitcase. Her stomach abruptly tried to turn over and she suddenly gagged.

There was a sound of crows flapping and screaming overhead. Moaning with a bad case of motion sickness and the mother of all headaches, she looked around. It was full night and there wasn't a bird in sight. "Why am I hearing crows?" She could still hear the crows as though she was sitting right in the middle of a squawking murder of them.

She closed her eyes and tried to think. "A murder of crows, a green flare and I feel like I want to throw up." She took several deep breaths and her stomach settled down. The sound of the birds began to fade as though passing away. She rubbed the back of her head and the ache seemed to be fading too. Her head shot up.

"Oh, my gods, the property barrier is green and I used a crow feather in the spell to mark a warning. Something big is trying to pass the property barrier!" Rowan got clumsily to her feet. "Gotta phone Rick." She grabbed her suitcase and levered it into the car's trunk. She slammed it closed and bolted toward the house.

A thunderous bong rang out. Pain flared from the base of her skull down her spine and she screamed. The night sky blazed bright lightning green and she heard a powerful rip of thunder. Her eyes rolled back in her head and her knees folded.

Rowan jolted awake lying facedown in the grass. "Gods, my head..." She rolled to her side, grabbed the back of her head and moaned. "What the hell just happened?" She looked around with pain squinted eyes. No sound of crows. "I heard them last time, why not this time?"

She rolled to her hands and knees and promptly emptied her stomach onto the grass. She gasped and spat. "The barrier. It broke my spell, that has to be why I passed out."

Her skin began to crawl. Something bad was coming. It was on the property and it was coming in fast. Whatever it was, if it was able to break through her barrier, it was definitely much too big for her to handle.

"The house... Got to get to the house." Moaning, she climbed to her feet and hurried to the back door. She had to call Rick, but there was no way he'd get here in time. *I think I'm in trouble...*

Rowan slammed the back door closed behind her and locked it. Rowan gasped for breath and tasted bile. She grabbed the cordless phone off the wall, then fumbled through her belt pouch to find the card with his number scrawled on it. He answered on the second ring.

"This is Rick "

"Rick!" she gasped out. Her stomach was trying to empty itself again. She grabbed her coffee cup from the kitchen table and stumbled to the sink for some water.

"Rowan? What's wrong?"

"The house barrier... Something's broken through it." She took a mouthful of water and spat it into the sink to get rid of the taste of vomit. "Something's here. Whatever it is—it's big and it's ugly, but I don't think it's another vampire."

"We're coming back right now. Get to the vault and lock yourself in!"

"I'm going! I'm going!" She left the cup in the sink and headed out of the kitchen.

"No!" Klaus's shout came over the phone, loud and clear. "Go to the top of the house! The creature after you can move through the earth!"

"What?" Rowan stopped in front of the door leading to the vault. "What's after me?"

"Never mind, just do what he says, get to the top of the house. Go to the storage room next to the TV room, there's a small balcony outside the big window. Wait for us there."

"Okay, okay..." She grabbed the stair railing and began to climb, pulling herself up the staircase. "How come I can still hear Klaus if you're on your way back? I thought he didn't like cars."

"We're not using the car."

Her stomach was tying itself in knots and she had the phone jammed tight to her ear, making it hard to hurry. "Rick? What's going on? Where are you?"

"We'll be there in a few minutes, just get upstairs "

Thumping came from the front door. "Open up—this is the police!"

Rowan stopped on the landing. "They're banging on the front door—they're saying, they're the police!"

Klaus's voice came over the phone. "They may well be. This creature can control the minds of others."

"Now you tell me?" Rick shouted. "Rowan, don't you dare answer that door!"

"No problem!" Rowan grabbed the railing and hauled herself up the stairs toward the third floor. The TV room was on the fourth. One more floor to go

There's a loud crunch. Something heavy hit the wood floor with a crash. Someone yelled. "She's on the stairs!"

"Oh, shit Rick, they're in the house!" Boots hammered on the staircase behind her. She tried to run faster and crashed to her knees on the fourth floor landing. She scrambled to her feet, turned the corner and bolted down the hall.

"Don't panic, just get to the balcony in the storage room—we're in sight of the house. Hurry!"

"I'm going, I'm going…" Rowan tore around the corner and grabbed the doorknob of the room right next to the TV room. "I'm there, I'm there "

"Stop or I'll shoot!"

She turned and saw two uniformed police officers on their knees pointing guns at her. The gun barrels yawned like black holes. Rowan froze with her hand on the knob. Every hair on her stood up and a fine trembling started all over her body.

"Put your hands on your head," one of the officers snapped.

Slowly, Rowan raised her shaking hands.

"Rowan? Rowan!" Rick shouted from the phone.

Very carefully, Rowan moved her thumb and shut off the phone. She put her hands on the back of her head and felt her heart trying to pound its way out of her chest. She was too terrified to think of a damn thing to say.

One of the officers got up and approached her. He holstered his gun, then grabbed the phone and threw it. It crunched against the wall. Her wrist was snatched, yanked behind her and a handcuff was snapped around it. He took her other hand and cuffed it as well. She didn't even think to resist. She knew that she had done nothing wrong and that these cops were not here to serve and protect, and yet everything in her was conditioned since childhood to respect the police.

Rowan blinked. There was something wrong with the police officer. She could feel through his skin that something was off, like he had soured. She couldn't smell anything but his clean uniform, but at the same time, something was definitely not wholesome or human about him.

The officer by the stairs holstered his gun. "We've got her," he shouted down the stairs. "We're bringing her down."

Rowan's elbow was grabbed in a tight hold and she was turned roughly toward the stairs. Rowan felt a hot wash of anger. "What are you arresting me for?"

The officer on the stair looked at her and smiled coldly. "We're not arresting you."

Rowan stared at the second officer. He looked perfectly normal, except for the flat leaden look in his eye, but a feeling of sour decay seemed to be oozing off of him. She felt her skin break out in a cold sweat and her stomach trying to turn again. The officer that had her elbow may have been off, but this one was rotted to the core.

Rowan was hauled down the stairs to the entryway. The front door was a splintered mess on the floor. *What the hell did they use? A Battering ram?*

They towed her over the fallen door, then outside. There were two police cars sitting on the drive with their turning lights sweeping across the front of the house and the lawn around them. The officer in front opened the back door to one of the cruisers

She dug in her heels. "What's going on? Where are you taking me?"

Something stepped out of the shadows directly to her right. It looked like a smallish bald man in a neat, dark suit but it was not even close to being human. The eyes were an inhuman red-gold, almost orange. There wasn't a hair on its head, not even for eyebrows. An invisible cloak of rancid skin-shivering power swirled around it.

She unconsciously pulled away. The officer's hand on her elbow tightened painfully. *This must have been what took out my barrier, but... What the hell is it?*

The creature walked toward her. It stopped less than a yard away and focused his blood-tinted gaze on Rowan. The bright red-gold iris sharply widened and swallowed the white. The dark pupil abruptly stretched and reshaped itself into serpentine slits.

Rowan felt a shiver of something cold and dank brush against her thoughts. *Eww, gross...* She took a startled breath and felt her gorge rise. The creature smelled of musty, moldy dirt. *What ever it is, it's been dead for a while.*

The police officer jerked her around by the elbow to face the left. A tall man dressed entirely in silver gray stepped out of the shadows and into the glaring house lights. Long blonde waves fell from his high brow and silver brows arched over stone gray eyes. The face was sharply angled as though hewn from stone and his skin was porcelain white. The ankle-length trench coat, worn open over a perfectly tailored gray suit, did nothing to hide incredibly broad shoulders. His shirt was a crisp white and a black tie was knotted neatly at his throat. He had his hands stuffed into the pockets of his coat.

Rowan's brows shot up. *He looks like an executive Viking...*

The man raised a silver brow and a small smile curled at the edge of his perfectly sculpted pale, lips. "I am Draugar." He nodded. "And you are a witch." The word ended with a sharp snap.

Rowan raised her chin. "What do you want?"

Draugar tilted his head toward the house. "It was your spell I felt seeking me, and your spell on this house, yes?"

Rowan nodded.

He nodded and his smile broadened. "I can make use of one such as you."

Rowan shook her head minutely. "Sorry, not interested. I have a job, thank you."

"I did not offer you a choice." His hand came out of his pocket and he made a gesture with his fingers too fast for Rowan's eyes to follow.

She heard a shuffling sound and saw the dead thing behind her walk clumsily toward Draugar. It stood beside the man in white, then turned to face her. The creature suddenly smiled. His teeth were serrated like a shark. He took a shambling step toward her and held out his hand. Rancid orange witch-fire curled around it.

Rowan jerked back and felt the officer's fingers bruising her arm. "What is it going to do?"

Draugar chuckled. "You will merely go to sleep. When you awaken, all will be well."

Rowan jerked back, but the officer's hold was unbreakable "Oh, hell no, I'm not letting that dead thing near me!" She felt her radiance blaze to life. Light bled from her skin and lit the ground around her. The officer holding her elbow released her with an inhuman hiss and stepped back.

Draugar raised his brows. "So you know that poor Rudolf is no longer among the living. Very perceptive." He held out a pale hand and his fingers brushed against the edges of her light. "How interesting." He smiled with tight lips. "No matter. Rudolf may be only a shambling corpse, but he still has his uses."

The dead sorcerer shuffled toward the edge of her glow. Rancid orange power ignited, then curled around his upraised palms.

Rowan backed away. Her radiance didn't seem to be bothering the creature all that much.

"Shoot her if she runs," Draugar called out. "Not to kill, only to hamper escape."

Rowan's eyes darted toward the police officers. They had their guns out and they were pointed at her. She froze in place. *Where the hell is Rick?*

"You are very strong but untrained," Draugar said calmly. "You will make an excellent student."

"Over my dead body," she snarled.

Draugar chuckled. "As you can see, death will not save you from me." He waved a hand at Rudolf.

The little sorcerer raised both hands and let out a string of arcane words Rowan didn't recognize. The creature shouted and his power lashed out. Rowan felt it contact, then slide across her light like sticky oil. His power spread until everything seemed tinted with that disgusting color. *What the hell is it doing? I've never seen anything like that...*

Suddenly, her sphere of light compacted inward. Her head began to throb under the pressure. He was crushing her magic around her. She gasped, then whimpered. The pressure steadily increased and she dropped to one knee, trying to make herself smaller. She desperately wanted to grab her head with her hands, but they were fastened behind her back. It was getting hard to breathe

"You cannot stand against Rudolf's power," the creature said calmly. "Release your spell and he will stop."

Rowan shook her head slowly. "I can't... I can't..." She gasped for breath. The pressure tightened. She wheezed, trying to get air in her lungs. She felt like she was slowly being buried under tons of earth.

"You will release it or you will pass out from lack of air to breathe." He chuckled softly. "Either way, I still have you."

Rowan fell and curled on her side. Her lungs pumped painfully for air and got nothing. *I can't breathe!* There was a rushing in her ears and darkness closed her vision into a small tunnel. Her eyes began to lose focus. She could hear her terrified heart pounding like thunder.

Somebody shouted from very far away. "No!"

Her power winked out.

Abruptly, the pressure crushing her was gone. Rowan lay on her side on the gravel drive and drew a long breath. Her mind was wrapped in a dark fog of fear. She sucked air into her starving lungs and coughed.

Someone turned her over on her stomach and she felt icy fingers close around both wrists. She blinked, but her eyes refused to focus, she couldn't see who held her. "Let me go," she began and coughed harshly. Icy cold seared both her wrists and she let out a sharp cry.

"Do not try to use your magic or you will be severely punished."

She jerked away but was hauled bodily off the ground by the armpits. An arm closed around her ribs, then tightened until her back was pressed against a body that seemed to be made of stone.

"Let her go."

Rowan's eyes abruptly cleared. She was facing Rick and he was standing in front of the broken entrance to his house. Rowan coughed. "Rick..." Her voice came out in barely a whisper. His overwhelming emotions washed into her through their mental link, flooding her with terrified concern colored by violent and bloodthirsty anger.

"Why should I?" The voice was calm, pleasant and right next to her ear.

Rowan looked up sharply; Draugar was holding her up off the ground with his arm wrapped tightly around her ribs. Fear squeezed her and she kicked out sharply. Draugar's arm around her chest tightened. She gasped for breath. He was squeezing the air from her lungs.

"Be still," he said softly and relaxed his hold.

Rowan drew a frightened breath. She threw a desperate look at Rick. It took everything in her not to scream for help. She could feel Rick's anger but it was hard to think past the gibbering fear in her own thoughts. There was nothing she could do. Her hands were still cuffed at the small of her back and she was being held off the ground, utterly helpless in the arms of something a hell of a lot stronger than she was.

Rick loosed a rumbling growl. "If you don't let her go, I will rip your throat out." His fingers lengthened into lethal claws.

A cloud of shadow coalesced at Rick's side and became Klaus. Rowan had never been so happy to see the gnarled vampire.

"Hello, Klaus." Draugar raised his free hand and signaled to the two police officers. They came trotting over to the cars. Draugar tilted his head to the side. "Rudolf?"

The gnarled visage of the dead sorcerer twisted into a nightmare parody of a smile, revealing the serrated points of his teeth. The little sorcerer took a step toward Rick and raised his palms. A dome of orange fire blazed to life, encircled the sorcerer, then spread to include Draugar and Rowan.

Rick took a step toward it then flinched back. Klaus stood perfectly still, his face completely without expression. His darkness boiled around him, but other than that, he seemed perfectly willing to merely watch.

Draugar frowned at Rick. "You are also vampire?"

Rick bared long white canines.

Draugar turned his gaze on Rowan. "You, a witch, willingly serve vampires?"

Rowan strained to take a full breath; his arm was squeezing too tightly. "It seemed like a good idea at the time," she wheezed out.

Draugar snorted. "You would be better served by remaining with me and learning to use your power than as a plaything for a vampire."

"I'm not a plaything." She shifted in his hold. The handcuffs were biting into her wrists and her feet were going numb from hanging from his arm.

Draugar turned his eye on the vampire. "You, vampire, are familiar to me," it said softly then raised a silver brow. "Holt... Rickart Holt, is it not?"

"Yes." Rick frowned. "Do I know you?"

"It has been a very long time." Draugar's face abruptly rearranged itself into the angular lines of a much older man with a neatly trimmed mustache. His long silver mane disappeared and was replaced by closely cut, iron gray hair. "Have I changed so greatly?"

"Mother of God," the vampire whispered. There was a shudder of horror in his voice. "Todt..."

Rowan looked over at Rick. His face was wiped clean of all expression but she could feel the acidic boil of hate churning within him through their mental link. "You know each other?"

A growl rumbled loudly from Rick. "It is because of Todt that I was damned before I ever became vampire."

Draugar's face remained that of an older man. He nodded. "So, you do remember me." His lip curled in a twisted smile. "As a soldier, your potential for exquisite violence manifested itself gloriously before you regained your human concept of morality."

Rick jerked his gaze away. "As a soldier, it was my job to kill." A muscle in his jaw flexed.

"You killed people?" Rowan said softly.

Rick's head shot up and his eyes sought Rowan's gaze. He'd heard her soft exclamation. "It wasn't my idea to be a soldier. I wanted no part of the war." Rick ground out. "I was conscripted straight out of college that summer. One minute I was walking to class, the next I was being stuffed into a bus under gunpoint."

Rowan blinked in confusion. *War? What war?*

Draugar smiled condescendingly. "And you were a very good, very obedient soldier."

"If I didn't follow orders, I would have been shot," Rick bit out venomously.

"Does he not sound innocent?" Draugar turned a silver eye on Rowan. "He was a Landser of SS-Sonder-Kommando Dirlewanger, one of the most ruthless penal battalions ever to serve the Fuhrer."

Rowan took a sharp breath. *The Fuhrer—as in: Hitler?* Rowan stared at Rick. "You were a Nazi?" she asked in a tight voice.

Rick looked at Rowan's white face. "Hell no, I was never part of that." He shook his head sharply and jabbed a finger at Draugar. "Todt's inhuman excuses for officers were Nazi, I was a Stabsfeldwebel, a Warrant officer one rank above master sergeant."

Rowan's heart hammered in her chest. *Rick was a* German *soldier during World War Two?* She looked at Draugar, then at Rick in shock. *Oh my gods, I don't even want to think about this…*

Draugar tilted his head to one side. "Out of curiosity, when I knew you as a mortal man, you did not kill others easily, but as a vampire, I know that you must drink blood to survive." The brows rose and a bloodcurdling smile spread across his face. "How do you justify the killing of others to survive? How do you live with the destruction of your own soul?"

Rowan shot Draugar a look of disgust. *Son of a bitch! What an ugly thing to say!*

Rick bared his fangs in a snarl. "Yes, I drink blood, but I don't need to kill for it." The growl in Rick's chest was very pronounced. "I haven't killed since I burned your camp to the ground."

Draugar's brows rose. "So, it was you that set fire to my camp, so long ago?"

Rick nodded. "It was both my sire and I."

Rowan looked at Rick. *He's never mentioned that he did anything with his sire. He said he didn't remember him.*

A nasty smile curved Rick's mouth. "The two of us hunted and killed as many of you as we could find. It was his idea to fire the whole camp afterwards. I had thought we'd gotten you and all your filthy abominations."

Draugar sighed. "If it will satisfy you, you did succeed in destroying all of my slaves."

"Good." Rick bared his teeth in vicious smile.

Good, Rowan thought in agreement. She reached for her magic, but it kept slipping just out of reach.

Draugar grinned. "However, the rest of your remaining militia compatriots died when the fire took the camp. Their deaths rest on your soul."

Rick flinched and glared hot daggers at Draugar. "I know." He wrapped his arms defensively around his body.

Rowan bit her lip. *Sadistic bastard!* She wriggled her fingers. *If I can generate my radiance, this guy will drop me, and hopefully knock out the orange field. Then I'll get the hell out of the way and let Klaus do his thing to this asshole.* Her arms were going numb and she couldn't feel her feet anymore. *If I can just get loose...*

Draugar tilted his head to one side. "I remember this other vampire, a Russian."

"A damned pity he didn't kill your ass."

Draugar nodded then smiled. "I'm afraid that it is time for me to leave you, pleasant as this conversation has been." His head tilted down.

Rowan followed his glance. Rudolf was on his knees. His head was tilted back with his eyes rolled back showing only the white. His mouth was slack and hanging open and his face had gone very sunken and gray. His hands hung limp at his sides.

"I'm afraid that Rudolf has not much more left in him, so it's time I set up his replacement."

Rowan's skin broke out in a cold sweat. Her head shot up and she glared at Draugar. "I am not going anywhere with you!" Abruptly, she found her magic. She felt the power surge under her skin—and turn into white-hot acid in her veins. She shrieked and continued to scream as fast as she could draw breath, thrashing in agony.

"I told you not to use your magic." Draugar said softly.

* * * *

"Rowan!" Rick lunged for the orange barrier. He struck it and hissed in sharp pain. Todt pressed a hand to Rowan's forehead. Her struggles and screams abruptly ceased. Her eyes closed and she collapsed like a rag-doll. Todt reached down and caught her legs under his other arm, lifting her up and cradling her like a child. Her red mane fell in a spill of shed blood against the stone gray of his sleeve.

One of the police officers scooped up the limp sorcerer and shoved him into the back of the first police car, then raced around to climb into the driver's seat. The second officer opened the back door to the car parked by Todt.

Todt's face abruptly shifted into the porcelain-pale, ruggedly handsome features of a Viking. His hair became spun silver and tumbled down past his shoulders. Todt shook his head, tossing his silver mane until it settled down his back. He shot a narrow look at the two vampires. "If I see either of you—the witch dies." He turned and shoved Rowan's unconscious form in the back of the waiting police car, then stepped in. The waiting officer closed the door and got into the driver's seat. Both police cars pulled away, crunching down the long gravel drive.

Klaus began to rise from the ground. "His sorcerer fades I can take him."

"No, Klaus!" Rick grabbed Klaus's wrist with clawed fingers. "I can't risk Rowan."

Klaus began to lift higher. "I must follow him—I will not risk losing him."

"No! Don't!" Rick grabbed the front of Klaus's robes to keep him from soaring after the cars. "I can't have you chase him, he will kill her. I've seen him kill for no reason at all."

Klaus twisted and caught both of Rick's wrists while continuing to rise, lifting Rick off the ground with him. "You do not have the power to fight me, you fool."

"I know," Rick hissed. Klaus was crushing the bones in his wrists. "You won't lose him, I can track her through my blood-bind." Rick eyed the second story window that was level with Klaus's head and twisted his wrists in Klaus's powerful grasp. "As soon as they are out of sight we'll follow them, we need to stay out of sight."

Klaus frowned and began to drop to the earth. "Very well. But my patience with you is very thin." He released Rick's wrists and Rick dropped half a story to the ground, landing lightly on his feet.

Rick rubbed his wrists then turned and watched the two police cars disappear behind the trees lining his drive. "So is mine."

∽ 𝔉𝔦𝔣𝔱𝔢𝔢𝔫 ∾

Arcanum

R owan took a deep breath and opened her eyes. She was staring at a cream-colored ceiling decorated with a relief of ornate sculpted vines and leaves painted over in white. She blinked. *Was I asleep?*

She turned her head to one side. She was lying sprawled across a large brilliantly colored Persian rug on the floor of a huge and empty room with tall windows heavily curtained in gold velvet, lining one whole side. There was an enormous white marble fireplace commanding the center of the wall by the windows. *Where the hell am I?*

She curled her legs under her and sat up. She groaned. Her body hurt like hell. Her stomach and chest muscles ached, her head was a throbbing mess and her hands and feet were tingling as though her circulation had been cut off. Her shoes and socks were missing. Rowan searched her waist and discovered that her leather cigarette pouch and her tarot cards were still attached to her belt. *Well, at least I can smoke if it gets too dull around here.*

She rubbed her sore wrists and discovered a finger thick bracelet of pale amethyst stone around each wrist. She held up her wrists. The bracelets were exactly the same. She twisted the slender stone and discovered that they would not go over her hand. She couldn't get them off. She rubbed at her tingling bare feet and found an amethyst bracelet around each ankle just like the ones on her wrist. *What the hell happened to me?*

Rowan's head jerked up, remembering the cops, the sorcerer and Draugar holding her like a doll. *Shit, I've been kidnapped by that monster I gotta get out of here.*

She looked around and saw a door on the wall opposite the row of windows. Rowan levered herself up onto her bare feet. She took two unsteady steps toward the door and bumped her nose smack, into a wall she couldn't see. Rowan jolted to a startled halt and rubbed her nose. "Son of a bitch! What the hell was that?"

She put out her hands. There seemed to be some kind of smooth invisible something right in front of her. She tapped it lightly with her knuckles and it made a sound like a window being struck. *Invisible glass?* She hit it harder with her fist and promptly bruised her knuckles. "Ow, shit."

She sucked on her knuckles, then put out a foot. Very carefully, she bent her knee, then kicked at the invisible glass with the ball of her foot, hard. She was knocked right off her feet and landed on her butt with a bruising thump. "Damn it!"

She rubbed at her sore foot, then got up. "What the hell is this?" She put out her hands and touched the smooth cool surface. "There has to be a way out." With both hands out, she traced a seamless circle all the way around the rug.

The door opened behind her. Rowan turned around and saw Rudolf limping unsteadily toward her. He was looking even more like a corpse than before. His skin seemed to be flaking off, and there were dark stains leaking through his coat. Rowan backed away from the sorcerer's approach. Rudolf stopped at the edge of the invisible glass. His orange eyes focused on her.

Rowan swallowed. He was giving her the serious creeps. She rubbed at the hair rising on her arms and brushed the bracelet. Her eyes dropped to Rudolf's wrists. He was wearing bracelets, too, but they were orange, the color of his magic.

She frowned. *My magic isn't purple* She blinked. It was when she sharing Rick's power. Rowan sucked in a breath. She must still be holding some of his power. Maybe she could still reach him? Rowan closed her eyes and opened her thoughts wide, seeking Rick's essence and felt nothing.

"I would not use your magic if I were you."

Rowan's eyes snapped open. Draugar was standing right behind Rudolf. She hadn't heard him come in. His long silver coat was gone, along with his jacket and tie. His white shirt was unbuttoned and open down the front, showing a long line of muscular and pale skin. He smiled and rolled one sleeve up over a muscular forearm, to the elbow. A warm wave of curious interest uncurled low in her belly.

Rowan jerked her eyes firmly up to his face. This was no time to let her libido get out of hand. "I thought that you wanted my magic?"

Draugar dropped his eyes and unfastened the cuff to his other sleeve. He began rolling it up. "Of course I want your magic, but only at my command." He glanced up at her. "If you attempt to use it without my permission, you will discover that it will cause you a great deal of discomfort."

Rowan's hands fisted at her sides. "What have you done to me?"

"At the moment your magic is contained. I'm sure you've noticed the bracelets?" Absently, he tapped a finger on the top of Rudolf's head. Rudolf abruptly collapsed into a sitting position.

Rowan closed a hand around the bracelet on her left wrist. She could feel her pulse racing under her fingers. "Is that what they do, block my abilities?"

"Among other things."

Rowan felt her breath hitch in fear. *Oh my gods, he took my magic!* Panic began to close around her heart and a cold sweat broke out on her lower back. She took a deep breath to calm herself. She had to stay clear-headed. *Don't panic.*

He raised a brow and frowned. "There is no need to be so distressed. They do not take your powers. You still have access to all your senses and abilities. You simply cannot use them without my express command."

Rowan felt the pressure around her heart relax. *Mother of us all, was I that easy to read?* She let out a breath she hadn't realized she was holding. "Then what the hell are they?"

"They are devices for control of your body." He smiled. "As long as you don't try to cast any outward form of magic or attempt to escape, you'll be fine." He stepped around Rudolf and walked onto the rug, right through the barrier as though it wasn't there, and continued purposefully toward her.

Rowan backed away in a hurry. He continued across the rug toward her until her back pressed against the barrier behind her. He reached for her and she ducked under his hand, scooting to the left. His hand closed tight around her upper arm. She jerked her arm and his fingers dug in painfully. "Ow, shit." *I am definitely going to have more bruises...*

His brows shot up and he abruptly loosened his fingers but kept a firm hold. "Forgive me, I have not dealt with someone purely human in a long time. I forget how fragile you are."

Why does everyone call me fragile? Rowan ground her teeth. "You could try asking me for what you want, instead of just dragging me around."

"Indeed?" He smiled. "Very well then, I want you to remove your clothes."

Rowan's mouth fell open. *Me and my big mouth!* She closed it with a snap. "What for?"

He tilted his head to one side and raised a brow in challenge. "I need to set the binding spell. It requires bare skin."

"Oh." She flinched. *Now I have to do what he asked or make a liar out of myself...* She swallowed. "Uh, all right."

Draugar blinked at her and his expression went carefully blank.

Rowan's brows shot up. *Well, damn, I think I surprised him.* Rowan tugged on her arm. "You're going to have to let my arm go so I can strip." To Rowan's amazement, he released her. Rowan took a deep breath and unbuckled her belt. She frowned at Draugar. "You don't have to stare. You have a barrier up, it's not as if I'm going anywhere."

He blinked then shook his head with a wry smile. "Of course." He turned to one side, presenting his cool profile.

Rowan rolled her eyes then turned her back on him. She opened her jeans and yanked her black T-shirt out of her waistband. *I can't believe I'm actually doing this.* She took a breath, yanked the shirt over her head, revealing her pink satin bra. She dropped the T-shirt on the rug. *First I'm doing favors for vampires and now this.* Rowan began to tug her jeans down. *How do I get myself into these messes?*

"Out of curiosity, does this mean that you will comply with all my requests?"

Rowan froze with her jeans around her hips. *Piss and firewater, what a question!* She peeled her jeans from her legs and dropped them on her shirt. "That is not something I can promise."

"Honesty?" He snorted. "How very unexpected."

"I'm one of the good-guys; I'm supposed to be honest. It's in the rules." Rowan stuck her thumbs under the waistband of her pink panties. She really, really did not want to take off her underwear. "Um, how much skin do you need?"

"All of it."

Rowan swallowed. "All of it?" Her voice came out in an embarrassed squeak.

"Lovely as your lingerie is, I require full nudity."

Rowan looked over her shoulder. Draugar was standing with his feet apart, facing her. His head was tilted to the side with his brow was raised and a tight smile curved his lips. He still wore his dress pants, but his shirt was a small crumpled pile of white silk on the floor. His arms were folded comfortably across his milk-pale and naked chest.

Rowan glared at him. *He's staring again!* She turned her head away in a huff. "Fine, all of it, whatever. And quit staring at me!"

Draugar's laughter boomed out.

Rowan flinched. *He's laughing at me?* Rowan squeezed her eyes shut then opened them and sighed. *Well, duh! He's going to be doing bad things to my nude body in a minute or two.* She struggled with the catch of her bra in the center of her back. *This is so fucked up. I should be fighting this guy tooth and nail.* She shook her head and dropped her bra on top of her clothes. *Oh yeah, like I can fight something as strong as that without getting myself seriously maimed or killed.* She pulled her panties down and stepped out of them. She dropped her panties on her clothes. Defiantly, she pulled her hip-length hair over her shoulders to cover her naked breasts and crossed her arms. *Now what do I do?*

"Come here." His voice was soft and dangerous.

Rowan turned around. He looked at her from head to toe and his face was serious. His head tilted and he frowned. She bit her lip, gathered the shreds of her courage and took a few steps toward him.

"Halt."

Rowan was jerked to a sudden stop by the bands around her ankles. "Shit," she hissed softly and teetered, off balance on her frozen feet.

He abruptly spat out a phrase she didn't understand. Her wrists were suddenly jerked out to the sides by the bracelets until her arms were stretched to their limits. "Ow, shit!" She gasped and pulled, twisting her wrists in the bracelets, but couldn't slide her hands free. "Son of a bitch!"

"Don't struggle, you will only harm yourself."

Draugar then said something else.

Rowan felt her feet abruptly dragged shoulder-width apart by the stone rings around her ankles and her knees buckled, tipping her forward. "Damn it!" The bracelets dug into her wrists, holding her upright. She fought to regain her balance.

Draugar closed the distance between them in two long strides. He reached out with both hands and gently pushed her hair over her shoulders to fall loose down her back. He stared down the length of her nude body. His eyes focused below her face.

Rowan felt the heat of a humiliated blush warm her cheeks. *He's staring at my breasts.* His hand closed on her shoulders and she flinched. His eyes flicked up to hers, then darted back downward. His fingers skimmed down to her full breasts, then lightly brushed her nipples. To her complete mortification, Rowan felt a jolt of sensual heat. Her nipples tightened and peaked. Rowan jerked away from him and pulled at the unmoving bracelets. *This is so not happening to me...*

His silver eyes looked up into hers. A smile curved his lips. "Very nice."

Rowan's temper suddenly flared hot. Fear and humiliation were swept aside. "Just set your damned spell, you sick bastard, then leave me the fuck alone!"

Draugar chuckled and pulled his hands away. He walked behind her. Rowan strained her neck to follow him with her eyes. He cupped the sides of her head in his hands and turned her to face forward. She felt his hands slide under her hair, then down to encircle her throat. She swallowed hard and felt her skin break out in a cold sweat. Was he going to kill her for her outburst of temper?

"Your skin is too cool and your pulse is too fast," he noted. "You're frightened." His comment sounded like an accusation.

Rowan snorted. *Well, duh...*

"There is no need to be so afraid."

Rowan barked out a short laugh. "Let's see, I've been kidnapped and I'm about to have a nasty spell put on me. What have I got to be nervous about?" She clamped her jaw tight and cringed. *When will I learn to shut up?* She sighed. Either he was going to kill her for her mouth or he wasn't.

"The spell isn't painful." His voice was soft as a kiss in her ear. "Parts of it will prove quite pleasant."

Yeah right, pleasant for whom? She felt his hands move to her shoulders then his fingers skimmed down her spine. Shivers followed the trail of his fingers, making the small hairs on her body stand up.

"The spell merely accesses your abilities for my own use."

Rowan blinked. *Was that supposed to make me feel better?* His fingers stopped at the base of her spine and she felt his palms splay across her hips at the top of her buttocks.

"Now that is interesting."

Rowan turned her head to look at him. His brows were drawn down in thought. "What?"

Draugar looked at her and a smile played at his lips. "It seems that the source of your magic is sexual."

Rowan felt her temper spike sharply in reaction to her fear. "I could have told you that, if you had bothered to ask."

Draugar's head tilted slightly. "Indeed?" He sighed softly. "As it is, this poses a bit of a problem."

"What problem?" Rowan felt hope pulse through her. *Anything that causes him a problem has to be good for me.*

Draugar shook his head with a small smile. "Nothing too difficult. Your magic needs sex—or more precisely, orgasm—to regenerate." He shrugged then began to walk in a circle around her. "That is simple enough to provide for, unlike Rudolf, who needs to eat human flesh about once a month."

"Rudolf eats people?" Rowan stared the hunched sorcerer on the floor. "You're kidding, right?" It looked like parts of him had flaked off onto the floor around him. He seemed to be quietly disintegrating right before her eyes.

"Unfortunately, no." Draugar sighed and walked around to stand before her. "Here in the United States, police procedure is quite sophisticated. Hiding the evidence of his kills has become something of a challenge." Draugar shook his head. "He was very careless on his last hunt. The police officers accompanying us tonight had traced him here. I was forced to take control of them."

"Gee, I feel so bad for you," Rowan said dryly.

Draugar snorted. "Yes, well, providing for your sexual appetite will be simplistic compared to providing for Rudolf's needs."

Primitive female fear spiked in her belly and Rowan swallowed. *I don't think I like where this conversation is going...*

Draugar smiled. "I just can't decide if I should find you a lover..." His smile broadened. "Or if I should take care of your needs myself."

Rowan felt a second cold sweat break out across her skin. "I really don't think that would be a good idea." Rowan was pleased to discover that her voice only shook a little. What frightened her more was the warmth building in her belly. She'd been using her power off and on around Klaus since this morning, then she'd fought off Rudolf's spell and *then* she'd nearly killed herself trying to escape Draugar. Altogether, she had used a huge chunk of magic. At the moment, her body's appetite was still under control, but if it got hungry enough, it wouldn't care where it got its satisfaction.

Draugar nodded. "You are probably right, given how your magic will be feeding from mine. I have no idea just how much power you'll take."

Rowan frowned. *I didn't take all that much power from the vampire, but then he drank my blood, too. Maybe they balanced themselves out?*

Draugar glanced at Rudolf. "Poor Rudolf is nearly gone..." He walked over to Rowan and cupped her face in his palms.

Rowan took a frightened breath. "What are you doing?"

Draugar smiled and his gray eyes became solid, flat discs of beaten silver. "I'm transferring his burden to you."

Rowan felt her heart trying to climb up into her throat. "I don't want it." She tried to jerk her head from his hands.

"Just a few moments more and we will be done." His eyes dropped to her mouth. His silvery power crackled around them, lifting her long red hair in a shimmering wind of power. Suddenly it surrounded, coalesced and soaked into Draugar's body. Holding her head still, he leaned close, and then his mouth pressed against hers in a kiss.

Rowan's eyes opened wide and she gasped in surprise. His tongue surged in to possess her and his rumbling arcane magic thrust deep into her throat, pouring into her. His tongue leisurely explored her mouth while his silver essence burrowed deep and swelled, filling her body.

She felt his magic entwine with her power, possessing her more intimately than sex. Her body unconsciously responded with a wet roil of ecstatic sensuality and she moaned. Moisture dampened her thighs and her nipples rose to hard, aching points. Rowan's eyes closed and tension built at a murderous rate as though she was about to climax. Her spine arched and she came up on her toes shuddering and writhing in her bonds.

Draugar tightened his hold on her head and angled his mouth, then locked his lips tightly to hers. He inhaled sharply and stole her breath.

Rowan's breath rushed out of her and she felt his power leaving her body in a shattering release that felt like orgasm.

With his lips locked firmly on hers, he wrapped his arm around her and held her tightly against his unyielding and cool body, keeping her locked to his mouth with one palm on the back of her skull. He swallowed her ecstatic screams.

Suddenly Rowan felt his retreating power pull on her magic. Interlocked with his, her power began to rush out of her mouth. He was unraveling her soul from within. *Oh Gods, he's taking my magic!* She whimpered and struggled in terrified reaction. She felt a chill, and shivered. She was getting colder while his body began to radiate heat. *He's killing me!*

The world faded to a muted and colorless gray. The world began to retreat. She stopped struggling and closed her eyes. *So, this is death...* Without her magic, she just didn't care anymore.

* * * *

Rowan blinked and stared at the ceiling. She was lying on the floor; she could feel the rug under her back. *What happened? I thought I was dead?* She shifted and discovered that her wrists and ankles were pinned by the stone bracelets to the floor. She could feel a tiny trickle of power within her, but she felt hollow. A huge something was definitely missing.

It's gone, he took it all; everything that makes me a witch. Tears started in her eyes and slid down her cheeks. *He took everything that makes me, me.* Her breath hitched on a soft sob. She turned her face into her arm.

"Your power is not gone, I have it. It will be returned momentarily."

Rowan lifted her head as far as her wrists would allow. Draugar was at the very edge of the rug where something very dead had crumpled in on itself in a small untidy heap of flaked ash.

Is that Rudolph? She watched. Draugar tapped the heap with his finger and it abruptly collapsed into a pile of fine gray ash. Rowan blinked. *I did not just see that happen...*

Draugar turned and strode over to her. In a single smooth motion he knelt at her side. "This is the last of the spell." He held his palms out over her head.

Rowan cringed away from his hands. "Don't destroy my mind."

Draugar gave her a fleeting smile. "That would be foolish of me. Your intelligence is what makes you valuable."

She blinked up at him. "What are you going to do?"

He frowned in concentration. "This will be swift and painless." He spoke again in a guttural tongue, his words harsh with grunts and growls.

Rowan felt a cool breath of magic brush through her hair. She bit her lip. *Painless, right, sure...*

Draugar threw a long leg over her and came down on his knees, straddling her hips. He arched over her, his hands pressed into the floor on either side of her shoulders. His silver eyes became bright, glowing with incandescent power. He smiled and settled his hips against hers.

Rowan gasped. Through the thin cloth of his trousers, she could feel that he was fully and heavily erect against the unprotected juncture of her thighs, the entrance of her body. Her nipples jerked to sudden attention and Rowan bit back a moan. Her body warmed, then roared to ravenous life under him, empty of power and literally starving to be filled. *Oh shit, oh shit...*

She arched up under him, helpless against her soul's overwhelming need. Her mouth opened and she cried out.

He dropped full length on top of her and his mouth took hers in a devouring kiss. Her hips rolled under him, begging for him to take her, starving for the thick hardness riding at the aching, hungry nether-mouth to her body.

She felt his hands move over her and the soft wind of power following his palms. His hands slid down her shoulders to caress her breasts. She writhed under his palms. A moan escaped her lips and he swallowed it. His hands moved down to her waist, then to her hips. He reached under her to cup the cheeks of her ass, lifting her against the delicious hardness that he denied her. The soft breeze wound around her body, caressing her like a soft cloth being drawn against her flesh, then abruptly dissipated.

Suddenly heat exploded low in her belly. She gasped. The sensation crested with orgasmic bliss, then uncurled like a great purring cat, spreading sensuously throughout her limbs. Rowan gave out a sudden sob of relief. Her magic was back.

"There," Draugar said softly. "It is done."

Rowan blinked up at him, her feelings caught between elation and fear. "Now what?"

Draugar raised a brow and a smile curved his lips. "Now you and your power are mine." He snapped his fingers.

Rowan felt her wrists and ankles released. Warily, she watched Draugar withdraw from on top of her body. He rose to his feet. Rowan refused to move, struggling with her feelings of both relief that he hadn't taken her blatant invitation and a stab of disappointment. *Gods he kills people for fun and I almost begged him to fuck me.*

She finally rolled to one side to sit up, facing away from him with her knees folded under her. *If he'd left off his pants I would have begged him to fuck me.* She wrapped her arms around her waist. *I almost did anyway.* She closed her eyes, feeling a rush of hot shame.

"Rowan?"

Cautiously, she turned to look at Draugar. He had not used her name before. "Yes?"

Draugar thrust out his hand and made an odd gesture. "Cast."

Rowan felt her power arc out of her in a shimmering ring and she gasped. *Oh, my Goddess! That isn't me! That's him!* Her magic swelled like a bubble into a gossamer and almost visible net of shimmering awareness. Suddenly she could feel the entire house and the property surrounding it. She could feel the two soured police officers standing by the front door and about half a dozen other people moving around in the huge house. Every one of them had a spot of taint to them. She reflexively felt within herself and discovered that she was clean of whatever was rotting within the other occupants of the house.

She frowned. "I'm not like the others," she said unthinkingly, out loud.

Draugar turned to look at her. "That is because you are mine. They were created by another."

Rowan cringed. *Can we ease up on the 'mine' crap?*

Draugar reached over and picked up his shirt from the floor. "And now I have to destroy them."

Rowan's mouth fell open. "Destroy them? You mean kill them?"

Draugar shrugged. "It was Rudolph's spell that held them. Now that he is gone..." He glanced at the pile of ash that still marred the rug. "His former slaves have been released."

Rowan's hands fisted at her sides. "So, you're going to kill them because they are reverting back to their original selves?"

Draugar snorted. "Hardly. What has been done to them is irreversible. Without Rudolf to control them, they will become increasingly uncontrollable and highly dangerous."

Rowan grit her teeth. "Dangerous? To you?" *I hope.*

"Not to me." Draugar smiled and shook his head. "I assure you, I am very difficult to harm." He sighed. "Rudolph's slaves are all eaters of flesh."

Rowan felt her skin grow cold and rubbed her chilled arms. "My Gods... What the hell are they?"

Draugar tilted his head to the side. "To borrow from your pop culture, I believe they are something you would call the living dead or zombies."

"Great Mother! Are you telling me that zombies are real?"

Draugar raised his brows and snorted in derision. "You know that vampires exist, how can you doubt these creatures?"

"I see your point." Rowan felt a shudder come over her. "And they eat people?"

Draugar shrugged. "These are not dead, but they are tainted and their bite is highly infectious. Left to themselves, they will hunt among the local population, making more of their kind until the entire town has either become one of them, or has been consumed by them."

"Oh my gods," Rowan said and shivered. The hair on her body rose. "And you have them for pets? Isn't that really dangerous?"

Draugar shook his head. "Not to me. I cannot contract their disease."

Rowan made a sour face. "Lucky you."

Draugar nodded. "Unfortunately, if their bodies are slain, say, by the local police, they do not fall immediately, but remain animate. Eventually, they become consumed by the taint that made them. In this condition they only last three days, but three days is enough to infect and massacre an entire town. I have seen it happen. Now that I can no longer control their actions, their destruction is necessary."

Rowan had to look away. "Or they'll kill the whole town."

"Indeed." Draugar tossed his shirt over his shoulder and headed for the door. "You will be safe in here, they cannot pass the barrier." He stopped when he reached the door and looked over his shoulder. "You may dress yourself, if you like." He smiled suddenly. "Although I would not mind if you remained as you are now. You are quite lovely."

Rowan's mouth popped open in surprise. "No, thank you!" She

leaned over and grabbed for her clothes.

Draugar turned the doorknob with his brow furrowed in thought. "I already have your soul," he said softly. "I am wondering what it would be like to have the rest of you."

Rowan whirled to face him with her clothes clutched defensively to her chest. "What exactly are you saying?"

"I am wondering if the possession of your body would be worth the price of a small amount of my power."

Rowan hunched behind her clothes. "When Hell freezes over!"

"I don't think I'll have to wait quite that long." He chuckled. "You were more than willing only a few moments ago." He opened the door. "I found myself quite tempted," he said and closed the door firmly.

❧ Sixteen ❧

Ensorcelment

"I have to find a way out of here before he gets back." Rowan struggled into her clothes with all due haste. She nearly screamed in frustration when she had to pull her T-shirt back off and then put it back on, right-side out. She didn't see her shoes or socks anywhere in the huge empty room. There was only herself, the rug she stood on, the heavily curtained windows lining the wall opposite the only door and the massive, ornately carved, marble fireplace against the right wall.

"Damn it, there has to be a way out." Hands out, she explored the smooth surface of the barrier that imprisoned her in the center of the vivid rug. She stretched as high as her hands would reach, but couldn't find the upper edge. In desperation she pressed her fingers along the bottom edge but it seemed to be sunk into the floor. She groaned and stood up to stare at what she couldn't see. "Piss."

Rowan dug into her hip pouch and pulled out a black clove cigarette and her lighter. "The damn thing's invisible. I could be standing in front of the exit and never know." The tiny gas jet of her lighter hissed. She lit the cigarette and exhaled the thick and pungent white smoke. "If I could just see this thing "

The white smoke billowed from her lips and abruptly curled to the sides and up as though it struck a flat surface. Rowan blinked, sucked another mouthful and blew more smoke. Briefly the smoke showed a smooth curving surface. "Well, damn, there it is."

Puffing on her cigarette, Rowan circled the entire circumference several times, looking for a seam, a crack, an imperfection It was smooth like glass and arched high over her head.

"Son of a bitch! I'm in a fucking bell-jar, like some damned china doll!" In frustration, she smacked the barrier with the flat of her hand. There was a soft hollow 'bong'. "Ow, shit!" She shook her smarting palm.

Groaning, she walked to the center of the carpet and flopped down to sit with her knees bent and her arms wrapped around her legs. Out of pure spite, she put her cigarette out on the expensive carpet, creating a nice black burn mark.

"This really sucks." She sighed and rested her chin on her upraised knees. *I can't be somebody's slave; I have a cat to go home to, and a job...* She blinked back the dampness in her eyes. *I have a life, damn it!*

Two more cigarette burn-holes later, Rowan felt a whisper against her senses. "What?" She lifted her head from her knees. "It's not Draugar, I can feel him upstairs along with two of the tainted things," she said thoughtfully. She closed her eyes to focus on the disturbance. "The rest of the um, zombie-things feel like they're migrating upstairs too, so it's not them." She tilted her head and reached out along the magical webbing around the property.

Something was moving along the house barrier that she was magically bound to. It was something familiar and dark. She frowned in concentration. The presence abruptly slid through the barrier and moved swiftly toward the side of the house that she was on. To her complete surprise, her nipples began to tighten and a warm curl of sensuality began to roil through her. *What the hell?*

The presence was suddenly on the other side of the curtained windows. There was a muffled sound of breaking glass. The curtain's shifted on the furthest window on the right, by the wall the fireplace occupied.

She groaned. "What the hell is after me now?"

Rowan?

Her name been projected directly into her thoughts. Rowan's eyes opened wide and she blinked. There was only one person who could do that. Rowan got to her feet and felt her heart beating in her throat. "Rick?"

Rick's dark head appeared between the folds of heavy velvet. His hair was tied in a long tail that fell over one shoulder. "Rowan?"

"Rick!" Rowan let out an explosive breath. "I am *so* glad to see you!"

"Glad to hear it." He grinned broadly. "Sorry I took so long." He pulled himself through the curtains and stood on the carpet. "I drove your car out here and I didn't realize that it was this far out in the middle of nowhere." He shook the skirts of his long midnight coat. Shards of glass scattered at his feet. He sniffed and frowned. "I leave you alone and you smoke up the whole place with your cigarettes."

"Like it's your house?" Rowan made a face. "Get over it."

He walked toward her and glass crunched under his feet. "As I recall, you smoked the hell out of my kitchen."

Rowan stuck her tongue out at him.

Rick snorted and shook his head. "Anyway, where are Todt and the short orange guy?"

"The orange guy, Rudolf, is dead. That was him." She pointed over to the ash stain on the carpet. "The other guy is upstairs killing zombie-things."

"Good, that sorcerer was a pain in the ass, and I was wondering where the cops had disappeared to." He stopped a few feet away from her. "Are you ready to get out of here?"

Rowan gave him a lop-side grin. "Sure." She put her hands on her hips. "As soon. I can escape the barrier he's put around me."

Rick's mouth fell open. "Barrier? Please tell me you're joking."

Rowan bit her lip and shook her head slowly. "Wish to the powers that I was..."

Frowning, Rick stepped onto the carpet that marked the boundary.

"Be careful, it's damned hard on the nose," Rowan said wryly. She rubbed her own nose in reflexive memory.

"I don't feel anything," he said softly and strode cautiously, right up to her.

Rowan stuck out her hand and felt the barrier just past his side. "You're inside it," she said softly. "Weird it doesn't seem to notice you."

"Good." Abruptly he grabbed her up in a hug, lifting her off the floor. She wrapped her arms around his neck. He buried his face under her red hair. "Damn, I was worried sick!"

She hugged him around the neck hard. "Me, too."

He pulled back. "Are you okay?"

Rowan sniffed and nodded. "Yeah, nothing broken."

"Good." He nodded sharply. "Time to blow this taco stand." He turned with her in his arms and felt a hard vibration go through Rowan.

"Ow, shit." She rubbed her shoulder. It had slammed into the barrier. "I still can't pass the boundary."

Rick frowned and let her slide down to stand on the rug. He waved his hands where she had made impact. "I still don't feel a damned thing."

"Can you hear this?" She knocked lightly on the smooth wall of magic. A soft bong followed each of her gentle strikes.

Rick's eyes widened. "Shit. I see what you mean." He frowned. "It's just a spell, right?"

Rowan nodded.

"Then there has to be a way to break it." Rick held out his hands, but still encountered nothing. "What would you normally use to break a spell?"

Rowan blinked then looked up at him. "I use my athame, and come to think of it…" She put out a hand and stroked the smooth surface. "Salt."

He turned to her and raised his brows. "Salt and your *what?*"

Rowan sighed softly. "My black handled ritual dagger. That's what I use to break spells." She tapped the invisible wall with her knuckles again. "But I've never run across anything like this before."

"Do you think it would work?" he frowned. "Just your dagger and salt?"

Rowan tilted her head to one side. "It's the only thing I can think of, at the moment." She shrugged. "It might not affect it at all, but then again, it might put enough of a crack in it to force my way through." She winced. "But, I don't have my dagger with me. Everything's in my red shoulder-bag and that's back at the house."

Rick looked at her blankly a moment, then suddenly smiled. "Does your shoulder-bag look like this?" He opened his coat and showed her a long-handled, red velvet bag slung across his chest.

Rowan laughed. "It looks exactly like that!"

"Good." He slid out of his coat, dropping it on the floor, then pulled the cloth handle over his head to hand her the bag. "Here, break this damned spell and let's get the hell out of here."

Rowan took the bag gratefully and dug into it. "Thank the powers that you thought to bring it!"

"Don't thank me, it was Klaus's idea to bring it." Rick shrugged back into his coat.

Rowan looked up with fully half her arm buried in her bag. "Klaus?"

Rick shrugged. "He said, and I quote…" Rick cleared his throat, frowned ferociously and proceeded in a guttural and hackneyed, Russian accent. "Take her bag of arts. The *ved'ma* will have need of her possessions to break what sorcery he has bound her with."

Rowan blinked. "You're kidding, right?"

Rick snorted. "'Fraid not."

Rowan's hand closed around the handle of her ritual knife. "Ah ha!" She pulled out her sheathed dagger. "I want you to wait over by the fireplace."

"By the fireplace?" Rick's brows knitted together. "What for?"

Rowan pulled out her bag of salt. The strings of a small blue bag were tangled to the ties. "I'm going to do this quick and dirty." She frowned at the small bag of frankincense, then looked up at him. "This spell is really strong and I have no idea what kind of aftershocks or explosion I'm going to set off if I actually succeed in breaking it. I don't want you to get hurt by accident."

Rick snorted. "I'm the big bad vampire, and you're the fragile human, remember?"

"Will you quit it with the *fragile* shit?" She untangled the small blue bag from the strings of her salt bag. Thoughtfully, she held the frankincense bag in her hand and somehow, she knew that she was going to need it. *If I'm going to need this, then maybe I need other things, too?* She shoved her hand back into the bag. "Give me what I need to pass through this barrier spell," she said softly.

"You're still more likely to get hurt than I am." He frowned. "Wait a minute, how much power are you planning on throwing at it?"

"Everything I can dredge up." Her fingers caught on more string ties. A breath of hope began to uncurl inside her. She pulled out her hand and found three more colored bags of herbs attached to her fingers.

"Everything? Isn't that dangerous?"

She rolled her eyes. "I don't have a whole lot of choice here. Once I start knocking on this thing, Draugar is going to know immediately and come running. I have to make a big enough hole to squeeze through on the first shot."

"And if you can't break it?"

Rowan bit her lip. "If I can't break it, then I need you to leave immediately."

"What? Oh, hell no!" He grabbed her shoulders. "I am not leaving here without you."

Rowan grit her teeth. "If you stay and get your ass killed, who else is going to rescue me? Klaus?"

"I am *not* leaving you here! How can you ask me to do that?"

"You don't have a choice and neither do I!" She jabbed a finger at him. "You have to be in one piece, upright and conscious to save me."

Rick winced then set his jaw. "Rowan, I'm not leaving you alone with him. You don't know what Todt is capable of."

Rowan set her jaw stubbornly. "Yeah, well, I'm learning "

"Rowan, I'm telling you right now, leaving you behind with that thing, is a really, shitty idea!"

"Look, I agree!" Rowan threw up her hands and he let her go. "Are you happy now?" She turned her back and shook her head. "But, if I can't break this spell, I have no one else capable of rescuing me." Rowan could feel her eyes beginning to water. "No one else even knows I'm here." She blinked, then rubbed the heel of her hand across her eyes. She turned to look at him. "I only have you."

* * * *

His hands clenched at his sides. "What if he takes you where I can't find you?"

"You will find me."

He winced at the absolute certainty in her voice. *I can't leave her. I won't* He took an unsteady breath. *I love her too much...* He blinked in stark surprise. *Love? When the hell did that happen?*

Abruptly he took a blindingly fast step and pulled her into his arms. She had a moment to gasp and then he kissed her. His mouth took hers and he desperately tried to say in his kiss what he was afraid to say out loud. That he loved her and that he was afraid. Afraid of losing her forever, and afraid of finally, finding her—after she had been changed into something that was no longer human.

He pulled back and held her by the arms. She was trembling under his palms. "I am not going to argue with you." He stepped back. "Do your hocus-pocus and let's get out of here." He strode for the massive fireplace and his shoulders knotted tightly.

Rowan watched him stride away and blinked. *Please Lady, don't let him do something brave and stupid, and get himself killed.* She closed her eyes against the sudden pain in her heart. *I couldn't take it.*

Draugar had warned her not to reach outside herself. Seated on the floor by the base of the barrier Rowan closed her eyes and turned her focus inward. This was not how she normally did magic. Normally she would stretch her power outward like questing fingers. Softly and politely she would use her magic to ask the elemental magics that breathed in all the swirling life around her to assist her in her need. Even her glowing radiance was in response to a call. Her brilliant glow was something that came from outside herself; a gift from the Goddess she served. What she was about to do was altogether different.

Gently, gently, Rowan summoned all the power she had from within. Warm and velvety, like a sleepy cat, it uncurled and moved through her. Affectionately, her power filled her to the brim until it spilled over and raised a soft wind that lifted her red hair from her shoulders. It moved through her and around her, playfully batting at the gossamer strands of spell weaving that bound it to the web around the house.

Rowan rose from the floor at the base of the barrier with her dagger in one hand and a fistful of odd herbs and resins in the other. She slapped her open hand against the barrier, ignoring the sting on her palm. Her eyes narrowed in determination and smeared the powdered herbs against the barrier, shaping an archaic symbol that meant: *door.* The symbol's shape stayed frozen in mid air, embedded in the barrier.

Rowan gripped her dagger with both hands and raised it. She took a deep breath, focusing her power into herself tighter and tighter. She braced both feet firmly and shouted the word for the rune she had used, the symbol that floated, embedded in the barrier right before her eyes. She stabbed.

The dagger sunk into the symbol with a distinct popping sound. Gripping with both hands, she jerked the knife downward. The barrier parted, ripping like taut fabric. Rowan's eyes widened. *Holy shit! It worked!* She jammed an arm through the hole, then her head. She shoved a leg through. The rip began to squeeze around her. The barrier was healing itself.

"Rick!" She waved her hand. "Quick, pull me through!" The barrier tried to squeeze her back into itself and she groaned. There was a blur of shadow and Rick suddenly had her by the hand.

"I've got you." He wrapped his arm around her and pulled sharply.

She fell gasping into his arms outside the barrier. The barrier suddenly became whole with a hollow wobbling sound. "Thank the gods." She struggled to stand but her knees were watery.

Rick brushed the hair from her face. "Are you okay?"

Rowan nodded. Everything felt a little fuzzy around the edges. "I'm just dead tired, gimme a minute to sit. I think I drained everything I had left." She took a heaving breath and shuddered with exhaustion. "I didn't have to break it. If we're lucky, he didn't feel the tear I made." She held up her wrists and showed him her bracelets. "Can you break these?"

* * * *

Draugar flung open the door to room where he was holding Rowan. "It is time to leave, I have destroyed the remaining revenants..." He stopped in mid-sentence and focused his silver gaze on Rowan. She was not within the barrier he had set; she was sitting on the floor by the fireplace.

Rowan tucked her hands behind her back and bit her lower lip.

He bespoke in his ancient language.

Rowan blinked but remained where she was.

His eyes glanced downward at her ankles. They were bare of his fetters. She had not only succeeded in slipping through his barrier, she had somehow loosed herself from his bonds. He raised a brow. "We have been clever."

Rowan gave him a small smile and a shrug.

"Silly fool." He pointed to the floor at his feet. "Come, now."

Rowan's body unsteadily rose to its feet and took a shaky step toward him. *Piss and firewater! The bracelets are gone, how the Hell is he doing that?* Rowan shuddered, fighting the powerful compulsion to obey. She grit her teeth and made her body stop.

"You should not be able to resist." He frowned. "I said come. Now."

She gasped, feeling her exhausted power well up in response. *He's trying to use my magic against me!* It took every ounce of her stubborn will not to take another step.

"I can barely feel you, your energy level must be very low," he said thoughtfully.

She took a ragged breath. "Gee, that's too bad for you."

Draugar sighed. "Regardless, we need to leave now." He strode toward the fireplace.

Rick flowed like living shadow from out of the deep recesses of the massive fireplace. "You'll have to go through me to get her." He stood between Draugar and Rowan and his body boiled with dark menace.

A gun seemed to appear in Draugar's hands. "There you are, Rickart Holt." The barrel yawned black and wide. "I've been expecting you."

Rick loosed an inhuman snarl and his long teeth gleamed in the room's dim light. "She's mine."

Rowan peeked around Rick's arm and projected to him. *It's not that I'm not grateful, but aren't we being a little possessive here?*

Rick turned a swift hot glance her way. *When you can stop bullets, you can have an opinion. Until then, I'm running this little scene.* He gathered himself for a lunge. "If you try to stop us from leaving Todt, I'm going to enjoy ripping you apart."

"Use caution, vampire," the Draugar warned softly. "Unlike the last time I shot you, these bullets are silvered and bespelled, and I am not limited by human reflexes."

Rowan turned to Rick in shock. "He shot you?" Rowan frowned.

"Wait, the scar on your shoulder "

"Yep, that was it." Rick's eyes narrowed. "It was a long time ago."
Rick snorted. "Even silver bullets won't kill me now, Todt."

"True." Draugar nodded. "However, the spell on them is enough to make you very, very uncomfortable. Personally, I would rather not damage you."

Rick blinked in confusion. "What?"

Draugar's lips spread in a condescending smile. "I would have you both."

Rowan frowned. "You want both of us?"

Rick loosed a deep rumbling growl. "Why the fuck would I want anything to do with the man that damned my soul?"

Draugar's lip curled. "You damned yourself."

Rick stabbed a finger at the draugar. "You ordered us into those Russian villages!"

"Yes, I did." Draugar cocked a brow at Rick. "However, it was your troop's creativity in obeying orders that damned you."

Rowan blinked. *What the hell are they talking about now? Russian Villages? Troops? Is this more World War Two stuff?*

"Creativity—my ass!" Rick crossed his arms over his chest. "You made us into insane killers with that stuff you had us drink right before we marched."

Draugar shook his head. "The drug only enhanced what was already within them. I needed to be sure that they would voluntarily act out their violent inclinations. If I remember correctly, you were particularly creative in evisceration..."

Rowan swallowed hard and refused to look at Rick. *Evisceration? Gutting people?*

Draugar sighed. "Even when I was your commander, I had such hopes for you. Your human conscience was your undoing."

Rick shook his head. "There was no way in Hell that I was going to put up with you drugging us into becoming psychopathic killers!"

Rowan swallowed and felt something unclench around her heart.

Draugar bared his teeth. "Which is why I shot you!"

Rick ground his teeth, then jabbed a clawed finger at Draugar. "You shot me because I discovered your other ugly little secret, that you were feeding us—your own troops—to those unholy things that called themselves officers!"

Rowan jolted. *What?*

Draugar snarled. "It could not be helped. My officers needed to be fed or they would have become uncontrollable. They could not feed on the innocent. They needed the unclean, those tainted by the corruption that comes from self-willed atrocities."

Rick folded his arms across his chest. "And no one noticed that you needed frequent replacements?"

Draugar smiled thinly. "Losses are expected during war. My entire core of officers needed only one every three days, far fewer lives than the average engagement."

Rowan's hands fisted at her sides. *Mother of us all! Is he saying that he had those zombie things for officers?*

Rick jabbed a clawed finger toward Draugar. "What was I supposed to do? Ignore the screams?"

Draugar shook his head. "You were under orders to stay away from the officer's encampment. That order was for your own safety."

Rick shook his head. "That was my friend being eaten alive on that table by your officers, I had to do something!"

"Your so-called friend..." The draugar's voice was a low snarl. "Had a way with small children or he would have never ended up on their table."

Rick visibly flinched. "My God," he whispered.

"So, you did not know of your friend's more interesting habits..." Draugar frowned thoughtfully then shook his head. "Your destruction was needless, you could have taken my offer instead and served me."

Rick hunched forward, teeth bared. "I could never be one of those..." Rick's hands were balled into white-knuckled fists. "Things."

"The officers were merely tools given to me." Draugar shrugged. "I wanted you for something altogether, different. Even as a mortal, power was within your grasp. You would have been safe from them as my apprentice in sorcery."

Rick snorted "And deal with you up close and personal, every day? Oh, hell no."

Draugar raised a brow. "And so, I was forced to shoot you."

Rick sneered. "What, I'm supposed to be grateful that you shot me?"

Draugar snorted. "I offered you swift, clean death rather than put you on their table to be eaten alive."

Rick rolled his eyes. "Oh, gee, thanks."

"As to our current arrangement…" Draugar raised a brow "…I have an enemy "

"We know," Rick said and bared sharp teeth.

Draugar snorted and shook his head. "Not that revenant vampire that dogs your heels…"

Rowan and Rick exchanged startled looks.

"He is of no concern, he cannot pass my boundaries." Draugar smiled at Rowan. "Rowan may be free of the barrier, but she is still tied to the shield, and directly to me. No, what seeks me comes from our past, Rickart. Perhaps you will remember him?"

Rick's lip curled in distain. "Like I give a shit."

Draugar's mouth set in a grim line. "You will give a great deal, when he comes to take you too. As it is, I can use you both."

"What? Both of us?" Rick frowned. "What the hell for?"

"When I delved into her magic I discovered something interesting. Your powers seem to be intertwined and the power the two of you generate together is very potent."

Rick grabbed Rowan's arm and took a step back from Draugar. "So?"

Draugar snorted. "Shall I spell it out for you? I need Rowan's sex-driven power at full capacity to break free of the binding set on me, and you're just the man to keep her there."

Rick jabbed a finger at Draugar. "You are one sick fuck!" He stepped backward, shoving Rowan behind him toward the broken window. "We're getting out of here now."

"Fool." Draugar shook his head and smiled. "Can't you tell that I already have both of you?" His eyes locked on Rowan's. "Cast," he whispered.

Rowan felt her power spool out in threads. She grabbed for it, but something held her back. It slid through her hold to wind around Rick in a webbing of magic.

Rick suddenly collapsed to his knees. "Son of a bitch!"

Rowan was pulled to her knees behind him by his grip on her arm. *Rick,* Rowan projected softly. *He's using his connection to me to get to you. I can feel him using my power to do it, but I'm nearly burned dry. If you try, you can resist him.*

Rick nodded slightly, then frowned in concentration. Staring Draugar in the eye, he got one foot under him and pushed slowly to his feet.

Rowan felt her power thin further. The world began to lose color and her heart sounded loud in her ears. Her power was nearly gone...

Rick took a single step back toward the broken window.

Draugar raised his gun. "Stop or I'll shoot," he said pleasantly.

"Fuck you," Rick said distinctly and took another step back. The gun went off with a powerful explosion. Rick's reflexes allowed him to twist sharply away from the bullet.

Rowan felt something hit her shoulder like a punching fist and she was spun backwards. The air was knocked from her lungs. She felt Rick grab for her and catch her in his arms. She sucked air into her lungs and felt something gnawing on her shoulder with big teeth. "Ow, piss!" she hissed and grabbed for her shoulder.

Rick hunched over her protectively. "Rowan, are you all right?"

Rowan stared at the blood on her hand. "No, I don't think so."

* * * *

Rick watched Rowan's eyes flutter closed and she groaned. He lifted

Rowan into his arms then whirled to face Todt. "You shot her!"

Todt's face was a mask of frustration. "I assure you, that was not my intent," he bit out.

The center window exploded and Rick leaped out of the way with Rowan in his arms to protect her from the knives of flying glass. Klaus unfurled in a mass of shredded darkness.

Todt jumped back and emptied his gun in Klaus's boiling darkness.

"You know that bullets will not work on me," Klaus hissed.

"Damn you." Draugar threw down the gun and his fingers elongated into curved daggers.

Klaus bared his serrated teeth and an inhuman howl escaped his throat. He drew a pair of long, black-bladed swords from nowhere, then launched himself at Todt in a blur of inhuman speed.

Todt abruptly sank into the floor like it was water.

Klaus dove for the floor after him and disappeared.

Rick blinked. "Okay, that was weird." He turned to look at Rowan cradled in his lap. Blood that smelled like sewage slithered from the bullet wound past his fingers. "Rowan honey, are you still with me?" Her eyes opened and they were dilated wide to black pits.

"It hurts," she said softly, then went boneless in his arms.

Rick looked up to find Klaus rising through the floor. His swords had disappeared.

Rick frowned. "Is he dead?"

Klaus scowled. "No. He has retreated into the earth where I cannot follow."

"He's escaped?"

"Yes." Klaus looked at Rick and frowned. "I smell blood that stinks of sorcery."

"It's Rowan's, she's been shot." Rick licked the wound and abruptly spat. The taste of her blood was painfully bitter and stomach-wrenchingly foul. There was no change; the wound continued to look angry and red.

Klaus appeared over Rick's shoulder. "You cannot heal her that way."

Rick nearly jumped out of his skin. "Shit, Klaus! Quit sneaking up on me like that!"

Klaus ignored his outburst. "The bullet has been bewitched. It must be removed or she will die from the poisonous spell."

Rick touched the edges of the bullet hole. Rowan moaned weakly and blinked her unfocused eyes. He dug a finger into the wound and pain stabbed him sharply. "Ow, shit!" He yanked his hand back. "It's like touching acid! Fucking son of a bitch...I should have taken that bullet."

"True." Klaus nodded. "The draugar meant it for you. It would have made you ill and very weak, but her, it will kill."

"I won't let her go." He stared into her unseeing gaze. "I'll make her one of us."

Rowan stirred and blinked up at Rick. "I don't want to be a vampire..."

"You're not dying on me," he said harshly.

"No! You must not turn her," Klaus snarled. "She must never be made vampire."

Rick bared his teeth at the elder vampire. "Why the Hell not?"

Klaus pointed his finger at Rowan. "What she will become will kill us all."

"What?"

Klaus paced before them. "She is a *ved'ma*. Ask her where her power comes from."

"Her power comes from sex, I already know that," Rick snapped.

Klaus curled his lip. "And she already feeds from your vampiric lust. Think fool! Do you imagine that the blood of a mere mortal will satisfy her as a vampire?"

Rick shook his head. "What the Hell are you saying?"

"Her unreasoning, new-born hunger will kill you before she can learn to control it." He bared his teeth. "Even then, her vampire appetite will be such that she will be the death of every mortal and immortal she encounters. Even one as old as I would not satisfy her."

Rick stared at the blood seeping past his fingers. "I won't lose her."

Klaus sighed. "Then you must retrieve the bullet and salt the wound."

"I tried, I can't touch it." Rick frowned. "Salt?"

Rowan gasped in his arms. "Salt breaks the spell..." She whimpered softly. "You need my athame to get it out."

"What does she need?" Klaus moved away, practically disappearing in the shadows.

Rick looked about on the floor. "Her magical knife."

"It's on my belt." Rowan drew a sharp painful breath. "Salt is in the red satin pouch inside my red velvet shoulder bag." Her eyes closed and she sighed softly.

"Damn it, Rowan, stay with me!" There was a thump. Rowan's red bag landed at his side.

"I cannot touch her things," Klaus whispered from nowhere. "You must do it."

"Fine, I'll do it..." He felt along Rowan's belt. "Where the Hell is that dagger?" Abruptly the black handle filled his hand. He pulled the sheathed, heavily carved dagger from where she'd tucked it at the center of her back. He set it on the floor beside him then grabbed the red velvet shoulder bag and dug though the bags, parcels, twists of paper and books that filled it. There were thousands of small cloth bags and the poor light made it hard to see the different shades.

"Salt, salt," he muttered and tangled his fingers on a string. He pulled his hand free and found that the strings were attached to a red bag. He opened the bag. It was full of white sand. He dipped a finger in the bag and tasted it. "Salt, good, great," he set the bag by his knee.

"Rowan?" She lay very still across his knees. "Rowan, honey?"

"Perhaps it is best if you leave her asleep," Klaus whispered from deep shadow.

"I suppose you're right." Rick ground his teeth and impatiently pulled the blade from the leather sheath. The black-handled dagger had a wide blade but a sharp point. "This is probably going to hurt."

"I would imagine so." Klaus was barely audible.

Rick took a deep breath and applied the point of the dagger to the ragged, seeping hole in her shoulder. Rowan moaned. He touched something metallic and felt a malevolent charge vibrate up his arm. "Shit, that is nasty," he muttered. Abruptly the blade began to blaze with light. He almost dropped the dagger in surprise. Rick frowned and squinted against the glare. The dagger's handle was growing warm.

"Quickly," snapped Klaus.

Rick dug and pried at the bit of metal. It came to the surface, glowing a rancid yellow-green. Rick grabbed for it with his fingers. Pain lanced hotly and he hissed. Using the dagger's tip, he dug it from the wound and flicked it, rattling, to the floor.

"Salt, salt," Klaus hissed.

Rick fumbled the red cloth bag open and sprinkled the wound.

"No, fool boy..." Klaus appeared at Rick's shoulder. "Use your fingers and pack the wound to break the spell. Her infection is not physical."

"You are not helping," Rick growled and poured half the bag over the gaping hole. He jammed a finger into the hole, shoving the salt in.

Rowan abruptly exploded in his lap, screaming. Salt flew everywhere. She thrashed and mindlessly struggled to dig the salt in her shoulder back out.

"Rowan! Rowan, it's okay, it's just the salt!" Rick fought to hold her down. "Shit, she's going to tear the hole bigger!"

"It is the spell she fights." Klaus crouched before the two of them. "Hold her head still."

Rick didn't think, he grabbed Rowan's head, and Klaus stared into her pain-widened eyes. "Sleep," he commanded.

Rick felt a slam of power and Rowan collapsed limply into Rick's lap. He darted a look at Klaus. "Will she live?"

"If she is strong." Klaus stood and brushed his hands down his robes. "You must leave. Now. Take her to the car and go home." He turned and strode for the deepest shadows.

"Why?" Rick rose to his feet with Rowan in his arms. "What's going on?"

Klaus turned to look at him. "Those whose will I serve are coming. If they find you, either of you, they will have no mercy." Klaus shattered into splinters of darkness and was gone.

"Klaus, damn it!" Rick shouted at the empty shadows. He sighed. "Thank you."

❧ Seventeen ❧

Segue

R owan was dreaming of snow

She walked in a forest of enormous and leafless trees. She could barely see through a falling curtain of bitter white. Her pale violet robes swept the snow at her feet and floated in a wind she didn't feel. The ground was soft and barely felt. She moved between broad trunks of trees that appeared suddenly and darkly. She slipped ghostlike through the endless half-light, hunting through the frozen forest of bare trees. She was looking for someone, but she had no idea who she was looking for.

Forever and forever and forever seemed to pass.

She frowned. "He has to be around here somewhere."

Abruptly she came to the edge of the trees and discovered an endless, rolling emptiness. The sky was the same color as the snow-covered ground. On the edge of the horizon she could make out a single tree. "There," something said within her. "He's there…"

Someone stepped out from behind a tree right beside her. A long coat of silver blew open in the wind.

Fear caught her breath. She stepped back into the forest.

The figure turned abruptly to look at her. Long ice-white hair lifted from a broad brow, revealing burning white eyes in a chiseled and brutally handsome face. He smiled. "There you are..."

* * * *

Rowan surfaced from sleep with a gasp. "Rick!" She blinked in the near dark. She was pretty sure she in Rick's huge bed in the vault. She could just make out the pillars. The mattress shifted under her. Rick leaned over Rowan with a grim smile. "I'm right here." He was fully dressed in a black T-shirt and dark jeans. He set his chin on his fist. "Welcome back. How do you feel?"

She tried to sit up and groaned. Everything hurt. She fell back among the pillows. "I feel like dog-crap." The blanket slid down and Rowan suddenly realized that she was naked. She grabbed for the blanket.

He brushed his hand across her brow. "You're supposed to feel like crap, you had a bullet in you."

"What?" She froze. "A bullet?"

"You got shot." He leaned over the other way and grabbed the remote control from the table by the bed. The light increased. "Don't you remember?"

Rowan blinked in the sudden light. "I think so. I remember the gun going off." She raised her hand and flinched from the stiffness in her shoulder and arm. She found a neat bandage taped on her shoulder. "Did you do this?"

Rick nodded. "I stopped at a drug store and bought some stuff to bandage you with, along with some antibiotic cream." He made a sour face. "Though I jammed so much salt in there, I doubt you'll get any kind of infection."

"Salt? You jammed salt into my open bullet wound?" Rowan winced. "In that case, I'm glad I don't remember." She shook her head and gave him a sour smile. "What day is it? When did we get here?"

"You got shot last night. You've slept the whole day away. It's Friday night." He sat down on the bed.

"It's only Friday? All that happened in two days?"

"Do you remember Klaus?" He leaned over and grabbed the white bag off the side table. "Here, you need to eat." He shoved the bag into her hands.

"I think, I remember hearing him." Rowan took the bag. "What's this?"

"Burgers and fries. They're about an hour or so old. If you're thirsty, there's a paper cup of soda on the table on your side of the bed."

"I'm sure it'll be just fine." Rowan dug a cold burger from the bag and her belly cramped. She was starving; she hadn't eaten anything since the sandwich yesterday afternoon. She took a huge bite. It was ice cold and tasted heavenly. She took a sip of the soda. *Mmm, flat watery cola.* She took another bite of the hamburger.

He frowned. "You don't remember telling me to use your athame to dig the bullet out?"

Rowan glanced up. "*I* told you to use my athame?"

"The bullet in you was cursed. I couldn't touch it." He looked down at his lap. "You almost died."

Rowan's mouth went dry and the hamburger turned to cardboard in her mouth. She grabbed for the soda and sucked on the straw so she could swallow. "Almost died?"

Rick nodded. "If Klaus hadn't told me to take out the bullet right there and then pack it with salt, you wouldn't be sitting here."

"Oh, my gods," she said softly then her brows shot up. "Wait a minute, you said Klaus? *Our* Klaus?"

Rick nodded curtly. "He basically saved your life."

Rowan frowned. "What for?"

Rick shook his head. "I haven't a clue."

She looked around. "Um, speaking of tall, dark and scary, where is he?"

He shrugged. "After I dug the bullet out of you, Klaus let us go."

He mouth fell open. She closed it with a snap. "He let us go? Just like that?" She took another bite of the cold hamburger.

Rick eased off the bed then turned his back to her. "Yeah, he told me outright, to pack you in the car and go home. Todt, or Draugar or whatever he's calling himself these days, escaped and Klaus went after him."

"Draugar escaped." Rowan felt a shiver that resonated to her core. She could still feel him humming on the edges of her power. "Shit, I need to reset the house barrier."

"You can do it tomorrow."

Rowan shoved the blankets. "But we're defenseless."

"Stay right where you are." Rick set a firm hand on the blankets. "I don't want you bleeding again. You haven't got the resources right now, and I don't think Draugar is going to come anywhere near here. Not with Klaus hot on his ass." He turned back and yanked his black T-shirt off, baring the sleek muscles of his back. "God, I'm tired. I haven't slept since you caught that bullet."

Rowan looked sharply away from the sight of Rick's naked back. "You haven't slept?" She heard the telltale jingle of a belt-buckle being unfastened.

"Or showered." He snorted. "I got the front door repaired, and brought your suitcases in from the car. By the way, thanks for taking that 'too-heavy-to-lift' spell off the suitcase. They're over by the foot of the bed. Anyway, I didn't want to leave you alone too long or fall asleep, in case you needed to go to the hospital. And then there's Klaus."

She turned to see his hands grab his waistband. "Has Klaus been back?"

"Nope." He began to jerk his pants down. He wasn't wearing underwear. "Looks like he's gone for good."

Rowan's body clenched hard with a different appetite and her pulse beat in her throat. A warm flush started creeping up her neck. *Not now, I don't need this now!* Rowan closed her eyes tightly and swallowed the cold mouthful of burger whole. She nearly choked on it.

"I'm going to go take a shower."

Rowan nodded with her eyes tightly closed. "Yeah, go do that."

"Rowan?"

"Yeah?" She swallowed hard. The bed dipped.

"I want you to shower with me."

Rowan's eyes popped open to find Rick stark naked and sitting much, much too close. "I, uh…" She swallowed and tried again. "I'll shower when I'm done eating."

"I can wait." He frowned. "And don't give me that look."

"What look?" Her voice came out in an embarrassing squeak.

Rick raised his brow. "Rowan, you're still not all that recovered yet. I don't want you falling in the shower, so finish your burger." His brows dipped in a frown. "I also need to check the condition of your wound, and that needs to be done in the bathroom. It's um, easier to clean up blood from tile than bed-sheets."

Rowan let out her pent-up breath. "Oh, okay."

"What?" He took a deep breath then his nostrils flared. "Ah, so that's the problem." A grin curved his lips.

Rowan looked at him suspiciously. "What?"

"It's time to use me as a sex toy, isn't it?"

Rowan blushed hotly.

He rolled his eyes. "It's not as if you can hide it." He raised a brow. "You're not still embarrassed over this, are you?"

"I, uh…"

He took the half-eaten burger from her fingers, then handed her the soda. "Drink."

Rowan automatically sucked on the straw.

He took the cup from her hand and placed it on the table. Gently he placed a hand on her shoulder. "You need to feed to recharge, and I need to feed, too." He pulled her close and tilted her chin up. "Get over it." He kissed her.

Rowan felt his mouth on hers and opened without thought. She felt a hot wave of primal lust rage through her and couldn't stop herself from sliding her hands into his hair and yanking him closer. She sucked on his tongue and nipped at his lips, kissing him as though starved.

Rick pulled back, breaking the kiss and grinned. "That bad, huh?"

Rowan was mortified. *Where the hell did that come from?* She swallowed and found herself licking her lips for another taste of him. "I'm not used to being this, um, out of control."

He nodded. "Yeah, that's pretty much what I figured. You're probably not used to using this much magic, either."

Rowan bit her lip. "No, I'm not."

He took her hands. "Look, we both have appetites that need taking care of."

Rowan gave him a tight smile. "That's one way of putting it."

Rick raised his brow. "So, why don't we take care of each other and enjoy?"

"I suppose you're right." She nibbled on her lower lip. "I'm sorry..."

"For what?"

Rowan flinched. "For Klaus and Draugar..."

He snorted. "You didn't invite that damned vampire into my house or ask to get kidnapped and shot."

Rowan raised her chin. "Yeah, well, I didn't get Klaus out either, and it was my spell that brought Draugar here."

"To draw Klaus out of the house." Rick gave her a wry grin. "Well, he's out now and you're safe."

Rowan felt a laugh well up and nearly choked holding it back. *This is so not funny.*

"Come on, let's shower." Rick took her hand. "We're both too nasty to touch each other right now." He grinned suddenly. "Though I'm sure I could handle it if you really need it now."

Rowan made a sour face. "No way in hell, Fang Boy. Definitely shower first." She slid her feet out from under the blankets and felt sudden exhaustion grab hold of her.

Rick scooped his arms under her legs. "I got you." He hefted her into his arms and stood.

Rowan grabbed for his neck. "I don't know why I'm so tired."

Rick rolled his eyes. "Heaven forbid, I just don't see why you're tired either." He gave her a sarcastic snort. "Gee, could it have been the kidnapping, then the spell you had to break through, and then the bullet you took, that was cursed, by the way?"

Rowan grimaced. "I see your point."

"Oh no, we're saving that for after!" Rick carried her into the bathroom, grinning.

Rick set Rowan on the toilet seat of the tiny bathroom. Carefully, he peeled the taped bandage from her shoulder. Rowan turned her head to see and Rick firmly turned her chin away.

"No, don't look." He frowned. "Luckily, the bullet was in the meat of your upper arm and not really in your shoulder, or you'd have broken bones."

She felt his fingers apply pressure and she hissed from the pain. "It feels like a really huge bruise."

"That's because there's a really huge bruise around it." He sighed. "It's only seeping a little blood and that looks clean." He sniffed. "No sign of infection, thank the Powers." He grabbed for the box of gauze and the hospital tape on the back of the toilet. "You'll probably be sore as hell for a while, but everything will be closed up with only bruises left by Sunday night."

"Sunday night?" Rowan's mouth fell open. "Look, I don't know squat about bullet wounds, but still, isn't that a little fast?"

Rick blushed. "After I dug all the salt out of you, I um, took care of your bullet wound my way."

Rowan swallowed. *His way? Does he mean that he used his mouth?*

"I only did it once, while it was still pretty fresh, but the bullet made a good-sized hole and I couldn't take you to a hospital." He glanced at her. "I couldn't think of a good explanation for how you got shot in the first place."

Rowan bit her lip. *I guess he did.* Oddly Rowan discovered that she wasn't really all that repulsed. *Well, I suppose it's good that I'm not in the hospital.*

"You feel better after a shower." Rick finished taping the new bandage on. "Then we need to talk."

Rowan felt her heart jolt in her chest. "Talk?"

"Yeah." He stepped into the shower and turned on the water. "Let's get you into the shower."

* * * *

The water pressure was heavenly. All Rowan had to do was lean against the wall and Rick massaged her in thick soapy lather with a facecloth. She groaned. "Gods, that feels good."

"Glad you approve. Hold still while I finish this off."

Rowan insisted on washing her own hair. Then Rick wrapped her in a towel and set her back on the toilet seat while he showered.

"Goddess, I can't believe all the weird shit in the past few days. You, Klaus, then Draugar and his house of horrors "

"Is that normal for you?" Rick's voice sounded odd from behind the shower glass.

Rowan shrugged and ran her fingers lightly over the bandage. "I get the occasional phone call to deal with weird stuff, but nothing this weird. Ghosts, usually, never bullets or vampires. I am going to have to do some fast tap-dancing to keep my job."

"So, stay here, with me."

Rowan blinked. *I did not hear him say that.*

Rick stuck his head out of the shower. "You could, you know."

Rowan bit her lip. "Could what?"

"You could stay here, with me. I have the occasional weird thing to deal with too, you know."

Rowan sucked in a breath. *He did say it. Oh, my gods* She shook her head. "I can't. I have a life to go back to. I don't want to lose my apartment, my job or my cat."

"I thought your job didn't pay all that well."

Rowan rolled her eyes. "It doesn't, but it's better than flipping burgers."

His eyes locked on hers. "Bring your cat, and your books, I won't mind. I have plenty of room."

Rowan felt a roaring in her ears. He really meant it. "I don't know," she heard herself say.

"Good enough for me." He pulled his head back behind the shower door.

Rowan opened her mouth, and then closed it. She closed her eyes. *Do I really want to live with a vampire?*

* * * *

Rick worked his comb through the impressive length of Rowan's hair then divided it for braiding. The bedroom's light made the dark red color of her wet mane look like he was plaiting thick ropes of fresh blood.

Rick pulled on her hair and Rowan grimaced. "Now why are we braiding my hair?"

"To keep it from getting tangled when we fuck."

Rowan cringed. *Gods, he makes it sound so coarse.* She wiggled back from the edge of the bed and it shifted precariously.

Rick grabbed a fistful of Rowan's soaking wet and half-plaited hair, and gave it a tug. "Hold still, damn it." He let go only to pull the braid tighter. "Quit wiggling so I can finish this."

"I am holding still." Rowan set her jaw. "You're pulling my head all around!"

"I'm almost done."

Rowan let out an exasperated sigh. "Thank the gods..."

He tugged the braid taut, and then wrapped the hair-elastic around the end. "Now you can wiggle all you want." He leaned back over the bed to set the comb on the night table.

The only mirror was in the bathroom so she couldn't see what Rick had done. She put her hands up to feel the intricate weave of the French braid. Her right shoulder was stiff and ached. She fingered her hair and looked over at Rick's neat, four-strand braid. *If my hair looks anything like that, I'm impressed.*

"The braids ought to keep us from getting snarled up together." The tight braid emphasized the strong column of his throat and the broad musculature of his shoulders. He stood up and pulled the red towel from his loins to show an impressive erection. The dim light shadowed all the planes and hollows of his lean form.

Rowan's body gave her a sensual and vicious kick in the groin. *I keep forgetting how beautiful he is.* Her body coiled tight with hungry anticipation. She swallowed hard.

Rick raised a brow. "Like what you see?"

Rowan nodded, completely unable to speak.

"Good." He grinned shamelessly and walked toward the bed. "And give me that!"

The towel wrapped around her torso was abruptly snatched away and thrown across the room. Her mouth was too dry to protest. Suddenly he was kneeling at her knees. She could smell the clean scent of soap and aroused male. His eyes were beaten copper and flame. His mouth was pale but lush and his lips parted.

"Game's over, Kitten." He set his hands on her knees, parted them, spreading her. He moved between them. "Kiss me." His voice was the barest of whispers.

Rowan leaned forward, placed her hands on his shoulders, and touched her lips to his. His mouth opened and she felt his tongue reach in to stroke hers. His tongue was cool, as though he had been drinking something cold. She could taste his toothpaste.

He turned his head and deepened the kiss, sucking on her lips and tongue. Heat flared deep and low inside. She caught the scent of her arousal and felt moisture gathering. He groaned and she felt his hands slide up her bare thighs to her waist, then higher. He cupped the fullness of her breasts. Rowan felt his thumbs rub against her nipples and jolted with sensual shock.

His mouth left hers and she made a soft sound of disappointment. He stared at her with eyes darkened in passion and licked his lips. His head dipped and he took her nipple into his mouth. Bolts of pleasure raced straight down to her core. She clutched his shoulders and moaned. He wrapped his arm around her waist, pulling her closer to the bed's edge. She felt his hand on her thigh and then his fingers touching her intimate and slick flesh. He slid a finger within and she arched up with the delicious invasion, wrapping her arms around his neck. His thumb stroked her clit. Her flesh caught fire and quivered with delicious hunger around him. Her breath caught in her throat and she bucked against his hand. His mouth released her nipple with a wet pop.

"You're ready for me right now," he said in a hoarse voice.

Rowan was unable to answer him; she was too busy writhing against his fingers. He pulled his hand away from her body and she moaned at the loss.

Rick pulled back completely, sitting on his heels while he sucked her flavor from his fingers. He stared at her flushed face and reddened lips. His head tilted and his eyes narrowed with intent. He rose from his knees and stepped away from the bed. "We need to be careful of your right shoulder, so lie down on your side, facing the bathroom."

Rowan began to recline and had the hardest time looking away. He walked back around the bed and Rowan tilted back on her elbow to watch him.

He unfolded a large, wine-red bath towel from the foot of the bed. "What I need is a rubber sheet," he muttered. "This will have to do." He came back to the bed and laid the towel out across the bed behind her. "We don't want the cleaning staff thinking I've murdered someone."

That's right. Rowan blushed ferociously. *His cum is bloody and makes a mess.*

Rick climbed on and the bed dipped sharply on its old springs. "Stay on your side and lay down."

Rowan dropped her head on the pillow.

He stretched out behind her and slid up, coming up on his elbow. He dropped a quick kiss on her temple. "Good girl." He pulled her braid up and coiled it on the pillow, then tapped her upper leg. "Bend your knee up."

Rowan lifted her knee, pressing her heel into the mattress. He drew closer, easing his legs between hers. His lightly furred thighs were rough against her smooth skin. His arm captured her waist and pulled her back against him. She felt the head of his erection brush her damp flesh and her body jumped in acute awareness. He pressed against her for entry.

"Hold still," he said in her ear.

Rowan's breath hitched in her throat and her body tensed. She felt his fingers slide down from her waist and dip between her thighs. He touched moist, inflamed flesh. An erotic bolt of pleasure made her gasp. Her neck arched back onto his shoulder. His hand moved to her thigh and gripped it. He thrust, sliding into her body in one long stroke. She let out a gasping breath and sheathed him.

He groaned. "I love the feel of you wrapped around my dick." He dropped from his elbow to grip her around the waist with both arms, holding her tightly. "Now, hold still and let me do the work." He thrust again, harder and deeper. His strokes continued in long, slow measured thrusts.

Rowan struggled against his strength, wanting more.

"If you don't hold still, you'll hurt yourself."

She worked to move her hips and her head thrashed. "I don't care, I don't care!"

"Damn it, Rowan." He grabbed a pillow, shoved it in front of her hips, and then pushed her over onto her belly, trapping her legs between his. He caught her hands and forced them both above her head to keep her from using them for leverage. The pillow raised her hips just enough to give him clear access to her pouting and moist entrance.

Rowan bucked her hips under him. He was too solid and far too heavy to shift. She let out a soft whimper. "I can't move."

Rick bit back a laugh. "That's the whole idea."

She strained to pull her wrists from his hands. "That's not fair!"

"It's perfectly fair." He used his free hand to position the engorged head of his cock against her wet cunt. "Just hold still and let me do the fucking." He thrust into her wet sheath and gasped. With her legs held tight together, she was a very snug fit.

Rowan moaned and shuddered beneath him. "Damn it!"

He pulled back and thrust again, deeper, then again. His thrusts became faster and harder. The wet slap of flesh against flesh grew loud in the small room and the smell of raw sex scented the air.

Rowan gasped and moaned. With each hammering thrust he shoved her closer to the sharp edge of ecstasy. The need for release coiled tighter and tighter until her body vibrated at a fever pitch. She felt a scream building in her throat.

"Fuck!" Rick gasped in her ear. "I'm about to lose it." He slowed his thrusts.

"No, don't stop!" Rowan fought under him. "Don't stop now!"

Rick groaned out a laugh. "Are you sure?"

"Damn you, vampire..." Rowan turned her face in the pillow to look at him and bared her teeth. "Fuck me!"

Rick grinned. "That sounds pretty sure to me." He released her wrists and rose up on his knees. Rowan got her hands under her to rise. Rick shoved a hand between her shoulder blades and pressed her back down into the pillows. "Stay down." He shook back his long braid "One prime fucking, coming up," he said softly.

Rowan felt one of his hands take hold of her hip. He tilted her onto her side and she looked up into his eyes glowing gold with passion and blood lust. His mouth was open in a breathtakingly sensual smile and his long teeth were plainly evident.

He released one of her legs and lifted it over his shoulder. "Bend your lower leg around mine." She crooked it under her. He dropped to his hands over her, trapping her on her side with one leg around his knee and the other crooked over his shoulder, wide open.

Rowan stared up at his open mouth. He was only a kiss away. She shifted her hips and frowned. "Damn it, I still can't move!"

"I know." He licked his lips. "But I can."

He thrust into her and she gasped. He was incredibly deep, but the position made it unexpectedly comfortable, too.

He raised a brow. "Feel good?" He pulled back and thrust slowly while circling his hips.

Feral lust clawed her from within and Rowan closed her eyes and moaned with molten delight trying to arch her back under him.

"I'll take that as a yes," he whispered. He dropped over top of her. His lips brushed the pulse beating in her throat and his arms framed her head. Her arms slid around his waist and pulled him closer.

"Oh, yeah," he said softly and slammed in, hard.

Rowan cried out under him, her fingers digging into his skin. With strong, even strokes, he held her perfectly still and fucked her. She struggled to move in counterstroke but could only tremble in delight as he took her with his maddening thrusts. She was hammered gasping and crying, to the yawning precipice of explosive climax.

He stroked her throat with his tongue searching for the fast-beating pulse. He held her thrashing head still with his palms and positioned his mouth. "Now," he whispered below her ear.

Her body jerked rigid and trembled on the edge. His lips closed on her throat and she felt the points of his teeth.

"Cum now." He thrust.

Rowan's mouth opened and her breath left her. Violent pleasure scorched her and swallowed her whole. There was a single moment of clarity and she felt Rick's body shudder with climax and his cock flex within her. His teeth pierced her throat. Two bright points of pain blossomed and then she was locked in a second vortex of vicious ecstasy so strong she thought she was going to pass out. Her magic burst upwards and power exploded over them, overwhelming them both in a grasping fireball of ruthless red-violet rapture.

* * * *

Rick collapsed face down, at her side and gasped for breath. "Holy shit, I was not expecting that." His head was spinning from the power of the blood he'd just swallowed and the resultant explosion of magic that had hit him like a locomotive.

Rowan moaned. *Mmm, I feel good...* She rolled onto her side and stretched like a well-petted cat.

Rick watched her actions with amusement. "Enjoying yourself?"

"Hmm?" Abruptly she rolled the other way and up against him. *I feel so good...* She pressed a small kiss on his throat and ran her foot up against his leg. "You're warm."

Rick caught her face in his palms. Her eyes were dilated to pools of almost solid black shimmering with violet power. "Of course." He pressed a kiss to her lips. "I just drank your blood. All the potency in it makes me warm."

She squirmed out of his hands and snuggled up under his throat. *You smell good...* She smiled up at him. *I feel so good,* tumbled over and over in her mind.

"Are you okay?" Rick intercepted her thoughts and felt a smile creeping across his face. *I think she's drunk from the shared power rush...*

She licked his nipple and he jumped.

"Hey!" This close to orgasm, he was still very sensitive. She went for his other nipple. He chuckled and grabbed her hands, then sat up abruptly. The world spun. "Whoa..."

He shook his head to clear it and discovered Rowan trying to climb into his lap. A look into her thoughts revealed simple repetitions of how good she was feeling. He choked on a laugh. "If sex puts you in this good a mood, I need to fuck you more often."

"Mmm, fuck," she whispered and licked her lips.

"Hello," he whispered. "Anybody in there?"

Rowan shook her head and let out a soft giggle. "Not right now."

"Tell me something I don't know." He blinked, grinned and dropped a kiss on the top of her head. She pressed kisses over his heart and he shook his head. *I think I like her this affectionate. I'm just surprised she can move at all after that with a bullet wound.* He frowned thoughtfully. *And a fresh vampire bite...*

He carefully took her arms and pinned her to the mattress on her back. He turned her head to the side and she made soft sounds of protest. The two jagged marks on her throat had already closed. They were still red and angry, but there was hardly any bruising. It had taken her all night to recover from the last bite. Somehow she was healing faster than before.

"Well, damn, that's different." He looked at the bandage on her shoulder and his brows lowered. Curiously, he peeled back the bandage. The hole was completely closed, pink and shiny with a fresh scar. It was definitely healing faster, too. *Her wound should not look this healed for another day or so. Could it be the sex?* He released her and she yawned, curling up among the pillows.

He snorted. "Now, you're tired?" He got to his feet and his knees felt a little wobbly, but not too bad. He left her on the bed and went to get something to clean them both up with. When he returned with a damp cloth, she was curled up and sleeping.

* * * *

Rowan awoke to the rich scent of Columbian coffee. Her stomach rumbled in interest and her eyes snapped open. She sat up with barely a twinge in her shoulder. The lights were up just enough to see the velvet bathrobe tossed over the foot of the bed. She looked up. Somewhere over her head, Rowan felt Rick's reassuring presence. He was doing something that had his complete attention.

His march of thoughts came to an abrupt halt. *Are you up, finally?*

Rowan grinned. "Is that coffee I smell?" she asked the ceiling and grabbed for the robe.

Yes, come on up and get some. It's two in the afternoon on a bright sunny Saturday, not that I can go out in it, but you can if you like. Rick was certainly pleased about something. *Oh, and we have some details to hammer out, but I think I have all your affairs in order.*

"Huh?" Rowan frowned. "All what affairs?"

So you can move in with me. Smug satisfaction shimmered through their link. *I have a mover ready to get your stuff on Monday, and I even located a possible job at the State Library by the University. They'd love to have you.*

Rowan tied the velvet belt around her waist and headed for the stairs. "Hey, wait a friggin' minute, Mr. High and Mighty Vampire! You got movers lined up and me a job? Those are my decisions to make!"

A flare of annoyance came from Rick. *You already agreed to move in, don't back out on me now.*

Rowan stopped halfway up the stairs. "I did? I don't remember "

Yes. You did. There was a bolt of possessiveness riding the shimmer of real anger coming from him.

Rowan grabbed the banister and climbed. "Of all the insufferable, high-handed, dirty tricks!" She reached the landing to find Rick leaning against the door.

"You are moving in with me, so I can keep an eye on you." He raised an annoyed brow. "Just give it up, will you?"

Rowan speared him with a look. "You had no right…"

He straightened and took a menacing step toward her. "I have every right."

Rowan took an alarmed step back and her heel thunked against the wall. She stopped and glared. "This is my life you're taking over!"

Rick nodded and closed the distance between them. "Yes, I am." He set his hands on the wall to either side of her shoulders, trapping her. He brought his face within inches of hers. His eyes were copper bright with heat. "And you know why?"

Rowan held her ground, such as it was, with her back to the wall. She was determined to be angry but it was difficult to be angry with someone who just saved her from a psychopathic sorcerer and a bullet. She took a steadying breath. "No. Why?"

A cool smile curled his lips. "Because you love me, stupid."

Rowan blinked. "I do?"

His eyes focused on her mouth. "Of course. I can tell." His lips captured hers in a searing kiss, devouring her, pressing her back against the wall.

Rowan moaned under his possessive kiss.

He broke the kiss to stare at her. "God, I almost lost you. You were bleeding all over the place, and there was nothing I could do to stop it. I could feel you fading right in my arms." He closed his eyes and pressed her against his heart. "I couldn't take it if something happened to you. Damn it, Rowan, you have to stay, so I can keep an eye on you. I don't think..." He took a harsh breath. "I don't think I can live without you."

She could feel fear and concern for her pulsing through their link threaded with determination. Her heart ached in her chest, echoing his feelings back with fear for him, concern for him She blinked in shock. She did love him. Rowan felt a hot tear slide down her cheek. She gave him a tight smile. "I guess you're right. I do love you."

"God..." He crushed her in his arms. "And I love you."

Rowan wrapped her arms around his neck. "Well, if it'll make you feel better, I'll try not to catch any more bullets."

Rick choked out a laugh. "Yes, that will make me feel lots better." He released her, and cupped her face in his palms. "I've been alive for over seventy years, and you are the very first woman I have been able to be completely honest with. You are the only person in my life who knows me as both a man and a vampire. Do you have any idea what it's like to have someone accept all of you?"

Rowan bit her lip. "I have some idea. Every man I know runs as soon as they figure out what my magic does to them. You're the only one who hasn't."

Rick grinned. "See? We were meant for each other."

Rowan smiled back. "I guess you're right."

"I'm right twice in a row?" Rick rolled his eyes. "I bet that sets some kind of record."

Rowan snorted. "Don't let it get to you're already swollen ego. I doubt it'll happen again."

"We'll see..." His expression became serious. "You're staying, right? With me?"

Rowan sucked on her bottom lip, then smiled. "I guess I'll have to, if I ever want to get any coffee."

Rick gave her a heart-stopping smile, and a swift kiss on the lips. "I knew if I held out on the coffee you'd give in."

Rowan arched her brow. "Oh, is that what you were doing? Blackmail?"

"Absolutely." He nodded and grinned. "Come on, let's get you some coffee."

Eighteen

Trapped

R owan was just finishing her second helping of eggs and her third cup of coffee when Rick's cell phone went off. He pulled the phone from his pant's pocket and waved for Rowan to finish.

"It's the office."

Rowan frowned. "Isn't it Saturday?"

Rick nodded and covered the phone. "An architect's job does not end on Fridays." He walked off to his study just opposite the living room, talking about permits and licenses.

Rowan shook her head and munched on a slice of toast. *Rick, the executive vampire...*

I heard that, Rick radiated from the study. Then a stream of utterly linear geometric thoughts laced with calm satisfaction followed.

Rowan grinned and chewed. *I guess he loves his work,* she thought as softly as she could.

A gentle shimmer of disquiet touched her power.

Huh? Rowan stopped chewing and listened inward. Her power was nestled deep within her, a purring and sleepy ball of warmth, with one ear twitching. Something had touched it, but not enough to alarm it. For some few minutes, she paid very close attention, but her power slumbered on without disturbance. The one twitching ear relaxed.

Unnerved. Rowan rose and set her dishes in the sink. *Draugar is still out there,* she thought very softly. She didn't want to disturb Rick, who seemed to be concentrating heavily on something complicated. *I better see about getting the stuff together to get the house barrier back up.*

Tying the velvet belt more securely around the overlong robe, she padded back down the hall headed for the vault stairs to find her red velvet shoulder bag. *While I'm at it, I'll pull out my tarot cards and see if there's anything else I need to know about, preferably before it happens.*

She walked through the door under the stairs and down the narrow steps to the vault. *Or are my cards still in the pouch on my belt?* She stepped through the vault door and into the dimly lit bedroom. *Okay, where did he put my bag? Come to think of it, where did he put my belt, and the clothes I was wearing last?*

Rick's orderly hum of thought came to an abrupt and startled halt.

Rowan looked up at the ceiling. "Rick?" She reached out for him...

Danger! screamed across Rowan's senses. Her magic abruptly came to hissing, spitting and enraged life. Her defensive light blazed up from under her skin and loose strands of her hair lifted in a wind of power and light. "Oh, my gods, Klaus must be back!" Rowan dashed for the stairs, her bag forgotten. "Rick!"

She had taken three steps when something monstrously powerful grabbed her blazing magic by the scruff of its furious neck, and immobilized it. Between one breath and the next, her light simply quenched. She gasped in shock, nearly tripping as gravity came crashing down on her. Her power was still there, she could feel its boiling fury, but she couldn't touch it. Something was blocking it.

Rowan? Rick suddenly projected in a cool controlled line. There was the tiniest shimmer of anger threading the thought flavored with an underlay of fear.

Rowan's head jerked up to look at the ceiling. "Rick? What's happening?"

Can you come into the study, please? An alarmed burst of fear followed, and he was gone.

Rowan grabbed the banister. "Rick?" She summoned every ounce of panic she had, and shouted in her thoughts. *RICK!*

A tiny shimmer of alarm replied, but nothing else.

Rowan stared up the stairs. Something was very, very wrong. And she was helpless; she couldn't touch her power. "Damn it! Whatever this is, I need help," she said without thought, and stopped. She took a breath in surprised revelation, and then another in silent wonder and hope.

"I need," were key words to a divine invocation, a request to the Powers that Be. Even the magically powerless could call on the Powers and be heard. Her inner power was not all she had. She was a witch, a high priestess to the Goddess. She had used common ordinary witchcraft for years before her magic had bloomed on the crest of her first boyfriend's orgasm.

Rowan looked back into the bedroom. She may have been cut off from her core magic, but she was far from helpless. Help was only an invocation away. Determination and a trace of uncertainty breathed through her. She pressed both hands over her heart and closed her eyes. "Blessed Mother of Magic, show me what I need," she said firmly, and desperately hoped. She opened her eyes and saw her red velvet bag, crammed full of her magical supplies, hanging on the newel post at the foot of the bed. She trembled in astonished relief, then grimly strode for the bag. "Sometimes, I just love being a witch."

Rowan shoved her hand in the shoulder bag and rummaged. "Blessed Lady," she said with far more confidence. "Give me what I need to deal with this problem," she said softly. She pulled out a tiny velvet bag, and of all things, her cigarettes with the lighter tucked into the box. She frowned at the bag and the cigarettes. She never kept her cigarettes in her velvet bag, but here they were, in her hand. Something in her soul told her that both the contents of the tiny bag and her cigarettes were exactly what she needed.

A grim smile tugged her lips. "Thank you, blessed Lady," she whispered. "I will not forget that I am a witch first, then a person of power."

Rowan felt a pull in her power. She looked back at the stairs. She was being called. She ignored the tug and opened the tiny bag. She found one silvered horseshoe nail and a piece of black yarn. Her brows shot up. "What is this?"

The pull on her power jerked her hard, and she gasped. She turned and headed for the stairs at a fast walk before she knew she was going to take a step. It felt as though her body was on remote control. Hastily, she closed the tiny velvet bag and tucked it into the robe's wide velvet belt at her waist. She trotted up the stairs so fast she tripped and barked her shin on a step. "Alright! I'm coming," she shouted in annoyance. "Ease off, will you? You're making me fall!"

The pull relaxed, but remained insistent.

"Pushy bastard." Rowan set her jaw, and moved up the stairs at a more human pace. She didn't know how she'd use the string, the nail and her cigarettes, but the Powers had provided, and they had never failed her. "And now you've pissed off the witch."

* * * *

Rowan stepped out of the door under the steps and immediately felt a hum of raw earth energy vibrating almost like a sound in her bones. *What the hell is that?* She turned left past the stairs, and stepped onto the cool marble floor of the study.

Rick was sitting at his desk, and his expression was coldly furious. She frowned. His eyes glanced to her right.

Rowan turned. Directly to her right in the corner and just out of casual sight, Draugar lounged comfortably, one knee folded over the other, in one of Rick's more modernistic chairs.

"There you are." He smiled.

Rowan's started then fear and anger blazed hot. "What the hell are you doing here?"

Draugar's brows shot up. "Collecting my property."

Rowan's brow wrinkled. "We don't have anything of yours..."

A growl came from Rick. "He means you, Rowan."

Rowan stepped back and looked over at Rick. "What?"

Draugar lifted his chin. "Actually, I'm here to collect both of you." He stood and lifted a hand toward Rowan. "Come."

Rick's eyes widened. "What?"

Rowan jolted forward. Her wrist was in Draugar's cool grasp before she knew she had moved that close to him. "Hey!"

"Be still."

Rowan abruptly stilled. In fact she was frozen in place unable to move a finger. Her heart thudded in her chest. *What the hell is going on here?*

Draugar pulled the collar of her robe down to expose the soft pink scar from the bullet hole. "You are recovering nicely. I'm quite pleased my bullet did not kill you. You may relax."

Rowan's breath exploded from her chest. She jerked her robe back onto her shoulder and shot him a glare. "Klaus told Rick how to remove your bullet."

Draugar nodded. "I figured he might. He's dealt with these before."

Rowan blinked in shock. *He knew Klaus would help?*

Draugar's eyes abruptly changed to solid silver coins. "Rebuild your original house shield."

"What?" Rowan's mouth fell open. "Mine?"

"Yes. Mine is very distinctive. Yours will be a far better disguise, should Klaus come by..." He smiled thinly at Rickart. "For a visit."

Rowan winced. *He meant: should Klaus come by for a snack. He must have known Klaus was feeding off of Rick.* She took a breath. "Okay, one house barrier coming up." She turned to face the center of the house.

Draugar released her wrist, and she felt his hand settle on her shoulder. "My barrier will lay under yours, to ensure that Klaus cannot enter, invited or not."

"Fine, whatever," Rowan muttered then closed her eyes and looked within. She felt her magic respond to her touch, like a welcoming cat rising under her hand. Focusing, she replayed the memory of her original ritual for the barrier spell: herb, feather, book and firelight. She silently replayed the mental twists and correlations in her inner psyche and loosed a rippling wave of magic that exploded out of her in a blazing ring of virulent green fire, invisible to the magically blind. The outward tide of magic gathered up the traces of her fallen spell repaired, sealed and rose in a protective dome of power. A bell rang, deep and true. The sound faded and crows called overhead

Rowan opened her eyes. "It is done."

Draugar chuckled softly. "That was certainly dramatic. From the feel of your spell, I'd say you've had in increase of power since your last visit with me."

Rowan bit her lip and looked over at Rick. When Draugar had first ensorcelled her, she had fed on Rick's power—before Klaus had forced Rick to drink his blood. Apparently the power in Klaus's ancient blood had boosted her abilities.

Draugar raised a brow. "You didn't use a formal ritual to raise this barrier."

Rowan shrugged. "I did the full ritual the first time. Once I do a spell the long way, I can run the whole spell in my imagination and get the same results."

Draugar stared in disbelief. "You are imagining the entire ritual?"

"It's called visualization, and I don't need to do the whole spell in my head. Once I do the whole ritual, I know all the short-cuts."

He frowned. "Short cuts?"

Rowan nodded and shrugged. "Well, yeah. I know what the spell feels like in my head, so I simply reproduce all those feeling and the spell happens."

Draugar shook his head. "We will discuss this at length, you and I, at a later time. Right now, I have more urgent matters to attend to."

He made an elegant gesture with his hand. "Cast."

Rowan gasped and her back arched. Magic blazed and loosed a second wave of vibrant power. The second spell slid under her original spell creating a gleaming net of shimmering perception. Every corner, turn, staircase and closet slid into awareness until she had a complete map of Rick's house and the property surrounding it lodged in her mind. Along with every bird and animal that moved on it.

Her body abruptly relaxed and she staggered a step. "Goddess..."

Draugar's hand on her shoulder steadied her. "Rowan, face me." His voice was calm.

Rowan turned to face him. *Now what?*

His flat silver eyes brightened. "Kneel and give me your hands."

Piss, he's raising power... She went down on her knees and lifted her hands. "You're going to put the bracelets back on."

Draugar took her wrists. "I don't want to waste your power on commands when there are more efficient ways to induce obedience." He tilted his head at Rick. "Rickart already wears them."

Rowan glanced over at Rick.

Rick's jaw clenched and a shimmer of worry transferred across their link.

"This will not be pleasant," Draugar said softly.

Rowan winced. *Great. So what else is new?* Earth power roared into her body and coalesced in a burning ring around her wrists. Her breath locked in her throat before she could scream. Lightning stabbed the back of her skull...

* * * *

Rowan awoke sprawled across Rick's lap with her head pounding viciously. "Gods, my head feels like someone drove a spike through it." She glanced around and winced. They were on the couch all the way upstairs in the TV room. The enormous TV was set to the news channel. The program was barely audible. "Great Mother, what did he hit me with? A baseball bat?"

Rick helped her sit upright. "The way you went down, I thought he had. You've been out for a couple of hours. Here." He put two white tablets in her hand, then reached over to collect a glass of water. "If I hadn't been wearing his damned bracelets." His voice deepened to a deep rumbling growl that she could feel, vibrating in his chest. "I would have ripped him apart right there." He set the glass of water in her hand.

Rowan's eyes were drawn to the thumb-thick bangle of dark crimson around his wrist. The bangles around her wrists were a deep blood-tinted purple. She frowned. *That's not the right color There's too much red.* She flinched away from the sight of their enslavement and squinted at the white tablets. "What's this?"

"Ordinary aspirin. I could feel your headache an hour before you woke."

Rowan popped the tablets in her mouth and gulped water. "Thank you." She gave him a pained smile. "You are the only man I know that thinks ahead of time."

He raised a brow, and his lips curved up on one side. "Was that a compliment?"

"Yeah." She returned his sarcastic smile. "Don't let it get to your head." She looked around sharply, then winced. *That was not a smart thing to do with a headache.* "So, what is Señor Psychopath up to now?"

Rick snorted, then glowered at the TV. "He's on my computer in the study. Hell only knows what he's doing. I brought you up here so I didn't have to look at him."

Rowan's fingers tightened on the half-empty glass. "Rick, one second I could hear you just fine, and the next everything just stopped. What happened?"

Rick swiped his hand across his chin. "He came up through the damned floor." He sighed and closed his eyes.

"Through the floor?" Rowan frowned. "Wait, didn't he sink into the floor of the other house when Klaus showed up."

"Yep." He pressed his fingers into his temples. "I think I remember Klaus telling us he could move through the earth." Anger laced with humiliation came through their link. "He came up through the floor like it was water, and then hit me with something, Hell only knows what, before I could get out of the damned chair." He turned his wrist over and the bangle shifted on his arm. "I woke up on the floor with this cool new jewelry."

"Can't you just break it? You broke mine before."

Rick gave her a sour smile. "Oh, I'm strong enough to, but he made sure to order me not to. Or break yours either." He snorted. "I tried anyway. Knocked me out cold for about a minute."

Rowan scowled. "Piss and firewater, there goes that plan…" Her eyes narrowed. "Through the earth…" She closed her eyes and reached out to feel the magical barrier she was maintaining. She could feel the study, and the glowing essence of Draugar stationed almost at its center—and the ground under the marble floor of the study. "The floor under the study is marble slab over earth. The Vault goes the other way, under the house."

"Yeah, so?" There was a trill from his pocket. Rick reached in and dug out his cell phone. He scowled at the crystal window. "Hold that thought." He opened the phone and jammed it to his ear. "Holt here."

Rowan slid off his lap so he could talk, then frowned at the cell phone. *Draugar lets him talk on the phone?* She rolled her eyes. *Oh, well it's not as if he can call the cops.* Rick was a vampire, with greater speed and strength than any human, cop or otherwise, and he was not fast enough or strong enough to deal with Draugar. The cops would be helpless. *We need something stronger than Draugar.*

She scowled. She didn't know of anything stronger than Draugar except *Klaus didn't seem to have a problem tackling him until he dove into the floor.*

She took a sudden breath, then dug for the tiny pouch she had collected earlier. Luckily, it was still tucked into the sash of her robe. She dug her fingers into the pouch and pulled out the piece of yarn.

Otherworldly chill vibrated through her fingers, Klaus's eldritch essence. Rowan blinked. *Mother of Mercy...* She could call Klaus, and he could remove their unwanted guest—if Draugar didn't sink through the floor, like last time.

The floor... She frowned and focused on the earth floor under the study. She propped her chin on her hand, thinking about the house she'd been taken to. The floor had been marble in there, too. If she remembered correctly, that floor had been set directly on earth just like the marble floor in the study here. Her brow furrowed. *But he walked through the door and took the stairs when he went after the zombies in the house...*

Maybe he couldn't go through wood, or... She frowned. Maybe he didn't like moving through floors that had an open void, such as a room, under him, like ice over a lake. But Draugar was over an earth floor in the study right now. Even if she called Klaus, as long as Draugar remained in the study, he could sink directly into the ground, and escape again.

They had to get Draugar out of the study, and keep him out.

Rowan dumped the single silver-dipped horseshoe nail out on her palm. *So, what am I supposed to do with this? This is about as good against Draugar as a common straight pin... Pinned... A ghost trap!*

Rowan bit her lip. Was it possible to pin Draugar in a simple ghost trap with her basic witchcraft? It would mean trapping and holding him somewhere other than the study long enough for Klaus to take him out. Could she even trap something as powerful as Draugar? If he broke out before Klaus got there, she'd be in real trouble. She closed her fist around the tiny nail. There was only one way to find out.

Rick abruptly ended his call and snapped the phone closed. He turned to Rowan. "You were saying?"

Rowan smiled grimly. "I think I have a plan to remove our problem. Ever heard of a ghost trap?"

* * * *

Rick listened, then stared at the thread from Klaus's robe in Rowan's palm. "No." He looked sharply away and crossed his arms over his chest.

"No?" Rowan frowned. "Why not? I'm pretty sure I can catch him. It's what I did with the sorcerer in the bar; I ghost-trapped him. Witchcraft is deific; it calls on the god-powers not my inner magic. I only need to hold Draugar long enough for Klaus "

Rick shook his head sharply. "No, no, absolutely no Klaus."

"No Klaus? Are you kidding?" Rowan set her jaw. "He's faster than you, and I'm just human. We don't stand a chance! Do you know someone else that can get this guy?"

Rick leapt off the couch. "You want to pit Klaus, against this guy in my house? Are you out of your mind? They'll destroy it!"

Rowan gaped. "We don't know what the hell he even wants from us, and you're worried about your damned house?"

Rick paced the floor. "I built this damned house stick by stick." He turned and pointed at the wall. "I even did the damned wiring and plumbing myself!"

"I swear I'll help repair the damage," Rowan said from gritted teeth.

"No." Rick shook his head. "There has to be another way. That, or we find a way to get him out of my house first."

"If we try this outside, he'll just sink into the ground."

Rick shook his head. "Not in my house." He jabbed a finger at Rowan. "I mean it."

Rowan set her jaw stubbornly. *Of all the stubborn, thick-headed, 'this is my house' vampire bullshit!*

Rick moved in a blur of speed. Suddenly he was leaning over her as she sat on the couch. "Promise me right now, that you won't call Klaus until I tell you."

Rowan crossed her own arms and glared. "Fine! I won't call Klaus. You can think of something, and we'll do that. But when you run out of ideas, let me know and we'll resort to plan 'K'."

Rick snorted. "Plan 'K'? That's original."

Rowan curled her lip. "You're making the rules, Fang Boy." She pushed him back and got off the couch, headed for the door.

"Where are you going?"

Rowan stopped in the doorway. "To get dressed." She turned and leveled a glare at him. "Is that okay with you?"

Rick glared right back. "Look, I just…" He stopped, dropping his head with a sigh. "Tell you what, I can have something on for dinner when you get back upstairs. Okay?"

Rowan felt her anger drain away. He was worried; she could feel the tension humming through their link. This was the second time someone had invaded his territory. *That has to be some kinda kick to the ego. I don't need to be on his case too.* She dropped her own head, then gave him a tremulous smile. "I'm sure what ever you make will be great. I like your cooking."

Rick nodded. "Right… Okay." He grinned suddenly. "Need any help getting dressed?"

Rowan rolled her eyes. "I'm sure I'll manage somehow."

His smile drained away. "Don't take too long."

Rowan tilted her head toward the door. "Trust me, I have no interest in jumping to that one's call in my underwear." She jabbed a thumb over her shoulder, indicating their unwanted guest downstairs.

Rick shoved his hands in his jeans pockets and looked down at his bare feet. "Want me to walk you down?"

Rowan took in his slumped shoulders and defeated stance. First Klaus, then her bullet, then Draugar… He'd had a hell of an awful week. *And now we're fighting.* Her heart thumped, aching for him. "Sure. I could use the company."

His head lifted.

She gave him a worn smile.

He walked over to her. "We'll get through this, somehow."

She wrapped her arm around his waist. "I know," she whispered back. "We always think of something." She felt his arms come around her and she pressed her cheek into his shirt to listen to his heartbeat.

They walked down the stairs side by side.

❧ Nineteen ❧

Plague

The kitchen was quiet but for the sound of scraping forks. "So, how's the pasta?" Rick asked softly from across the kitchen table.

Rowan swallowed the forkful in her mouth and swiped a napkin over her lips. "I think I can truthfully say, that this is the best pasta and mushrooms I have ever eaten."

"Really?" Rick grinned.

Rowan nodded and took a sip of the ginger ale by her plate. "Absolutely. And the garlic bread isn't bad, either."

He snorted. "Your T-shirt had me worried."

"Oh, this?" She leaned back in her chair displaying yet another black T-shirt blazoned with the phrase: 'The Fastest Way to a Man's Heart: Six Inches of Cold Hard Steel' in harsh silver letters. She grinned. "You can relax. Dinner definitely made a favorable impression on my temperament."

"Are all your T-shirts that violent?"

Rowan nodded. "All my favorites are." She dug her fork into her pasta.

Rick shook his head and lifted his glass. "What am I going to do with you?"

Rowan grinned broadly. "Oh, I'm sure you'll think of something."

Somewhere outside a crow was calling. The crow's harsh voice was joined by another, and then another.

Rowan turned to look at the hallway leading to the front of the house. "Do you hear that?"

"Hear what?" Rick set his glass down and frowned.

"Crows..." She listened intently. She could clearly hear a small flock of crows calling from somewhere near the front of the house. "A bunch of them..."

"No, I don't hear a thing." Rick looked toward the back door. "We're half an hour past dark, birds shouldn't be awake."

"If you can't hear them, then..." Rowan's memory provided a stark reminder of the last time she had heard crows calling at night. A sky full of crows had called right before the house barrier had fallen to Draugar's sorcerer. She was receiving a warning. "Shit." She set her fork by her plate of pasta, stood up and looked toward the front of the house.

"Rowan, what's going on?"

"We're about to have company." Rowan felt the awareness of the house barrier shiver. Points of movement pressed against the farthest reaches of the barrier. "We're about to have lots of company."

Rick rose out of his chair. "People, as in: humans?"

"I'm not sure." She focused her awareness on the barrier. The movement coalesced into six bodies stopped at the front gate. She frowned in concentration. "It feels like people... Yes, humans. I think..."

"You think they're human? You're not sure?"

"They're definitely people, but I'm not sure they're human. They don't feel quite right." She frowned. They felt vaguely familiar. Not familiar as in: she knew them, but familiar as in: she'd felt this type of being before. She had the distinct impression that they were basically human, but there was something wrong with them. They felt rotted.

Rowan's heart slammed in her chest. "Rick?"

Rick came around to her side of the table. "Rowan, what is it?

What's wrong?" His hand closed on her arm. "Rowan, your skin is ice cold."

She stared at him in shock and fought to get in a breath. The hair was lifting fast on her entire body. "They're human, or they were. They're dead," she said in a voice she could barely get out of her throat. She began to shiver. "All of them. There are six dead people moving at the front gate."

Rick's mouth fell open. "What?" His voice was barely a whisper.

"Both of you, get in here now!" Draugar called from the study.

Rowan gasped at the strength of the pull. She nearly knocked her chair over in her haste to obey the command. It took everything in her not to break into a run.

* * * *

Draugar stood by the desk in the center of the study, shrugging into his long coat.

Rowan bit her lip. "We've got company."

Draugar nodded curtly. "Yes, I know. I'm tied to the barrier as well." He turned to look at Rick. "Time to earn your keep, vampire. We have some minor eradications to accomplish." He fastened his belt.

Rick set his hand on Rowan's shoulder. "What about Rowan?"

Draugar shot Rowan a stern look. "You are forbidden to set foot outside the door."

Rowan scowled "Hey!"

Draugar shook his head. "This is work for those of us who know how to kill."

Rowan sucked in a breath. "They're already dead."

"Yes, unfortunately. I only hope they have not had time to make more."

"More?" Rick face paled. "What do you mean: more?"

"Then these are zombie things?" Rowan could barely breathe past the lump in her throat. "Like the ones in your house?"

Draugar nodded. "Oh, yes. However, these are dead. Once they are in this condition, they become highly contagious. If we're lucky, they came here first."

Rick scowled. "These things are yours?"

"Not quite. I must have missed one of Rudolf's victims."

Rowan's mouth fell open. "They're Rudolf's? But he was toasted by you, two days ago."

Draugar shrugged. "He must have wounded someone on his last hunt, someone who finally died. I'll know as soon as I see them." Draugar strode from the study and headed for the front door.

"Wait who's Rudolf?" Rick followed Draugar into the hall.

Rowan followed at Rick's heels. "The little orange sorcerer guy."

"Oh..." He frowned at Draugar. "So, why would they come here?"

Draugar turned around to face them. "Because creatures of sorcery are always drawn to power." He looked at both Rowan and Rick. "The two of you are irresistible lures to such as they, especially you, vampire."

"Me?"

Draugar nodded. "These creatures in particular are drawn to the corrupt. They feed on it, as well as on living flesh."

Rowan raised her brow at Rick. "Told you... you were drawing the weird shit."

Draugar snorted. "Do not underestimate your own lure, witch. The bracelets show that your power is being stained by the vampire."

Rowan swallowed hard. *Stained? As in corrupted?*

Rick gave Rowan's shoulder a gentle squeeze. "What do you want me to do?"

Draugar smiled. "I'm going to teach you to use your latent power to cast fire."

"Thanks, but no thanks." Rick smiled grimly, then crossed his arms over his chest and extended his fingers. Armored plates formed in a blur of motion over his skin, spreading to cover his hands, and extending his fingers into long curved blades. The armor plating rapidly formed up his forearms. He flexed his bladed fingers. The plates made a soft metal snicking sound as they shifted on his hand.

"I'll do just fine without your sorceries."

Draugar raised a brow. "Impressive, and very useful I'm sure, against ordinary humans. However, fire is the only way to destroy these. If you hack them apart, the pieces have a way of grafting themselves back onto their bodies. Of course it's never quite right, but that does not seem to bother them much." He smiled thinly. "Calling a fire hot enough to turn them to ash is our only option to keep the damage they can cause to a minimum."

Rowan shook her head. "Wait, you took out all the ones in the house by yourself..."

"Yes, but I destroyed them one at a time; they were not attacking en masse." He opened the front door. "It's you and the vampire they want, I have nothing they can use."

Rick scowled. "Aren't you worried that I'll use the sorcery you teach me on you?"

"You can try if you like." Draugar raised a silver brow and gave him a cool smile. "However, fire will not harm me." He held the door open, then looked back at Rick. "Do you have a gun?"

"Yes."

"Get it."

Rick turned away then turned back. "I thought you said fire was the only way to destroy them?"

"It is. But a gun is useful for disabling their ability to attack, long enough for you to set them on fire." Draugar lifted his chin. "Fetch your gun."

Rick turned on his heel in a very military about-face, then sprinted for the vault.

"As for you..."

Rowan turned to face Draugar. "What?"

Draugar frowned thoughtfully. "I want you in the securest room in this house."

"The vault." Rowan flinched. She hadn't meant to say it out loud.

Draugar nodded. "That will do. I'll have Rick lock you in."

Rowan gasped and took a step back. "I don't need to be locked in the vault!"

"As long as you continue to maintain the barrier, they will remain outside the house, however…" Draugar took a step closer, "…you are too valuable to leave to chance."

"But the vault?" Rowan "Are you out of your mind? I don't know how to open it!"

"I can retrieve you through the earth, should something should untoward happen to the vampire."

Rowan's hands fisted at her sides. "What do you mean 'untoward'?"

Draugar sighed. "Calm yourself. I have no intention of seeing Rickart harmed." He pulled a large semi-automatic pistol from his pocket. A pistol that looked hauntingly familiar. "I will have Rickart maintain telepathic communication with you. This way, you can keep a watchful eye on your lover from within, and he can let you know when to move the barrier within the property line." He jerked the sliding barrel open with an ominous and loud ratchet, and looked down into it.

Rowan shook her head. "You want me to move the barrier in?"

Draugar nodded. "I do not want to light our bonfire in the street." He snapped the gun closed with a heavy click, then popped out the bullet case, and checked his count. He slammed the case back in the gun's handle then smiled. "This eradication will not take long. When we are done, we will all sit down and discuss travel arrangements."

Rowan swallowed. "Greece?"

Draugar shook his head. "I'm afraid I have a pressing appointment in California."

Rick was suddenly at Rowan's side. "What's in California?"

She jumped. "Gods, you scared me." Then she saw what was in his hand and scooted a step away. It was a large, black high-tech pistol.

"Automatic?" Draugar asked politely, ignoring his question.

Rick gave him a half grin. "If it needs to be. I have a pair of spare clips for it, but if I use it on automatic, they empty in three seconds."

"Good. I want you to lock Rowan in the vault." He smiled. "For safe-keeping."

Rick nodded. "Good idea." He took Rowan's elbow.

Rowan's mouth fell open. "Hey! Not you, too?"

Rick rolled his eyes. "It's the safest place for you." He tugged her elbow. "Come on."

Rowan dug in her heels. "But, the vault? Isn't that a little over-kill?"

Draugar frowned. "No arguments, we do not have time for them. Go."

Rowan went.

* * * *

Rowan stared at Rick from the other side of the vault door. "Rick, I can't get out of here if something happens to you. I don't know how to open the door."

Rick drew the door closed until she could barely see his face. He sighed. "The door is on a time release. Once engaged, if I don't open it, it unlocks at exactly seven PM."

Rowan let out a breath. "Oh, okay."

Rick's head came up and his eyes were coins of molten gold. "But if something does happen, call Klaus immediately."

"But?"

"Immediately." He closed the door and the lock engaged with an echoing clank.

Rowan stared at the closed door, and shivered.

* * * *

Rick lunged back up the vault stairs in a blur of unnatural speed. The front door was open and Draugar was standing out on the night-darkened lawn. He turned to look at Rick with burning silver eyes. "Rowan?"

"She's locked in."

Draugar nodded. "Good." He turned to survey the long lawn.

The breeze shifted and Rick gagged. "God, they're dead all right, I can smell them rotting. What in Hell's name, are they? They can't be natural."

"They're not. They are called *strigoi*, after the Rumanian walking dead. They are a plague of death alchemically engineered by the monster I am trying to escape from."

"Klaus?"

"No, Klaus's master." Draugar turned to regard Rick with a calculating gaze. "You should be quite familiar with them."

"Me?"

Draugar nodded. "Remember the feast you attended?"

"Feast?" Rick swallowed hard. "The Nazi officers... They were these *strigoi*?"

Draugar nodded. "Living *strigoi*. These are dead. Back in the war, Kaminski's entire Russian brigade and Dirlewanger's penal battalion were also these creatures. One bite and a living human becomes part of the collective mind of the herd. Once that human dies, it rises and becomes this. Now you know why I had the flame-thrower troops follow them on the battlefield. I didn't want the dead rising. They would have infected and eradicated all of Russia and Europe in less than a year."

Rick stared in horror. "And still you unleashed these things on towns and villages."

Draugar shot him a cold stare. "And then burned those same villages to the ground to keep the rest of the outlying villages and towns safe. Do not mistake me; I abhor them, and their creator. They are a death-plague, an abomination against life itself. I destroyed them whenever I found them."

Rick shook his head. "Then what the hell were you doing with them?"

"Following orders." Draugar sighed. "My function was herd-master. I controlled the dominant minds of the herds, the Nazi officers, Kaminski and Dirlewanger. By controlling them, I controlled their individual herds." He looked toward the distant trees. "Fully half your troop was already infected when I had you transferred to my camp." He raised a brow at Rick. "You may not believe this, but I was trying to keep you from being bitten by your fellow officers."

Rick scowled. "You're right, I don't believe it. Especially since you put a bullet in me."

Draugar shook his head. "At the time, it was unavoidable." A blaze of white fire formed in his outstretched hand. The white fire elongated then coalesced into a metal rod as thick as his thumb and about same length as his forearm. "Take this."

Rick took the rod. "What is it?"

"A silver rod. Gold is the easiest medium to focus and direct power through, but silver is more resistant should someone else try to redirect your charge. I need you to maintain the blaze once its started. If we are lucky, they will run straight for it, missing us entirely."

"Shit, you're going to scorch my lawn!"

Draugar gave him an amused smile. "Would you rather they got into the house?"

"Fuck, no!"

"I thought not." Draugar pointed at the rod in Rick's hand. "I will draw the magic from you to cast fire, but you have to grasp it and maintain the blaze by keeping the power steady. More specifically, do not point the rod anywhere but at the fire you start. Understood?"

"Yeah, sure, whatever..." Rick turned a sharp look at Draugar. "Wait a minute, are you telling me that they run *to* fire? Not away from it?"

"Yes, rather like moths." Draugar said dryly then pointed with a long finger over toward the trees. "Point the rod at the crest of the hill and keep it pointed there. Do not waver or you will set fire to your entire lawn and possibly the house."

Rick nodded and pointed the rod. "Right, okay."

"Prepare yourself." Draugar spat out a phrase.

Rick stiffened and fire blazed on the grass where the rod was pointing. "Shit!" He kept the rod pointed at the one spot.

"Do you have it? Can you feel your power in your mind?"

Rick frowned. "I think so. Yes."

"Good. I am releasing control to you."

Rick gasped and the blaze leaped up as tall as the house. He frowned and the blaze moderated to a small bonfire.

Draugar chuckled. "Good. Contact Rowan and have her bring the barrier in to there." He lifted a long finger and pointed at the crest of the slope below the house.

Rick opened his mind. *Rowan?*

*   *   *   *

Rowan opened her book-filled suitcase on Rick's bed. The Gods only knew how long she was going to be stuck in here, she might as well do something with the time she had.

With ruthless determination she thumbed through the titles until she found the Grimoire, the spell book, she was looking for. Sooner or later, Rick was going to change his mind about trapping Draugar and calling Klaus. She wanted to make damn sure she had a ghost trap strong enough to hold Draugar.

Rick's presence washed across her thoughts. *Rowan?*

Rowan stared up at the ceiling. "Rick?"

Yeah, hang on. I want to get a tighter connection. Rick's presence in her mind strengthened. *Can you see this?*

Rowan suddenly realized that she could see a hill, and a fire. The night was oddly well lit, and in color. There was an odd blue wash to the sky. Even the trees in the distance gave the impression of grays and browns. It looked as though movie techs had filmed during the day and darkened the film to pretend that it was night. "Yeah, I see it. Is that a fire on your front lawn?"

Yeah, I'm maintaining it. Hang on I want to get a little closer. His presence bloomed until she felt as though she was being wrapped in a tight full-body hug.

The view changed subtly and she heard sounds. Small movements became very apparent. The wind shaking the distant winter-bare branches, and ruffling the yellowed grass in the lawn kept taking her attention. She had almost the feeling of a breeze sliding through her hair. No wait; it was his hair "Wow, it feels like I'm almost inside your skin."

Humor slid across their connection. *You're seeing through my eyes.*

"Then this is what the world looks like to you? Weird." Rowan could almost smell his skin, and the soap he had washed with. She sniffed. It wasn't an actual scent, but the impression was very strong. She could also feel the subtle shifts in his power as he fed and controlled the fire.

"Wow, nice job on the fire-casting. So what's up?"

Thanks! Oh and Draugar needs you to move the Barrier in—to here. The view focused on the crest of the hill only a few yards away.

"Okay—but I have to move the entire barrier, all the way around the house, does he know this?"

I'm pretty sure he does. There was a wash of bitterness. *He seems to know every other damned thing*

Rowan frowned. "That's awfully close. In fact, you're going to be outside my barrier."

Tell me about it. His grim humor washed across her senses. *Don't worry about me, I'm not exactly helpless and I won't be that far from the barrier.*

"Just be careful."

Oh, I will... A streak of pure testosterone-driven male possessiveness washed from Rick. *I won't leave you alone with him.*

"Good." Rowan reached into her center where her power was still, but awake and alert to the barrier with only a tail twitch of movement. She stretched out along the power strands maintaining the barrier around the house. "Okay, here we go." Curling her hand, she pulled in, and the border moved closer to the house.

The points of energy pressing against the barrier followed. Some came slower than others, but they all followed the wall of energy inward, toward the house.

"Rick they are headed your way."

"Okay. Keep that wall tight. He paused and Rowan felt him peek from her eyes. *What are you doing?*

Rowan bit her lip. "Research. You know, just in case."

Rick's suspicion slid across the link. *Okay, but don't do anything, not right now.*

Rowan sighed. "I'm just doing prep-work. That's all."

Okay... His view slid out of focus.

"Rick?"

I'm still here. Humor threaded across their link, and grim alertness. *I just need all my attention to deal with this.*

"Be careful."

You already said that. She could sense his grin.

"Well, I'm saying it again." She bit her lip. *I love you,* she added softly. *I just got you, I don't want to lose you.*

I love you, too. The barrier slid past him and he was outside her senses.

Rowan felt the shimmer of rot that signaled the dead people approaching the new border of her barrier. She could just make out Draugar's white earth energy humming just outside her borders, and a warm, yet cool shimmer that was Rick. *At least I'll know if something goes wrong.*

Rowan opened her book to the page she was looking for, then dug a piece of parchment from her folder and pulled out her colored pens. "Might as well get busy with this ghost trap."

The drawing was complicated, but the spell itself was really simple. A very fast shift in her mind would activate the trap, but she would need the intricate mental maze that the drawing represented to hold a being as powerful as Draugar in place. Very carefully, she made changes and additions to the original puzzle, in case this particular spell had been used on him before. It stood to reason, Draugar was old. Someone had to have used something like this at least once on him. She did not need him solving the puzzle as soon as it caught him.

"I just hope he doesn't figure out my changes in the puzzle before Klaus can get to him."

* * * *

Six shambling figures lurched from the shadows of the trees at the bottom of the hill. Slowly, they lurched toward the ring of light cast by the floodlights around the house. Their eyes reflected glints of scarlet flame.

"Here they come." Draugar drew his gun from his pocket. "Do not allow yourself to get bitten, I have no idea what their bite would do to you. They would not normally affect a vampire as they are already animated corpses; you however, are still living..."

Rick frowned at the fire he was maintaining. "How did you know?"

Draugar raised a silver brow. "I have destroyed a number of vampires in my lifetime. I know the difference." He turned and pointed his gun at the first shambling figure to step under the floodlights. "Use extreme caution with these creatures. I'd hate to have to destroy you."

Rick slanted a gaze toward the silver-haired sorcerer. "Yeah, me, too..."

The figure stepped into a light. It looked three days dead, with blue-gray skin and flat blue-white orbs for eyes. At one time, it had been female. It was wearing the filthy remains of some kind of blue-green hospital uniform. The creature's mouth opened and thick black ichor dripped from its lips. The firelight gleamed on a plastic tag that dangled on a string around its neck.

Rick choked. "Holy, shit! Is that a nurse?"

"My guess would be a morgue attendant. These creatures do not rise from death until the following day. Very likely Rudolf's wounded died, and was brought to a morgue, where it killed the attendant on rising. Stay alert, here it comes."

Suddenly the creature burst into a loose-jointed jog, straight for the fire. It dove right in and went up like a torch without a sound. The night was briefly scented with the odor of roasting meat. The magical fire crackled and the entire figure crisped to black ash in seconds, then collapsed in a small pile of gray dust.

Rick shuddered. "It just waltzed right into the fire, and turned to ash. It didn't even make a sound, like it couldn't feel the fire."

"I don't believe they can feel pain. If we are lucky, they will all end themselves as swiftly. However, that is doubtful." Draugar's gaze remained on the tree line bordering the lawn. "Here come the rest."

The next shambling figure did not come alone. Two more followed at its heels. All three were in very poor condition. Hunks were missing from their bodies. Their clothes were heavily stained, and barely recognizable.

Rick frowned at the remains of clothing. "More hospital workers, I think..."

"Stay alert!" Draugar shouted as the first creature veered around the fire straight for Rick.

"Shit!" Rick lifted his gun and took out the creature's knees in a small burst of bullets and an explosion of gore.

The creature dropped to the ground and crawled. The other two walked straight into the fire and crisped in seconds.

"Pay attention!" Draugar snarled. He walked over to the crawling thing and grabbed it under the arms.

The thing grabbed a mouthful of Draugar's sleeve.

Draugar wrested his arm free and lifted it.

Rick took a step toward him. "It bit you."

Draugar tossed it into the fire. "I told you, they have no effect on me. Pay attention to that fire."

The grass showed broad scorch marks where the blaze had

moved with Rick's shift in attention. "Piss, I'm going to have to re-sod..."

"Worry about your property later. We still have two more; the one in the poorest condition and Rudolf's original kill. Rudolf's victim will be the hardest to destroy, as it will retain much of its intelligence."

"How do you know?"

Draugar raised a brow. "If it can hold five others, it is still quite lucid, for a *strigoi.*"

A young man in jeans and a leather jacket crested the hill. He looked whole, even clean. Only the reflected gleam of fire in his eyes, the gray cast to his face, and the subtle scent of rot gave what he was away. He looked at the fire and then at them.

"You are different," he said in a voice that barely carried. "What are you?"

Rick sucked in a breath.

Draugar nodded toward Rick. "What we are is not your concern. You on the other hand..."

The young man focused on Draugar. "Do you know what happened to me? What I am?"

Draugar kept his gun trained on the young man. "You are dead."

The young man frowned. "But I don't feel dead."

"Don't you?" Draugar motioned with his gun. "How much do you really feel? How much do you remember?"

The young man's expression showed confusion. "I remember nothing I feel I do feel." His eyes focused on Rick. "I feel hunger."

Rick lifted his gun.

The young face settled into grim lines. "You want to kill me."

"You heard him." Rick tilted his head toward Draugar. "You're already dead."

"Your kind only walks for three days," Draugar said softly. "In the meantime, everyone you encounter will die."

Confusion washed across his face. "I want I want my life back."

"There is no cure for death." Draugar pointed at the dancing flames. "Walk into the fire. You can feel it calling to you."

"I walk, but…" The young man stared at Rick. "I'm dead?"

"Yes." Draugar took a step, pulling the young man's attention from Rick. "You know that what you are is unnatural. End it now, before you spread your infection to others."

The young man shook his head. "No. I don't want I'm not ready to…"

Draugar took a step closer to him. "You will drop where you stand on your third day. It is the nature of your kind."

The young man focused on Draugar. "To kill yourself is wrong."

"To kill others is worse," Rick called out.

The young man's head shot up. With inhuman speed, he bolted toward Rick.

"Idiot!" Draugar shouted and fired his gun.

The *strigoi* staggered on a broken knee, but kept running.

Draugar tossed his gun away then lunged for the *strigoi* in a blur of speed. He tackled him to the ground. Limbs flailed. The night echoed with vicious snarls.

Draugar rolled up onto his feet with the young man in a strangle hold. "You are dead. You know you are dead. You must be destroyed before you infect others."

Black drool spilled from the young man's lips. "I won't walk into the fire."

"Then I will carry you there myself." Draugar dragged the struggling creature toward the fire.

Rick gasped. "Draugar, what are you doing?" His fire leapt high and broad.

"Hold that fire steady, Rickart!"

Rick brought the blaze down and Draugar walked straight into it. The fire lifted Draugar's white hair and his long coat flared. The young man struggled a moment, then stilled and became a figure of black ash. The ash disintegrated and fell from Draugar's arms. Draugar brushed his palms against each other and walked out of the fire.

Rick stared. Draugar was utterly untouched.

Draugar turned to Rick and bared his teeth in rage. "Don't ever do that again, you idiot! When dealing with those, don't ever call attention to yourself! Did you want to get bitten?"

Rick jerked his gaze away. "My apologies." Movement on the hill's crest caught his attention. "There's the last one."

Draugar turned. "Good." He sucked in a breath and staggered.

Rick turned to look. "Draugar?"

Draugar dropped to his knees, clutching his heart. "Get the last one into the fire." He collapsed on the grass and was still.

Rick took a step toward Draugar, then stopped. "Shit."

The creature came crawling up the hill dressed in the tattered remains of hospital-type uniform. It was missing a leg below the knee.

Rick stared at Draugar, then back at the approaching creature. "Fuck the lawn." He pointed the silver rod at the creature and the fire lunged across the grass for it. The creature blackened to ash and was gone.

Rick shut down his power, quenching the fire. The night went dark and still.

❧ Twenty ❧

End Game

Rowan heard a heavy metal clunk. The lock on the vault door had disengaged. Rowan quickly folded the piece of parchment up and stuffed it into her back pocket. The nail was still in the tiny pouch in her front pocket. She slid off the bed. "Rick?"

I'm upstairs. Rick's thoughts wavered with an odd mixture of concern and annoyance.

Rowan pushed at the vault door and it swung open. "The vault door just unlocked."

I told you it's on a timer. Humor slithered across their link. *It must be seven.*

"Oh, I didn't realize you put me in here before seven." Rowan turned to look around the bedroom. "There's no clock in here. Um, can I come up now?"

Sure. A crackle of confusion threaded his thoughts. *Um, Draugar's passed out.*

Rowan took the stairs two at a time. "What happened?"

I have no idea. We're in the living room. I put him on the couch. Rick's confusion was a strong overlay to his thoughts. *We had one more thing to kill. He said to get it into the fire, then he just dropped.*

Rowan walked through the study and into the living room.

Draugar was sprawled across the long modern couch facing the fireplace. Rick was in one of the chairs with both guns on the floor, to one side of his chair.

Rowan pulled her parchment from her pocket. *He's passed out and not in the study. Now would be a good time to pin him and call Klaus. If he gets here fast enough, there won't be a fight in your house.*

Rick studied Draugar for a long minute.

Rowan could not tell what he was thinking.

He looked over at Rowan. *Do it.*

She moved swiftly to the side of the couch, crouched down and shoved the paper under the couch while pulling out her cigarettes. She lit one and walked to the back of the couch. She knelt with the silvered nail in one hand and her lit cigarette in the other. She stabbed the nail into the couch, blew smoke on it then whispered: "Blessed be."

Draugar jerked on the couch.

Rowan walked over to Rick's side and dug out the black thread. Closing her eyes, she reached into the thread with her senses. She couldn't actually call—Draugar's magic prevented any outward magic. Gently, she presented an invitation. A black and oily vibration pulsed up her arm. She gasped, and opened her eyes. She looked at Rick. "I think he's close."

Draugar groaned and sat up on the couch. "That was unfortunate."

Rick leaned forward in the chair. "What happened?"

Draugar wiped his hands down his face. "An assassination. I was not expecting it."

"What?" Rick's brows dipped. "Who was killed?"

"No one you know, but someone important to me." Draugar set his elbows on his knees and rested his head in his hands. "It means that the trip to California has been cancelled. It will take seven days to know where I am supposed to be."

Rick's mouth fell open. "Seven days?"

"That's how long it takes to transfer the responsibility to the next in line. Never mind, it would take too long to explain. In short, I have seven days of relative freedom, so I will leave you until then..." He leaned forward as though to stand, then stopped.

Draugar frowned at the two of them then focused on Rowan and her lit cigarette. He looked up at her with eyes that blazed with wrath. "Witch...Tell me what have you done. Now."

Rowan answered before she could stop herself. "It's a ghost trap."

Draugar sat back on the couch and his lip curled. "What did you hope to accomplish? Your small magics cannot hold me for long."

Rowan set her jaw. "It should hold long enough."

Draugar's eyes narrowed. "Long enough for what?" He scowled. "Klaus." He dropped his head and chuckled. "He cannot pass both your barrier and mine."

Rowan lifted the eldritch thread from Klaus's robe. "He can if he was already inside them when the spell was cast."

"What?" Draugar straightened and snarled. "You had better hope that Klaus is not already on his way back to Russia. If I get free before he gets here, both of you will be punished severely for this. "

A dark chittering that was more an unnerving feeling than sound echoed in the back corner of the living room. Darkness pooled and rose.

"I think you should have more concern for yourself." Klaus stepped from the dark corner.

Draugar caught Rowan's gaze and his expression was bitter. "Hello Klaus, that was quick."

Klaus shrugged. "I was nearby."

Draugar's expression darkened. "Did you bring the chains?"

Klaus moved to Rick's side. "Do you think they are necessary? Your heir is dead."

Draugar looked at the floor. "I felt the passing."

Rowan frowned at Klaus. *Heir? What the heck were they talking about?*

Klaus gave Rick a significant glance.

Rick sighed and got up out of the chair.

Rowan looked at Rick and her brows rose in question.

Rick shook his head and walked out of the living room.

Draugar sat back on the couch. "Without chains, how do you intend to deliver me?"

Klaus tilted his head. "You can go willingly."

Draugar raised a brow. "Even on the plane?"

Klaus sighed. "I can request it."

Draugar nodded in defeat. "So be it."

Rowan stared from one to the other. What was going on between these two? This sounded more like a cop talking to a criminal than anything else; were they enemies, or not?

Rick walked back into the living room with a glass full of red liquid in his hand.

Rowan frowned. *Rick?* she sent. *You're feeding Klaus?*

Rick shook his head. *Not now.* He handed the glass to Klaus.

Klaus upended the glass too fast for Rowan to see. He handed the empty glass to Rick and focused on Rowan. "Release him from your spell."

Rick set the glass on the floor and scowled at Draugar. "Have him release us first." He held out his wrists where the ruby bracelets gleamed.

Draugar stared sullenly at the far wall. "You may break them."

The bracelets crunched under Rick's hand. He was more careful with Rowan's bands.

Rowan walked behind the couch and drew on her cigarette. She released a breath of smoke on the nail. "Go in peace."

Draugar snorted in sour amusement then rose smoothly from the couch. He turned to face Rick and Rowan to give them a bow and a mocking smile. "Thank you for the hospitality." He folded his arms across his chest and regarded the ragged vampire. "Take me home, Klaus. I am tired."

Klaus moved to his side and darkness swallowed them both to

shatter into rags of smoke.

Rowan blinked. "They're gone." She turned to Rick. "Do you think it's over?"

"Over enough for me." Rick groaned. "God, I have to re-sod my lawn. I have a business party here next weekend!"

Rowan gaped. "A business party?" She shook her head, trying to jump from one subject to the next.

"Yep. And gimme that." He tugged the cigarette from her fingers and tossed it into the fireplace. He slung his arms over her shoulders. "A business party for my fellow architects, and you get to be hostess."

Rowan shook her head. "I'm a librarian, I have no idea how to be a hostess for a business party!"

Rick pulled her into a close embrace. "I'm sure you'll figure it out. You're clever."

Rowan frowned. "There are limits to my cleverness."

"Really?" He leaned down and took her mouth in a swift kiss. "Can we test those limits?" His hands slid under her shirt. "In bed?" His palms closed on her breasts. "Now?"

Rowan's thought scattered as her body reacted hungrily. Her nipples came erect with violent haste. A wet throb in her core made her knees tremble. She groaned and dug her fingers into his shoulders.

Rick's tongue caressed her throat as his fingers tugged on her aching nipples. "Mmm, so I was right, it is time for me to play sex toy."

Rowan gave him a smile that was all appetite. "Do we have to use the bed?"

Rick grinned right back. His eyes ignited to copper flame. "What did you have in mind?"

Rowan grabbed the hem of her T-shirt and pulled it off. "I was thinking; the floor looks comfy."

Rick's brows dropped. "The floor looks comfy? It's hard wood."

Rowan licked her lips and reached for her bra clasp. "If I'm on top it won't matter to me."

Rick grabbed the hem of his shirt. "Who says you'll be on top?" He yanked the shirt off.

Rowan released the clasp on her bra. "I do."

Coming Soon to Extasy Books:

Burning Shadows
Enchantment in Crimson
Book Two

"Um, I know this is kinda late to be asking this, but do we have something to call this ghost from? Something that belonged to him or something from his grave?"

"Oh yes." He stopped and waved her into an opening in the wall to the right. "We have the king himself."

"Whoa!" Rowan nearly tripped. A heavily carved wooden sarcophagus was sitting in the center of the stone-lined room. Rowan walked around the body-sized box. The wood was scarred and black with age. "This is…" She swallowed. "This is the King's body?"

He nodded. "*Knyaz* had me remove it from the cathedral four decades ago. No one even knows it is missing."

Rowan looked up. "He stole his own ancestor?"

He gave her a tight smile. "Among other thing…"

"What's it doing here?"

"That in none of your concern."

"Fine, whatever…" Rowan shrugged, then frowned. "You mean he's had the body for four decades and he hasn't been able to raise the ghost in all that time?" She shook her head. "I don't get it, it's not hard to raise a ghost; it's basic witchcraft. People do it by accident all the time."

"The problem is not calling on the ghost. Every conjuration has been successful. The problem is that the ghost has proved fatal to the conjurer before the question of his demon could be asked."

Rowan stared at the box. "I see…" She squinted at the deep carvings. They looked like some form of weird writing. "In that case, I bet there's a booby-trap."

His brows shot up. "A what?"

Rowan dropped her coat on the floor then her scarf. "Some kind of magical trap designed to kill the person that calls the ghost." She walked back over to the sarcophagus and rummaged in her red velvet bag. Her hand came free with a pair of small leather packets. Both held silver-dipped horseshoe nails. She frowned. *Why these?* They were used primarily to set boundaries. Her brows shot up. "Did the other witches cast a circle?"

He tilted his head. "A few."

"Did they make a circle around the box and then a second one around themselves?"

He nodded. "That too."

"Okay…" She stuffed her hand back in her bag. "Give me what I need," she said under her breath and dug into her bag. Her hand promptly tangled in the silk scarf wrapped around the crystal spectacles. Rowan continued to dig through the bag, but couldn't untangle her hand from the scarf. Frustrated, she pulled the scarf and spectacles out. She looked at the sarcophagus holding the dead king and frowned. The decorative carving all over the box was in fact writing. *I wonder if the spectacles can read this, but* She looked over at her watcher then at the sarcophagus. *Fuck it, this is my life we're talking about here.*

Rowan unwrapped the spectacles and set the wires over her ears. She stretched to peer at the top of the box. The carvings came into focus and slowly began to rearrange themselves into legible script. Oh yes, this was writing all right.

"What are you doing?" His voice sounded suspicious.

"Reading." Rowan frowned. "How many witches used blood in their spell?"

"All of them."

Rowan yanked the spectacles off. "Then I found your problem." She gave him a tight smile and rewrapped the spectacle in the scarf.

"The coffin clearly warns against shedding blood anywhere near it."

He stepped away from the wall. "You read that, just now?"

Rowan snorted and shook her head. "I told you before that I could read this stuff."

"So you did." He crossed his arms and stepped back to lean against the wall. He frowned at Rowan. "However, that was not medieval Ukrainian."

"So?" Rowan scowled. "Do you want me to raise this ghost or not?"

He gave her a tight smile. "By all means."

Rowan dug into her bag and pulled out a black cigarette then lit it. She drew on her cigarette, then looked over her shoulder. "You may want to wait outside the doorway, I'm going to need room to work."

He looked at Rowan. "You're using a full ritual? I thought you did not require one?"

"Normally, for raising a ghost, I don't." Rowan nodded grimly. "But, I'm not in the mood to take chances with a ghost that kills."

About The Author

I have lived in seven states and spent two years in England. I have been an auto mechanic, a security guard, a waitress, a groom in a horse-stable, in the military, a magazine editor, a belly dancer and a stripper. These days I work as a copywriter/editor for an adult entertainment Internet Company. I write promotional material for my company and my non-fiction articles are published in Klixxx Magazine and AVN Online magazine. I guess you could say that I write for a living.

Why do I write? I write to keep my sanity. For me, writing is more than a passion—it's an *obsession*. The stories crowd into my head. I write them down so I can get some peace.

Where do I get my ideas from? Rampant curiosity. I play the game of 'What If?' with everything I encounter. Everything I do and everything I see, triggers a story to be told. I am a voracious reader of Romance, Science Fiction, Fantasy, Horror and Erotica, so naturally my stories follow along the lines of what I want to read.

383190